# "I LIKE IT MUCH BETTER
# WHEN YOU SMILE, SAM."

Leaning forward, Kate brushed her lips across his. "Goodnight, Sam."

"You shouldn't be kissing me, Kate." His arm tightened around her shoulders.

"It was just a little goodnight kiss. It wasn't meant to be anything more."

"My mind understands that. But my body doesn't comprehend a word you're saying." His voice became husky and low. "And demands that I should be enjoying more of your kisses."

"Oh, my." Kate forced a tremulous smile. "I think you're making far too much out of one goodnight kiss."

"It's not the goodnight kiss that's causing me so much turmoil, Kate." His fingers skittered across her cheek. "The turmoil comes from knowing that you want more than just a goodnight kiss, too."

# Someone Like You

## SUSAN SAWYER

AVON BOOKS ◆ NEW YORK

SOMEONE LIKE YOU is an original publication of Avon Books. This work has never before appeared in book form. This work is a novel. Any similarity to actual persons or events is purely coincidental.

AVON BOOKS
A division of
The Hearst Corporation
1350 Avenue of the Americas
New York, New York 10019

Copyright © 1996 by Susan Sawyer
Inside cover author photo by Mary Schamehorn
Published by arrangement with the author
Library of Congress Catalog Card Number: 96-96028
ISBN: 0-380-78478-5

First Avon Books Printing: August 1996

AVON TRADEMARK REG. U.S. PAT. OFF. AND IN OTHER COUNTRIES, MARCA REGISTRADA, HECHO EN U.S.A.

Printed in the U.S.A.

RA 10 9 8 7 6 5 4 3 2 1

To my editor, Christine Zika,
who planted the seeds for a story about
Kate and Sam—
with my heartfelt gratitude for your
patience and guidance
in nurturing this story into full bloom;
and to my agent, Pamela Ahearn,
who is everything an agent should be (and more)—
with my deepest appreciation for your wise counsel
and your persistent belief in me.

# Acknowledgments

Special thanks to Suzanne Newman, vice president, Marketing and Public Relations, The Medical Center of Central Georgia; and to Marilyn Ashmore, director of the marvelous Hay House— for introducing me to the delights of Macon, Georgia, and providing invaluable assistance with my research for the setting of *Someone Like You*.

# Prologue

**K**athryn Carey gazed across the wide expanse of land behind the stately Georgia mansion and frowned. "Sam should have been here by now," she mumbled, nervously clutching the fragile stems of her wedding bouquet.

A white lace veil, caught on the wings of a warm July breeze, fluttered across her face. Unaccustomed to wearing bridal attire—especially a piece of bothersome lace that tickled her nose and clouded her vision—Kate flung the veil over her head and peered across the grounds once again.

To her left was a tiny cottage that served as a children's playhouse. A miniature version of Hopewell House, Kate's family home, the little building was a child's delight, a frequent setting for imaginary tea parties and games of pretend. But the small cottage was silent this afternoon.

Kate's gaze quickly shifted to the spring-house, then wandered beyond the smokehouse and barn to the grove of trees bordering the Hopewell property.

But Samuel Springer was nowhere in sight.

Kate heaved a frustrated sigh. The wedding guests would be arriving at any moment now, expecting to witness the most glorious wedding of the summer season in Rome, Georgia. But how could a wedding take place without a groom?

"Sam's probably down by the creek, fishing or reading one of those boring old books of his," she muttered irritably. "I'd wager he doesn't even know what time it is."

Ripping the lace netting from her fair hair, Kate dashed across the yard. After tossing her veil and bouquet on the porch of the small cottage, she picked up her skirts and headed for the creek.

A few moments later, she spotted Sam. He was sitting on a smooth boulder beside the water, one hand casually draped over a wooden pole. The tips of his bare toes were dangling over the gurgling stream, and the sleeves of his shirt were rolled up to his elbows. His auburn hair was wild and tangled, like he'd just tumbled out of bed.

She crept closer to the boulder. Sam was sitting very still, as still as a marble statue. His head was tilted forward, his chin was resting on his chest, and his eyes were closed . . .

The revelation hit Kate like a thunderbolt. Fishing wasn't the reason for Sam's tardiness. The scoundrel was *sleeping!* And how could he sleep so peacefully, knowing everyone was expecting him to marry her?

"What do you think you're doing, Samuel Springer?" she demanded, storming up to him.

His head jerked up. "Wh-Wh-What the devil is going on here?" he asked, blinking in confusion.

"You know what's going on, and don't you deny it!" Kate yanked the fishing pole from Sam's hand, tempted to smash it over his head and pound some sense into his brain. "You know what day it is!"

"It's my fishing day." He scowled. "And you're disturbing it."

"It's also Saturday, the twenty-seventh day of July."

"And the year is eighteen hundred seventy-two. What difference does it make?"

Exasperated, Kate rolled her eyes heavenward. "Doesn't the date mean anything to you?"

"Should it?" he taunted.

"Of course it should!" she wailed. "It's our wedding day!"

Feigning regret, Sam slapped the heel of his

palm against his forehead. "How could I have forgotten?" he groaned. "You haven't talked about anything else for weeks."

"Well, we can't waste any more time talking about it now." Kate tossed the fishing pole onto the creek bank. "If we don't hurry and get back to the house right now, all the guests will be wondering where we are, and—"

"You're gonna have to find someone else to marry today, Kate," Sam snapped.

He bolted to his feet, retrieved the pole from the mossy bank, and stomped back to the creek. Plopping down on the boulder, he cast the line into the water. Then he leaned back and yawned, acting as if he hadn't a care in the world.

Kate glared at him in stunned disbelief. "I can't believe you're doing this to me! I've been decorating the playhouse and getting everything ready for the reception all morning long. Why, I even got Aunt Dorinda to bake a cake for us."

"Cake?" Sam's head snapped up. "What kind of cake?"

"Your favorite." She licked her lips and grinned, praying she'd finally stumbled across the bait that would lure him back to the playhouse with her.

"Applesauce raisin with vanilla icing?" he guessed.

Kate nodded, her smile fading away. "But

you have to show up for the wedding if you want a piece."

"I'm not going to any wedding today, Kate, not even for a piece of Aunt Dorinda's cake." Sam shrugged. "Besides, I don't remember agreeing to be a part of this stupid plan of yours."

"But you never said you *wouldn't* marry me!" Distraught, Kate plopped down beside him on the boulder. "And if you didn't want to get married, you should have said something before now."

"You wouldn't have listened, even if I'd shouted to high heaven," Sam argued. "You're always too caught up in all your little plans to pay attention to anything I have to say."

"That's not true!" she denied hotly. "If you'd told me you didn't want to marry me today, I could've scheduled the wedding for another afternoon."

"It wouldn't have done any good." Sam heaved a weary sigh. "I wouldn't have agreed to marry you, no matter what time or date or place."

Cringing, Kate fluttered her lashes and blinked back the surge of moisture swelling in her eyes. "I wasn't trying to make you do something you didn't want to do, Sam. Honest, I wasn't." Her voice faltered, and her lower lip trembled. "I th-th-thought we c-c-could have a g-g-good time, and—"

"Those tears of yours aren't gonna change my mind about marrying you, and neither is that little pout on your lips," he warned gruffly. "I know all your tricks, Kate. And just because you know how to get your own way with everyone in town doesn't mean you can get your way with me!"

Sam never intended to snap at her so harshly, but he couldn't seem to help himself. Everyone catered to Kate Carey's whims, and he was determined not to fall prey to her charms.

It wasn't that he resented Kate, nor the love everyone bestowed so freely upon the girl. On the contrary, Sam figured he would be grateful to Kate and her family for the rest of his life. After all, Kate's older sister, Julia McRae, and her two elderly aunts, Odelphia and Dorinda Hopewell, had opened their home—and their hearts—to him at a time when no one else would.

Still, Kate had become something akin to a pesky little sister to him over the years. Pampered and spoiled, she was accustomed to getting her own way with everyone who knew her.

Except Sam, of course. He took great delight in refusing to succumb to her wishes. And whether he was snatching ribbons from her hair or dangling worms in front of her nose, he was always looking for new ways to tease and torment her, if for no other reason than to make her squeal and squirm.

But Kate's beguiling charm made it difficult for anyone—including Sam—to deny her heart's desires. Sam secretly adored the girl, though he couldn't bring himself to admit it to anyone.

At that instant, Kate tugged on the sleeve of his shirt. "Quit being such an old fuddy-duddy, Sam," she scolded. "Everyone knows we're only pretending to get married today. It'll be like a fancy tea party, where everyone gets dressed up, says nice things to each other, and pretends to have a good time while they're trying not to spill anything on their Sunday clothes."

Sam glowered at her in disbelief. "Haven't you heard one word I've said? I'm not playing any more games with you, Kate. Good grief, I'm fourteen years old! I'm a man now, and I'm too old to be playing games with little girls any longer."

"But I'm almost grown, too!"

"You're barely eleven. Almost a baby."

"I am *not* a baby!" Kate's deep-set green eyes blazed with anger. "Why, I'm even an aunt! And if I'm old enough to be an aunt, I'm too old to be a baby."

"But being an aunt doesn't make you old enough to marry anyone," Sam pointed out solemnly. He turned away from her, staring into the murky waters of the creek once again. "Go find another groom for your wedding, Kate. I'm sure Daniel Young or Edward Sprayberry might marry you."

Kate wrinkled her nose in disdain. "Daniel is nice, but I don't think I'd like to marry him. And I can't possibly marry Edward, either. I'm older than he is. Besides, I don't want to marry just anyone. And since you and I know each other so well, I figured—"

"I'm not going to marry you, Kate." The line of Sam's jaw hardened. "Not today, not tomorrow, not ever. Because I'll never marry someone like you."

Sam steadied himself, expecting her to lash out at him, maybe even pound her fists into his arm. Kate usually retaliated when he refused to give in to her demands. But this time, she remained silent, frozen, glaring at him in stunned disbelief.

A long moment passed, filled with an awkward silence, before she pursed her lips together and tossed back her head.

"That's fine with me," she announced crisply. "I thought getting married would be something fun for us to do, since we're always arguing and fighting. But getting married isn't nearly as much fun as I thought it would be."

"Getting married isn't supposed to be fun," Sam muttered under his breath.

"You're just saying that because you're an

old stick-in-the-mud." She surged to her feet. "Your idea of fun is sitting around here, catching your stupid old fish and reading those stuffy old books of yours."

"I happen to like fishing." Sam bristled defensively. "It gives me the chance to study in a quiet place. Besides, I'm going to be a lawyer. And future lawyers need to read as many books as possible."

"Future lawyers need some friends, too." Whirling, Kate headed toward the creek bank. "But you're acting like you don't want any friends. You're the meanest person I've ever known in my whole, entire—"

"Then why did you want to marry me?"

The question stopped her cold. She turned her head, peering over her shoulder at him. "I just wanted us to be friends, Sam," she admitted wearily. "I've always tried to be your friend, even when nobody else would, and I thought you might like pretending to marry m—"

"You know I've never liked games of pretend, Kate." Sam heaved a frustrated sigh. "Besides, when I decide to marry someone, I'll be the one who does the asking. After all, the man is supposed to be the one who brings up the subject of marriage."

A heated blush rose to her cheeks. In an obvious attempt to soothe her wounded pride, she threw back her shoulders and lifted her chin. "Well, you could ask me to marry you a million times, and I'd never consent to your proposal. I'll never marry someone like you, Samuel Springer!"

With that, she spun around and stomped up the creek bank, marching back to Hopewell House in a rush of fury.

# Chapter 1

*July, 1882*

**"I**'m delighted you could attend our little party at Hopewell House this afternoon, gentlemen." Standing in the shade of a blossoming magnolia tree, Kathryn Carey flashed her most disarming smile at the group of men clustered around her.

"Your *little* party?" Chuckling with amusement, a bespectacled young man scanned the crowd of guests milling across the well-manicured lawn. "I'd say you have at least two hundred people on hand today, Miss Carey."

Kate quickly surveyed the throng. "Why, I do believe you're right, Mr. Hightower." Fluttering her thick, dark lashes, she swept her gaze over the band of men clamoring around her. "Of course, I might have been inclined to pay more attention to my arriving guests if I hadn't been captivated by the charms of six of the

11

most attractive gentlemen in all of Rome, Georgia."

Chortling, Kate's faithful flock of adorers beamed with delight. Sputters of laughter were still rippling through the group when a stocky man with a receding hairline edged his way to Kate's side.

The man's gaze roamed over the length of her petite frame, studying the dips and swells displayed by the drape of her white gown with blatant approval. Shifting his gaze higher, he boldly admired the alluring hue of her deep-set green eyes and the thick, golden curls tumbling over her shoulders.

"Attending your aunt's seventy-fifth birthday celebration is truly an honor, ma'am," Thaddeus Ballard proclaimed. Grasping Kate's hand, he pressed his lips across her slender fingers.

With a graceful ease, Kate pulled away from the man's hold. Judging by the lustful gleam in his eyes, she suspected that Thaddeus Ballard was much more interested in pursuing her than celebrating Odelphia Hopewell's birthday.

"I'm flattered to know that you hold such high regard for my dear Aunt Odelphia, Mr. Ballard," she finally managed to say.

At that moment, a bearded man bounded up to Kate, presenting her with a bouquet of magnolia blossoms. "It's a privilege to have the pleasure of your company for the afternoon, Miss Carey.''

Another gentleman, struggling to shove his way to the front of the group, sighed in frustration. ''But some of us don't particularly enjoy sharing Miss Carey's company with everyone in town,'' the man grumbled.

''Maybe all of us could have a few moments of privacy with her this afternoon,'' George Hightower suggested. Glancing over at Kate, he adjusted the rim of his thick spectacles. ''Would you be willing to spend some time—possibly a half hour or so—with each of us, ma'am?''

Kate absently fingered the mauve ribbons woven through her hair, ribbons that matched the hue of the satin sash that was cinched around her waist. ''Well, I'm very willing, but—''

''Don't be ridiculous, Hightower,'' Thaddeus snapped. ''Why should anyone give up the chance to enjoy Miss Carey's company for an entire afternoon?''

''Maybe some of us don't enjoy watching you slobber all over her hand,'' George shot back, his face reddening with fury. ''Why, you've been fawning over Miss Carey like some love-smitten fool all afternoon. The rest of us haven't had the chance to—''

''Now, now, gentlemen,'' Kate broke in, hoping to curb the tension sizzling through the air.

"There really isn't any reason to bicker over me. Even though I would like nothing more than to spend the rest of the afternoon with you, I'm afraid it isn't possible."

Groans of disappointment rumbled through the group. "Why not, Miss Carey?" one of the men asked. "You're the reason why we're here."

"I'm afraid I can't possibly neglect my duties as hostess for this afternoon's festivities. If I ignore the rest of my guests, everyone will think I'm being dreadfully rude." Kate curled her lips into a beguiling smile. "And if I don't give anyone else the chance to enjoy the company of the most charming and handsome gentlemen in attendance today, everyone will think I'm being terribly selfish, too."

"All of us have been rather thoughtless, I suppose." George heaved a sigh of resignation. "We should've realized that other people would be making demands on your time this afternoon."

"Perhaps we'll have the chance to catch up with you later," Thaddeus suggested.

"I truly hope so." Smiling graciously, Kate turned to leave. "Enjoy yourselves, gentlemen."

Picking up her skirts, she breezed across the lawn. Unaware of the admiring glances that were following the sway of her bustled gown,

Kate scanned the scene in front of her with interest.

At the moment, dozens of people were huddling around the linen-draped tables scattered throughout the yard, filling their plates from the sumptuous assortment of foods.

Others were gathered in small clusters, sipping on freshly squeezed lemonade and chattering amiably with their friends and neighbors. The soft strains of a string quartet drifted over the gathering, harmonizing with the hums of conversation and laughter buzzing through the air.

Kate plunged into the midst of the throng, offering a gracious smile and a word of welcome to each guest who crossed her path. But after greeting guests for more than an hour, she was longing for a brief respite from the heat of the summer afternoon.

Slipping away from the crowd, Kate climbed the steps leading up to the verandah and sauntered over to a small refreshment table. She had just dipped a ladle into a punch bowl brimming with lemonade when a male voice rumbled in her ear.

"Pardon me, Miss Carey, but—"

Unaware of anyone standing behind her, Kate nearly jumped out of her skin. The ladle slipped from her grasp, clattering back into the depths of the bowl.

She whirled around and looked up into the

face of a strikingly handsome man with a dark mustache. "Why, Mr. Moulton! I didn't realize you were here."

"I didn't mean to startle you, Miss Carey. But when I saw you standing here all by yourself, I couldn't resist seizing the opportunity to talk with you for a moment. I've been trying to catch up with you all afternoon."

"I suppose I've been rather difficult to catch until now." Kate smiled. "So have you been enjoying our little gathering here at Hopewell House?"

"Very much so." Augustus Moulton drew in a deep, steadying breath. "But I would like nothing more than to serve as your escort for the remainder of the afternoon, Miss Carey. It would be a privilege for me, I can assure you."

"I'm truly flattered by the offer, Mr. Moulton, but I'm afraid I must decline. If I yielded to the temptation of allowing you to serve as my escort today, I'm afraid I would be terribly distracted from my duties as hostess. I'm sure you understand."

"Of course, Miss Carey." A shadow of disappointment flickered across his face. "Another time, perhaps."

He hesitated for a moment, appearing as though he wanted to say more, before he turned and walked away. Sensing that she'd not seen the last of Augustus Moulton, Kate retrieved the ladle from the punch bowl and poured a generous serving of lemonade for herself.

She was savoring the first sip of the drink when she noticed an attractive couple heading toward her. Watching Julia and Tyler McRae as they strolled across the verandah, Kate paused for a moment to admire her sister and brother-in-law.

With her chestnut-brown hair piled into soft mounds over her head, Julia possessed a youthful appearance that belied her true age. Observing her sister's new hairstyle, Kate was convinced that a newcomer in town would never suspect that Julia was sixteen years her senior.

But it would be impossible for anyone to overlook the love that flowed so freely between Julia and her handsome, dark-haired husband. At the moment, Tyler's arm was draped across Julia's narrow shoulders, and his eyes were glimmering with a mixture of affection and pride as he gazed down at his beautiful wife.

As the couple stepped up to the refreshment table, Kate's lips curled into a teasing grin. "Well, it's about time you two came out of hiding. I've been wondering where you've been keeping yourselves all afternoon."

"Oh, we've been around," Julia replied vaguely, amusement shimmering from her eyes. "In fact, we couldn't help but notice that you were chatting with Augustus Moulton a few moments ago."

"Ah, yes, Augustus Moulton." Kate took a sip of her lemonade. "A very handsome man, Augustus."

"And he certainly seems interested in you," Julia remarked.

"He's been rather persistent in his requests for my company lately," Kate admitted. "As a matter of fact, Augustus has pursued me so much in the last few weeks that it's becoming rather difficult for me to disregard him. I'm beginning to think the man has decided to follow me wherever I go."

"Then maybe you should allow him to call on you," Julia suggested. "He's quite a catch, from what I hear."

"And he has plenty of good qualities about him," Tyler pointed out. "He's educated, wealthy, and—"

"Boring," Kate finished, stifling a yawn.

"I don't understand, Kate." Julia's green eyes narrowed in confusion. "Any other young lady of twenty-one would be thrilled to have the most eligible bachelor in town pursuing her."

"But Augustus Moulton simply doesn't interest me, Julia."

"No one interests you for very long," Tyler observed candidly. "From what I've seen this afternoon, every unattached man in town is clamoring after your affections. What more do you want, Kate?"

"A little excitement in my life." Kate idly fingered the rim of her glass. "It seems like my world has become one endless round of parties and teas, charity balls and church socials."

"What a pity." Tyler shook his head in mock dismay. "And to think I actually believed you've been enjoying yourself all this time."

"I never said I wasn't having any fun, Tyler. Who wouldn't enjoy attending every social event in town? It's just that . . ." Kate paused, returning her empty glass to the refreshment table. "I need a challenge in my life. I need a sense of purpose, a source of fulfillment, a cause to support. I want my life to consist of more than simply deciding which gown to wear to an afternoon tea and figuring out new ways to avoid the likes of men like Augustus Moulton and Thaddeus Ballard."

An expression of bewilderment flickered across Julia's face. "But I thought attending all those teas and socials provided you with plenty of material for your society column."

"Gathering information for my weekly newspaper column isn't as challenging as it used to be. All you have to do is report what you see and hear." Kate sighed. "And after you've reported on one church picnic, you've reported on all of them."

"Have you tried to approach your stories

from a fresh angle?" Julia asked. "It might make your work more interesting."

"I've covered every angle I can possibly think of. What I really want, more than anything else in the world, is to cover the real news in town—fires, politics, business deals, and the like. But that grumpy old Carter Jackson won't hear of such a thing."

Tyler went rigid. "You've talked to Jackson about this?"

"I've tried." Kate fingered the band of embroidered roses that bordered the scooped neckline of her white gown. "But he wouldn't listen to anything I had to say. Do you realize he had the nerve to actually dismiss me from his office yesterday?"

Tyler paled. The publisher and editor of the *Rome News-Tribune* was one of the most influential men in Georgia. "Good God, Kate, what happened?"

"I just told him I could liven up the front page of that stuffy old newspaper of his with some juicy news stories. But he didn't like my idea at all."

Tyler groaned. "How absurd."

"But that's not the worst of it," Kate continued on. "He said he'd throw away his printing press before he'd allow a pretty little thing like me to work for him as a real reporter. That's a man's job, he claims. He wants me to keep writing my columns at home and dropping them off at his office every week. Why, that old grump wouldn't even consider letting me have a space at the newspaper office! He said I'd distract everyone else from their work."

"I can't imagine why," Tyler mumbled cynically.

"If you ask me, *he* was the one who was distracting everybody, getting all red in the face and escorting me out the door. Why, I was so humiliated I wanted to strangle him!"

"But you didn't. . . . Did you?" Tyler probed.

Kate bit back a smile. "Don't worry, Tyler. I'm certain that grumpy old man will eventually recover from my visit to his office."

"Jackson will never let me hear the end of this," Tyler muttered. "Everyone in town— including Carter Jackson—holds me accountable for everything you say and do, Kate." He scowled. "Trouble is, no one seems to remember I'm not the one responsible for fathering you."

"But everyone knows you're the one responsible for spoiling me," Kate countered, unable to resist teasing her brother-in-law. Tyler had shamelessly pampered her since her childhood days, and she knew he couldn't deny it.

He and Julia had practically raised Kate as their own, lavishing her with love and attention over the years. Living under the same roof with Tyler, Julia, and the elderly Hopewell sisters, Kate figured she'd been showered with more affection and caring than most people could expect to receive in a lifetime.

Though Kate possessed only vague memories of her late father, a Methodist minister, and no recollection of the mother who'd died giving birth to her, she'd always known that she occupied a special place in her brother-in-law's heart. Even now, Kate could detect the familiar bond of affection glimmering from Tyler's vivid blue eyes.

"I'm not the only person in the world who's been wrapped around that little pinky of yours, Kate," Tyler claimed, the corners of his mouth twitching with amusement. He nodded toward a trio of young men who were lingering on the steps of the verandah. "Just take a look at your suitors. They're so anxious to please you that they're willing to do anything to win your affections."

Kate rolled her eyes heavenward. "Those three young men aren't suitors of mine, Tyler. None of them have ever called on me."

"But they're ready and waiting to leap at your every beck and call," he pointed out. "They're just like everyone else who has ever known you. To be honest, I can't think of anyone who hasn't been victimized by that delightfully naughty charm of yours, Kate."

"Then your memory must be failing, Tyler." Julia glanced at her husband and smiled. "Don't you remember Sam?"

"Good God, how could I have forgotten?" Tyler chuckled. "And where in the hell is that scoundrel, by the way? I haven't seen him all afternoon."

"He probably stayed in Macon just to spite me." Kate laughed. "After all, I'm the one who sent an invitation to him, requesting the honor of his presence for Aunt Odelphia's birthday. And Samuel Springer has never done anything I've asked him to do."

"Don't remind me." Tyler groaned, feigning despair. "I still haven't recovered from the strain of trying to keep the two of you from murdering each other when you were children. You and Sam were quite a mismatched pair, growing up together here at Hopewell House."

"But you and Julia managed to settle most of our disputes quite nicely, as I recall," Kate said.

"It wasn't always easy," Julia conceded. "Even though you and Sam aren't related, Tyler always said he'd never seen a brother and sister who could fuss and fume like the two of you."

"And they still hold the record," Tyler insisted. "Our own brood may get into squabbles at times, but the disagreements between Rebecca, Jeremiah, and Emily are mild compared to the constant fights that erupted between Kate and Sam."

"No one else ever teased and tormented me the way Sam did," Kate mused aloud, grinning at the memory of the red-haired, freckle-faced boy who had irritated her beyond all reason.

"And if Sam were here, he would insist that you were constantly provoking him." The wistful smile on Julia's lips faded away, replaced with a troubled frown. "I suppose Sam must have good reasons for not being with us today. He has always adored Aunt Odelphia, and I don't think he would intentionally disregard her birthday."

"He never acknowledged the invitation to our party for Aunt Odie," Kate recalled. "Do you think he could have misplaced it?"

"More than likely, his schedule simply wouldn't permit him to make the trip," Tyler speculated. "I suspect he can't just pick up and leave Macon on a moment's notice. After all, he has a thriving law practice to consider now."

"And the responsibility of caring for that precious daughter of his, too." A touch of sadness clouded Julia's eyes. "Raising a little girl—all by himself—couldn't be easy for him."

"Sam should know that we're here for him if he needs us. After all, we're the only family he's ever had." Kate's heart swelled with an ache of sorrow. "I only wish I knew why he hasn't come back to Hopewell House since Abigail's funeral. We haven't seen anything of him in the last six months."

"He may not be ready to face us yet." Tyler's

voice was somber and strained. "A man has to wrestle with his grief in his own way."

"And the process of mourning can't be rushed for anyone," Julia added. "Sam will have to come to terms with losing Abigail in his own time, I'm afraid."

"Still, it might have been good for him to be here with us today." Turning, Kate swept her gaze across the lawn. "I'm certain Sam would have enjoyed himself. It looks like everyone is having a wonderful time."

"Several guests have already thanked me for inviting them." Julia gazed fondly at her sister. "You should be quite proud of yourself, Kate. Not many young women have the talent to put together a social event as large—and as successful—as this one."

"Thanks, Julia." Listening to the snatches of laughter and conversation drifting up from the crowd, Kate straightened the folds of her gown. "I suppose I should be getting back to our guests now."

"We'll catch up with you when it's time to serve Aunt Odie's cake," Julia said.

Kate scooped up her skirts and breezed across the verandah. The three young men languishing on the steps sprang to their feet, nearly tripping over each other as they scrambled to escort Kate into the yard.

Watching Kate's admirers clamoring around her, Julia rested her head against her husband's shoulder. "What are we going to do with my precocious little sister, Tyler?"

"I don't think we can do anything with her, my dear. Kathryn Carey has a mind of her own."

Julia sighed. "Sometimes I think she'll never settle down. Every man in town is vying for her attention, but she doesn't seem interested in any of them."

"That's because all of them are too eager to please her. She's never cared for anyone who buckles beneath the pressure of all her demands. Personally, I think Kate needs a man with some backbone, someone who knows how to stand up to her when no one else will."

"Sounds like you're talking about someone like Sam." Julia laughed. "Honestly, I don't think anyone has ever been able to rile Kate's temper like Samuel Springer."

Chuckling, Tyler nodded toward the throng of suitors assembled around Kate. "Apparently, we don't have to worry about anyone provoking Kate's temper this afternoon, my dear."

At that moment, a buggy rattled over the well-worn drive leading up to Hopewell House. When the vehicle halted beside the mansion, the driver leaped down and scurried to assist the passengers from their seats.

Tyler's smile faded away as a tall, auburn-haired man emerged from the buggy, cradling a little girl in his arms.

"But, then, maybe we do have a reason to worry," Tyler mumbled, a troubled frown creasing his brow.

# Chapter 2

$\sim$ ◌ ◌ $\sim$

**S**tepping down from the buggy, Samuel Springer tightened his hold around the child nestled against his chest.

"We're at Hopewell House now, Caroline." Even though Sam knew full well that his daughter wasn't listening to anything he had to say, he couldn't resist the urge to tell her about their arrival. "We're finally here."

He glanced down at the red-haired tyke, and his heart rolled over. Caroline had drifted off to sleep just as the train had chugged into the Rome depot. Now, deep in the throes of a belated afternoon nap, the three-year-old was oblivious to the sounds of voices and music and laughter drifting over the grounds.

"Where would you like your baggage, sir?" the hack driver asked, retrieving a pair of traveling bags from the back of the buggy.

"Just leave everything here with me. I'll take

care of getting my bags into the house a little later.''

The driver deposited the bags on the ground, then accepted Sam's generous payment for his services with an appreciative smile. ''Enjoy your visit, sir.''

Sam grinned. ''I don't intend to do anything else while I'm here, I can assure you.''

Chuckling, the driver tipped the brim of his hat and returned to the buggy. Just as the vehicle lurched forward, returning to the main road, Sam heard an outbreak of applause and laughter from the front lawn.

Curious about the commotion, Sam edged his way across the drive and halted beside a row of neatly trimmed hedges to peer across the grounds.

Dozens of guests were assembled on the lawn. Clapping and cheering, the visitors were focusing their attention on a tall, reed-thin woman with a crown of silver curls. The woman was ambling through the throng, working her way toward a table near the verandah.

In center of the table was a six-tiered cake, adorned with thick mounds of icing and dozens of blazing candles. As Odelphia Hopewell approached the festive setting, the chatter and noise from the crowd faded into a respectful silence.

''Oh, my.'' Odelphia's thick spectacles shimmered, reflecting the glow of the candles. "Is all of this for me?"

"Don't worry, Odie." Dorinda Hopewell waddled up behind her sister. "No one expects you to eat all of it by yourself."

A smile tugged at the corners of Odelphia's mouth. "Are you suggesting I should share my birthday cake with everyone?"

"Offering a slice to each guest would be very considerate of you." Dorinda edged closer, examining the decorative icing on the cake with a critical eye. Short and plump with an insatiable sweet tooth, she rarely passed up the chance to indulge in her favorite pastime of enjoying rich, sugary desserts.

"I suppose I should share it," Odelphia conceded. "After all, it's an enormous cake."

"You'll probably have lots of leftovers, even after everyone has the chance to sample a slice or two." Dorinda heaved an exaggerated sigh. "And I certainly don't want you to worry about having to eat the rest of it all by yourself."

Odelphia feigned concern. "But what will I ever do with all the leftovers?"

"Well, I suppose I could assume personal responsibility for what's left," Dorinda volunteered. "After all, I wouldn't want you to be shouldering any unnecessary problems today."

"How very thoughtful of you, Dorie." Odelphia affectionately patted her sister's round shoulder. "It's a relief to know I won't have to contend with such a tremendous burden this afternoon."

Dorinda's plump cheeks blossomed with color. "It's the least I can do, considering it's your birthday and all."

Chuckles of amusement rippled through the crowd. "Happy birthday, Miss Odelphia!" someone shouted.

"Blow out your candles now, Miss Odie!" another guest urged.

"And don't forget to make a wish!" a third voice rang out.

Heeding the advice of the throng, Odelphia drew in a deep breath. Leaning forward, she squeezed her eyes shut and let out a whoosh of air.

"Try again, Miss Odelphia," someone shouted.

Odelphia's eyes fluttered open. Dismayed to discover that not a single candle had been extinguished, she heaved a disgruntled sigh.

At that instant, a boy with dark hair scrambled up to the table. "I'll help you, Aunt Odie!" Jeremiah McRae offered.

An attractive girl trailed closely behind the lad, tugging on the arm of her younger sister. "Emily and I can help, too," Rebecca McRae volunteered.

Odelphia laughed. "Apparently, I need all

the help I can get. I just don't have the wind to blow out seventy-five candles by myself." She motioned for the youngsters to form a circle around the table. "Let's give it a try, my dears."

Odelphia and the McRae children clamored around the cake, huffing and puffing until all of the flames had been extinguished. Curls of smoke were drifting up from the smoldering wicks when the crowd broke into a round of applause.

The silver-haired Hopewell sisters quickly plucked the remains of the candles from each of the tiered layers. Then they set to work, sharing the tasks of cutting and serving the cake to their guests.

Through it all, Sam stood motionless, quietly absorbing the sights and sounds and smells swirling around him. He recognized several familiar faces in the midst of the throng. For several moments, he savored the mouth-watering scents that wafted from the delectable assortment of food on the tables. And he couldn't ignore the easy flow of laughter and conversation drifting through the crowd.

But most of all, he became acutely aware of the camaraderie between friends and neighbors, the sense of warmth and caring that had been absent from his life for far too long.

God, how he'd missed this place.

Somewhere along the way, somewhere in

the midst of the living hell that his life had become, he'd forgotten how much Hopewell House—and the family who resided here— meant to him.

But as Sam stood in the shadows of the stately old mansion, dozens of memories rushed through him, memories that reminded him why he loved this place so.

Recollections of his first visit to Hopewell House danced through his mind with vivid clarity. Ironically, it had been the occasion of another party, a celebration in honor of Kate's seventh birthday.

At the time, Sam had been a frightened ten-year-old, struggling to fend for himself after his mother had abandoned him. Arriving at Hopewell House for Kate's birthday dinner with an empty belly and a scant knowledge of family life, he'd been overwhelmed by the plentiful platters of food and the generous servings of love and devotion that had been passed around the table.

A few days later, the warmth and caring of that family changed the course of his life forever. Appalled to discover that Sam was living alone, Julia had promptly removed the boy from the squalor of the abandoned shack that had been the only home he'd ever known.

Even now, some fourteen years later, Sam knew he would never forget the afternoon when Julia and Tyler had rescued him from that horrid place. His life had taken a new direction on that day—starting from the moment Julia had announced that he could live at Hopewell House for as long as he wanted—or needed— to stay.

"This is your home now, just like it's mine," she'd told him. "And I promise to take care of you as long as you're here. You'll always have a warm bed and plenty of food."

But Julia and her loved ones had provided Sam with more—much more—than the basic necessities of life. Within a short time, Sam realized he'd been plunged into the center of a family who cared for each other in ways he'd never imagined possible.

Over the course of the next seven years, the elderly Hopewell sisters became the doting grandmothers he'd never had. Julia wedged a permanent place in his heart, replacing the mother who had abandoned him. Somewhere along the way, Tyler filled the shoes of the father he'd never known. And Kate became something of a pesky little sister, both charming and infuriating him with her precocious ways.

By the time Sam set off on his own, he was a confident, self-assured seventeen-year-old, eager to pursue his dream of obtaining a law degree. He moved to Macon, Georgia, and became a student at Mercer University.

During his days at the university, Sam maintained close ties with the family who'd raised him as one of their own. But traveling back and forth between Macon and Rome became increasingly difficult after his graduation from law school.

Between establishing a successful law practice in Macon and starting a family of his own, Sam had little time to spare for visits to Rome. In recent years, trips to Hopewell House had become nothing more than fond memories to Sam.

But now that he'd finally returned to his childhood home, Sam regretted that he hadn't take the time to visit more often. "You fool," he muttered under his breath. "Why in the hell haven't you been here before now?"

He shifted uneasily, glancing across the lawn once again. His gaze aimlessly wandered over the crowd until the familiar features of a petite young woman snared his attention. *Kate.*

Studying her, Sam couldn't deny that the little girl from his childhood memories had grown into a beautiful young lady.

At the moment, her hair was glistening like spun gold beneath the dappled rays of sunlight. Ribbons were woven through the soft mounds of hair on the crown of her head and streamed through the clusters of ringlets that tumbled over her shoulders and cascaded down her back. The rosy hue of the hair ribbons was repeated in the sash cinched around her waist and in the border of roses embroidered along the flowing hem and the scooped neckline of her white gown.

A group of admirers—ranging from young schoolboys to stately gentlemen—huddled around Kate, vying for her attention. She chatted playfully with the little band of adorers, bedazzling them with her charm and beauty.

Sam chuckled under his breath, regarding Kate's admirers with a mixture of pity and amusement. Little did they realize that she'd been fluttering those thick, dark lashes, flashing that winsome smile, and enchanting everyone around her, since the day she was born.

"The poor saps," Sam mused aloud. "They have no idea of what they're getting themselves into."

Sam suspected he knew, better than most, what lay beneath that dazzling package. Lurking behind that provocative smile was a pampered beauty who'd never known the meaning of hard work. A precocious charmer with a stubborn streak, Kate rarely yielded to any man's authority—especially if she was bent on having her own way.

Of course, Kate possessed some redeeming qualities, too. She cherished her friendships, lavishing her dearest friends with her overly generous spirit and staunch loyalty. Blessed with sharp intelligence and a quick tongue, she could match wits with debaters who were far more experienced than she.

And no topic or conflict was too risqué or difficult for Kate to tackle. During his childhood, Sam had spent endless hours sparring with her about everything from the weather to the minister's Sunday sermons. In fact, arguing with Kate had been Sam's favorite pastime during the days of his youth.

But debating about anything more controversial than the shape of the moon held little appeal for Sam now.

He heaved a weary sigh. After three, long years of contending with Abigail's wandering eye and fiery temper, Sam figured he'd dealt with enough conflict and discord to last a lifetime.

Though his marriage had been nothing short of a nightmare, learning about the circumstances of Abigail's fatal accident had destroyed what little was left of Sam's fledgling belief in the power of love.

Worse yet, the injustice of it all had gnawed away at Sam like a festering sore. Since Abigail's funeral six months ago, Sam's bitterness and anger had mounted with each passing day. And in recent weeks, he'd buried himself in his work, shutting himself off from anyone other than Caroline.

But from the moment he'd arrived at Hopewell House, Sam felt something stirring deep within him, something akin to a faint glimmer of hope. Once upon a time, Hopewell House had once been a safe haven for him, a heavenly refuge from the cruelties of life. Never had he felt so wanted and loved as when he had resided here.

Now, gazing around the familiar grounds, Sam felt that little thread of hope tugging at his heartstrings once again. Would this visit give him the chance to escape from his problems, if only for a little while? Could he recapture those wondrous emotions of love and acceptance, all those feelings of warmth and security, that had been generated here long ago?

He wasn't looking for anything more than a few days of peace, a chance to forget about everything other than the one good thing that had resulted from his disastrous marriage . . . *Caroline*.

Sam glanced down at the sleeping tyke nestled against him, the precious treasure that destiny had entrusted into his inept care.

His gaze roamed over the tangle of carrot-red curls and white satin ribbons spilling across his shoulder, then settled on the angelic features that warmed his heart like nothing else could. Still fast asleep, the child's pink-tinted lips were slightly agape, and her cheeks were splotched with a rosy hue.

An ache squeezed his chest. Beneath all those ruffles and ribbons was a little girl who desperately needed the strength of a mother's love to guide her through the rough passages of life.

Sometimes, Sam thought Caroline resembled a little lost angel who was struggling to find her way in the world. For the life of him, he couldn't remember the last time he'd seen a glint of excitement dancing in those wide, solemn eyes or heard a squeal of delight gurgling from those rosy pink lips.

He gathered her close. Risking everything—even his own life—would not be too great a sacrifice for his daughter. There was nothing he wouldn't do for the child.

At that moment, Julia and Tyler rushed up to greet him.

"We're so glad you're here, Sam!" Julia exclaimed, stretching up on her toes and planting a kiss on his cheek.

"A visit to your old stomping grounds has been long past due, son." Tyler clapped him on the shoulder. "It's good to see you back."

Though Sam had expected that Julia and Tyler would greet him with open arms, the warmth of their welcome overwhelmed him for a moment. "It's good to be here again," he finally managed to say. "Getting away from Macon for a few days will be good for Caroline and me, I'm certain."

"Our doors are always open whenever you can visit, Sam. There's always a place for you

and this adorable daughter of yours at Hopewell House." Julia brushed a hand over the
toddler's wayward curls, her eyes glowing with
affection for the child.

"I suppose I should've sent a wire or a note
to let you know that we were coming, but . . ."
Sam paused, slightly embarrassed by his negligence. "But to be honest, I didn't know about
Aunt Odelphia's party until last night. The
invitation got buried beneath a stack of paperwork on my desk. Caroline and I hopped on
the first train out of Macon this morning, trying
to get here in time for the start of the party.
And we might have succeeded if we hadn't
been delayed for a few hours in Atlanta."

"I suspected something like that had happened." Julia's smile faded away as her gaze
drifted back to Caroline. "Poor child! She must
be exhausted after that long train ride. Let's get
her settled inside the house so she can finish
her nap."

"Sounds like a good idea to me," Sam
agreed.

After Tyler retrieved Sam's traveling bags,
the trio turned, heading for the house. But
they'd taken only a few steps when Julia placed
a hand on Sam's arm.

"Go ahead and join the rest of the guests,
Sam. I can take Caroline upstairs for you," she
insisted. "The party will be winding down

soon, and I'm certain Kate will be anxious to know that you're here."

"Thanks, Julia." Grateful for her thoughtfulness, Sam carefully placed his daughter into Julia's capable hands, then turned to join the celebration on the grounds.

# Chapter 3

"**M**ay I freshen your lemonade, Miss Carey?" The young man's high-pitched voice warbled like the chirp of a canary. "I would be honored to fetch another glass for you."

Seated in a white wicker chair on the lawn, Kate bestowed a gracious smile on the anxious young man. "I truly appreciate your thoughtfulness, but I believe I've had my fill of lemonade for one afternoon."

"Oh." The young man's shoulders drooped, and his face clouded with disappointment. "Well, then . . ." he mumbled, staring down at the ground, obviously not knowing what else to say.

"But there is something else you can do for me," Kate added hastily, attempting to ease his dismay.

His head snapped up. "Anything for you, Miss Carey."

"Since my empty glass has become quite useless . . . perhaps you could dispose of it for me?"

He nodded with such vigor that Kate feared his neck might break. "It would be a pleasure to grant your request," he insisted.

The young man beamed with delight when Kate surrendered the glass to him. Turning to leave, he cast a triumphant smile at the remaining gentlemen in Kate's loyal following who were still huddled around her, vying for her attention.

As soon as the young man departed, Thaddeus Ballard edged forward. "I noticed your first piece of cake was rather small, Miss Carey. Would you care for another slice?"

"What a deliciously tempting idea," Kate mused, sighing with exaggeration as she pretended to consider the matter. "But as I recall, Aunt Dorinda offered to assume personal responsibility for any leftover cake. My aunt is a generous woman, mind you, but sweets have always been her downfall. And something tells me she isn't eager to share the remainders of that scrumptious birthday cake with anyone at the moment."

She nodded in the direction of her aunt, who was guarding the meager remains of the tasty confection like a protective watchdog. Kate's attentive audience followed the direction of her gaze, chuckling with amusement as Dorinda licked a generous dab of icing from her fingers.

With her admirers momentarily distracted, Kate shifted uneasily in her chair. Though flattered by all the attention from her faithful admirers, she couldn't deny that she was becoming increasingly bored with the mindless jabber and frivolous sentiments whirling around her.

Worse yet, her cheeks were aching from the strain of keeping a constant smile on her lips, and her feet were throbbing from the pain of wearing slippers that were far too small.

Kate restlessly peered across the lawn, inadvertently catching the gaze of a handsome, mustached man who was standing a few feet away from the rest of her admirers. Apparently encouraged by their brief moment of eye contact, he boldly stepped forward, breaking through the circle of men surrounding Kate.

Kate's heart sank as the man approached. All afternoon, Augustus Moulton had been keeping a watchful eye on her. And though his dauntless pursuit of her was quite admirable, Kate had no desire to spend any more time with him.

Not that Augustus was threatening or offensive. On the contrary, his manners were impeccable, his demeanor pleasant, his features quite handsome.

But nothing could compensate for the man's lack of personality. Augustus Moulton was as personable as a dead tree. An overwhelming urge to yawn seized her every time she heard that expressionless, flat monotone of his.

Now, as Augustus neared, Kate frantically searched for a way to avert another encounter with him. As soon as she spotted Maggie O'Neill in the midst of the crowd, she breathed a sigh of relief. Surely Augustus wouldn't be brazen enough to intrude upon a woman's conversation with her best friend!

Kate surged to her feet. "As much as I've enjoyed your company, gentlemen, I'm afraid I mustn't neglect the rest of my guests any longer. So if you'll pardon me . . ."

The men sighed with disappointment as Kate picked up her skirts to leave. Carefully side-stepping Augustus, she threaded her way through the maze of guests. As she neared a willowy young woman with reddish-brown curls in the midst of the crowd, she picked up her pace and rushed forward.

"There you are!" Kate exclaimed, greeting her friend with a warm embrace. "I've been looking everywhere for you, Maggie. Thank goodness you're here!"

"For heaven's sake, Kate!" Maggie's eyes twinkled with amusement. "You're acting like you haven't seen me for years."

"And what's so wrong with that?" A slight

pout formed on Kate's lips. "I'm truly glad to see you, Maggie."

"But I suspect you're not as genuinely thrilled as you'd like for me to believe."

Kate feigned innocence. "Whatever gave you that idea?"

"I know what you're trying to do, Kate." Maggie laughed. "I've seen Augustus ogling you all afternoon, and I know you're pretending to be deeply involved in a serious discussion with me so you can avoid him."

"Am I so . . . transparent?" Kate asked in a wounded tone.

"It's not easy to fool your best friend," Maggie consoled sympathetically. She lowered her voice to a whisper. "And, apparently, fooling Augustus isn't easy, either," she warned just as Kate sensed the presence of someone standing behind her.

"Good afternoon, ladies," a voice rumbled in a tone as flat and dry as a barren desert.

Kate inhaled a deep, steadying breath and planted a bright smile on her lips. "How nice to see you again, Mr. Moulton," she murmured, slowly turning to face him.

He acknowledged the remark with a cordial nod, then directed his attention to Maggie. "May I borrow your friend for a moment, Miss O'Neill? I promise to return her to you, safe and unharmed, within a short while."

"I'm certain Kate and I can finish our conversation at some other time." Maggie pressed her hand over Kate's, squeezing her fingers in a gesture of sympathy and support, before turning to leave.

As Maggie disappeared into the crowd, Augustus extended his arm to Kate. "Shall we find a quiet place to talk?"

Kate nodded toward the rose garden, Aunt Odelphia's pride and joy. Rows of colorful blossoms, carefully nurtured and lovingly tended by Odelphia, lined the garden pathway that stretched along the west side of the house. Located some distance away from the center of the festivities, the spot offered seclusion from the roar of the crowd. "No one should disturb us in the rose garden," she suggested.

"A wonderful idea," Augustus agreed.

Kate placed a hand around his outstretched arm. Falling into step beside him, she forced herself to view the situation in a positive light. Enduring a few moments alone with Augustus Moulton wasn't the end of the world, after all. She would simply listen to whatever he had to say and politely express her opinion on the matter. Then she would conclude the brief discussion with a gracious smile and return to her guests. Within a few moments, the entire ordeal would be over and forgotten.

Enjoying the fragrant floral scents drifting through the air, Kate entered the garden with Augustus. After sauntering along a winding

trail lined with dozens of blossoming rose-
bushes, they paused beside a wooden bench.
"Your persistence in persuading me to spend a
few moments with you this afternoon has
aroused my curiosity, Mr. Moulton," Kate admitted freely.

"I've been quite anxious to talk with you
since our conversation on the verandah," Augustus conceded, a troubled frown wrinkling
his brow. "But I hope my aggressive manner
has not offended you in any way."

"I've always believed that boldness is an
admirable trait," she assured him.

The compliment seemed to ease the rigid set
of his shoulders. "I appreciate your willingness
to steal away with me for a few moments, Miss
Carey. Engaging in a private discussion with
you on the front lawn seemed quite impossible,
considering that several hundred people were
demanding your attention. It was hardly an
appropriate place for discussing a personal
matter."

"But no one can overhear our conversation
now," Kate reminded him in a quiet tone.
"Please proceed, Mr. Moulton. I'm quite anxious to hear what you have to say."

He inhaled a deep breath, as if summoning
up his courage to begin. "As you know, Miss
Carey, my father's expertise in financial matters
has permitted the Moulton family to lead a
comfortable life. After attending Harvard Uni-

versity, I joined my father's business, and I am proud to say I have been quite successful in my endeavors . . ."

The monotonous timbre, never once varying in tone or volume, had the potent effect of sleeping powders on Kate. Struggling to keep her lashes from drifting to a close, she forced herself to focus on his handsome face.

But as Augustus droned on, her gaze strayed over his shoulder. Just as she glanced across the yard, a blurry image seized her attention.

". . . and I am fully prepared to assume the financial responsibilities and obligations of establishing a household . . ."

There was something familiar about the distant figure, something she couldn't put into words. Curious, Kate narrowed her eyes.

". . . and no other woman has ever intrigued me as you have, Miss Carey . . ."

The figure came into sharper focus. A man was crossing the lawn, a tall, handsome man wearing a black suit. There was a bold confidence in his stride and an air of determination in the set of his broad shoulders.

As he approached the garden, his features became more visible to Kate. His hair was a rich, dark auburn, and he looked just like . . . like *Sam*.

". . . and I've discovered that most of my thoughts are centered around you . . ."

Somewhere in the recesses of her mind, Kate

became vaguely aware of Augustus's voice drifting around her. But she had no idea what he was saying. She was too surprised by Sam's unexpected arrival to comprehend anything that Augustus had to say.

When Sam paused at the edge of the garden, Kate seized the opportunity to observe him while Augustus continued his monologue.

During Kate's childhood, she'd never viewed Sam as anything other than the holy terror that he was. In recent years, she'd watched him become a devoted husband and father. A mere six months ago, she'd seen him as a broken man mourning the loss of his wife.

But now, she realized that the passage of time had transformed an ordinary freckle-faced boy into a breathtakingly handsome man. Gone were the youthful air of innocence, the boyish stubble of whiskers, the unlined face.

Somewhere along the way, Sam's striking features had been seasoned with the mark of maturity. The angles and grooves of his face had become rugged, chiseled, strong.

Gazing at him, Kate noticed that his dark brows were bushier, his jawline more defined. He was thicker through the neck, more muscled in the body. And the hue of his hair, once a bright red, had darkened into a deep shade of auburn.

Yet, some things about him had not changed at all. His eyes were still as green as a meadow in summer. The width of his shoulders bore the same, proud stance. The curve of his mouth still held the boyish charm that she remembered so well. And there was the same hint of belligerence in the stubborn set of his jaw that she had always found unsettling.

". . . and if you grant your permission for me to call on you—"

"I realize this is a most awkward moment to interrupt you, Mr. Moulton," Kate cut in smoothly, "but a dear friend of mine has just arrived, quite unexpectedly. If you'll pardon me for a moment . . . ?"

But Kate didn't wait for a reply. Before Augustus could open his mouth, she was halfway across the garden.

Approaching Sam, she couldn't help but admire the finely tailored lines of his dark suit and brocaded waistcoat. A silk cravat of forest green, draped around the wing collar of his snowy white shirt and held in place with a tie pin, emphasized the emerald hue of his eyes.

Their gazes locked and held as she glided to a halt in front of him. "Well, it's about time you got here," she scolded, unable to suppress a smile.

"Better late than never, so they say." He took both of her hands into his, grinning down at her with amusement. "Still breaking hearts, I see."

"It's a pleasant way to pass the time, especially now that I don't have you around to pester anymore," she taunted. "I was beginning to think you weren't coming today, you know."

"So you've been watching—perhaps even waiting—for me?"

Slightly ruffled by the thread of confidence woven into the question, she leaped at the challenge to goad him. "I've been waiting for your arrival with bated breath all afternoon, Sam! Why, I've done nothing but watch for you. Ever since the party started, I've spent every moment of every hour, every second of every minute, waiting, watching, hoping you would suddenly appear in the crowd—"

"Liar." Amusement twinkled from the depths of his outrageously gorgeous green eyes. "You've been too busy to miss me."

Kate laughed, enjoying the moment until she heard the shuffle of footsteps along the garden path. No doubt, Augustus had grown weary of waiting for her return. Once he caught up with her, she suspected he wouldn't hesitate to request another private meeting. And she sensed the requests wouldn't stop until she agreed to listen to the rest of his boring monologue.

But Kate couldn't bear the thought of contending with Augustus again. She hadn't the slightest inclination to reciprocate the man's feelings for her. Nibbling on her lower lip, she hastily considered her options. What if she feigned a sudden illness? Or succumbed to a fainting spell?

A bout of dizziness, however, would only provide a temporary solution to a permanent problem. If she hoped to discourage Augustus from pursuing her in the future, more drastic measures would be necessary. Perhaps he would concede defeat in his quest to snare her affections if she expressed an ardent interest in another man . . .

Seized by a sudden thought, she glanced up at Sam. Would he cooperate with her? After all, he'd never been the cooperative sort. Instead of complying with her request without protest, he'd probably launch into a heated debate, taunt her with bothersome questions, or deliver a lengthy sermon about the perils of her scheming ways.

But the sound of Augustus's approaching footsteps convinced Kate to cast aside all of her doubts and fears. Desperate to ward off her approaching suitor, she lunged forward and hurled her arms over the broad expanse of Sam's shoulders.

Genuine surprise flickered across his face. "I didn't expect this kind of welcome from you, Kate. You must be happier to see me than I thought. It's almost seems like you're truly pleased that I'm—"

"Shut up, Sam." Kate laced her fingers together behind his neck. "Just shut up and kiss me."

The shuffle of boots moving across the winding pathway snared Sam's attention. He looked up, glancing behind Kate, and an expression of sudden understanding dawned across his intriguing features. "Trying to make your suitor jealous?" he asked, returning his gaze to her face.

"No," Kate snapped impatiently, anxious to move ahead with her plan. "I'm trying to convince him that any further attempts to catch my attention will be totally senseless. I want him to believe that I'm interested in someone else so he'll stop following me everywhere I go."

"I see." He arched one eyebrow. "And you're using me as a decoy in this little game of yours."

"Not unless you're willing to participate," she mumbled, unable to hide her mounting irritation. At any second now, Augustus would be standing beside them. She couldn't afford to waste precious moments arguing with Sam. Infuriated, she stared straight ahead, focusing her stony gaze on the broad width of Sam's chest.

"I don't mind lending a hand," he assured her smoothly. "But I suspect that kissing you won't be an enjoyable experience for me, knowing how you treat your admirers after you've grown weary of them. Something tells me that you'll cast me aside without a second thought, just like the rest of your heartbroken suitors."

"Then you can *pretend* that you're enjoying yourself," she ground out, rapidly losing her patience with him.

"But you know I've never been very good at games of pretend," he reminded her, his voice a low, taunting whisper.

She snapped up her head, intending to voice a scathing reply. But Sam didn't give her the chance to utter a sound. Any response that might have crossed her lips became smothered beneath the pressure of his mouth grinding into hers.

The shock of the unexpected move turned Kate's world upside down. Jolted by the jarring contact, she reeled in confusion. Yes, she'd asked for a kiss from Sam, a kiss that would discourage any further advances from Augustus. But never in her wildest dreams had she expected anything other than a few pecks across the cheek or a light brushing of his lips across hers. Never once had she fathomed that Sam would kiss her like this.

His lips were seducing hers with masterful skill, devouring the contours of her mouth with such fervent persuasion that Kate melted beneath the heat of his sizzling touch. He angled his head to one side, gliding his mouth across her lips over and over again with hot, moist strokes.

Sam was kissing her like she'd never been kissed before, scorching her lips with the heat of his mouth and igniting fiery flames of desire in places far deeper. When his tongue slipped between the curve of her lips and surged into her mouth, Kate feared her knees would buckle beneath her.

Swooning, she clung to his broad shoulders for support. He pressed his hands along the curve of her spine, drawing her closer against him. All the while, his lips clung to hers, relentlessly demanding more.

As his tongue swirled around hers, Kate felt as weak and giddy as if a lightning bolt had seared through her. He was kissing her with the passion of a man possessed with an insatiable desire for the woman in his arms. It was senseless, it was endless, and it was the most provocative, mind-boggling moment of Kate's life.

And it also made Kate realize just how very little she knew about kissing. None of her suitors had ever demanded anything other than a simple, flirtatious kiss from her. And most of the kisses had been over before she had the chance to close her eyes. Never before had she been kissed by any man like this.

Sam's arousing touch was awakening a response that both amazed and alarmed her. Kate couldn't explain why her pulse was racing so furiously, why her heart was thundering in her chest, why everything around her—all the noise and music and laughter—seemed very distant and far away.

Was this truly Sam who was kissing her? The same Sam who'd yanked on her braids and stolen her hair ribbons? The Sam who'd wounded her pride when he'd refused to marry her beside the playhouse so long ago?

Waves of confusion swept over her. Sam wasn't supposed to ignite all these feelings of desire in her. Someone else, maybe. But not Sam. Not the man who had been like a brother to her for most of her life.

The moment his arms loosened, she slithered away from his hold. Edging back, she planted her hands on her hips and glared at him. "You scoundrel! You weren't supposed to kiss me like . . . like . . . like *that!*"

He had the audacity to laugh. "And just how was I kissing?"

She lifted her chin and haughtily returned his gaze. "Like some love-starved maniac!"

"But it apparently achieved what you wanted to accomplish," he noted, his gaze drifting meaningfully across the narrow pathway behind her.

Slowly turning her head, Kate looked over her shoulder. To her surprise, Augustus Moulton had vanished. For the first time during the course of the afternoon, the dark-haired admirer was not standing behind her.

But her dismay over Sam's unsettling kiss overshadowed any joy she might have felt over Augustus's disappearance. Her lips were still tingling from the blazing heat of that kiss, and she didn't understand why.

She crossed her arms over her chest and frowned. "A kiss on the cheek would have sufficed, Sam."

"But it wouldn't have been very convincing. I dare say your admiring suitor wouldn't have departed so quickly if he'd witnessed the sight of someone bestowing a chaste peck on your cheek."

She knew he was right, but she couldn't bring herself to agree with him. "Well, you didn't have to resort to such despicable tactics," she grumbled.

His eyes narrowed with suspicion. "And just how were my tactics despicable?"

"It was the *way* you kissed me, Sam!" She floundered, groping for the right words. "It was much too bold, much too . . . *convincing*."

"Wasn't that what you wanted me to do?" he asked with mock innocence.

"Of course not!" She yearned to slap that impudent grin from his lips. "I never asked you to kiss me like we were long-lost lovers who had just been reunited!"

"So you didn't *like* the way I kissed you?" he pressed on.

"I never said that," she denied, feeling a heated flush rise to her cheeks. "But it was entirely inappropriate!"

"I suppose you should know all about inappropriate kisses." There was a touch of smugness, a hint of playful teasing, in his tone that infuriated Kate beyond reason. "Considering you've probably been exposed to a great deal of suitors who were anxious to steal kisses from—"

"All of my suitors are well-versed in the proper way to kiss a lady," she informed him, bristling with defiance. "They treat me with the utmost respect, and they never take advantage of me. And never once have any of them kissed me so . . . so . . . so savagely!"

All traces of amusement vanished from his lips and eyes. "That's the way I kiss, Kate." His voice became gruff and low. "It's the only way I know how to kiss a woman."

"Well, you didn't have to act like you were enjoying yourself so much," she muttered.

"For God's sake, Kate, *you* were the one who wanted me to pretend like I was having a good time!" His face reddened with fury. "What did you expect?"

"I expected something milder. Something not so wild and heated and passionate and—"

"Damnation, Kate!" he roared. "I gave you exactly what you asked for."

"No, you didn't. You took advantage of the situation," she countered hotly. "I'll know better than to ever ask you to kiss me again."

"You don't have to worry about me kissing you anymore," Sam assured her. "I wouldn't even consider the thought. I'll reserve my affections for a woman who will appreciate me more than someone like you!"

They were still standing face to face, glaring at each other in frigid silence, when Tyler quietly stepped up beside them.

"Well, I see you two are having a pleasant chat," he observed, nearly strangling on his laughter.

"Sam started it," Kate claimed.

"Kate aggravated it," Sam declared.

"I see." Tyler's gaze swung from Kate to Sam and back again. "For some strange reason, I feel like I've stepped back in time. Do either of you ever remember having this conversation before?"

Visions of childhood spats and squabbles flashed through Kate's mind. But as she stood there, glaring at Sam, the absurdity of the situation hit her with full force. And when she detected a twitching motion at one corner of Sam's mouth, she burst into laughter. "Dear heavens, you would think we were children again!"

"Pitiful, aren't we?" Grinning, he shook his head in disbelief. "Five minutes together, and we're ready to strangle each other."

"At least you're here. I will give you credit for that," she teased, curling a ringlet around her finger. "And what about Caroline? Is she here, too?"

"She's upstairs, finishing her afternoon nap. I suspect she should be awakening soon." Sam's smile faded away. "Something tells me I should check on her. Waking up in a strange place might be frightening for a little girl all by herself."

"Then we'll see you back at the house," Kate said.

As Sam retreated back to Hopewell House, Tyler held out his arm to Kate. "Shall we return to our party now?"

Nodding, Kate fell into step beside her brother-in-law. The crowd was waning now, and she sensed that the party would be over soon.

Inhaling a deep, steadying breath, Kate swept across the grounds to bid good-bye to the remaining guests.

# Chapter 4

〜〜・⚬⚬〜〜

**T**wilight was settling over Hopewell House by the time the last of the guests had bid their good-byes, climbed into their buggies, and driven away from the mansion.

Kate ambled across the lawn, grateful that the staff of Tyler's hotel had furnished the food and the service for the festivities. Between the chefs' mouth-watering delicacies and the efficiency of the workers who were now clearing the grounds, Kate had no doubts why The McRae had garnered a reputation as the finest lodging and dining establishment in all of Rome.

Satisfied that the party had been a smashing success, Kate retreated into the house for the evening. Just as she entered the foyer, Sam clambered down the stairs, holding a little girl in his arms. Two chubby fingers were wedged into the child's mouth, and her eyes were wide with wonder.

"Looks like you have your hands full, Sam," Kate observed with a wry smile, gliding to a halt beside the staircase. "I can't believe how much Caroline has grown in the last six months."

"She's getting to be a handful—in more ways than one." Chuckling, Sam shifted his daughter's weight from one arm to the other. "She's been refusing to take her afternoon naps this week. But by the end of the day, she's so exhausted that she falls asleep at the dinner table."

Kate affectionately tweaked the end of the child's nose. "I never liked to take naps, either, Caroline. I was afraid I might miss something. Your daddy was a devious little rascal, and I suspected he might play a trick on me while I was sleeping."

"Don't believe anything this woman tells you, Caroline." A glimmer of amusement sparkled from Sam's eyes. "Kate was the mischievous one. She was always getting me into trouble."

"Me—mischievous?" Kate blinked with mock innocence. "You're one to talk, Samuel Springer."

At that instant, Caroline squirmed beneath the tight grip of her father's arm and lunged for his cravat. Coiling the ends of the silk fabric around her fingers, she unbeknowingly tightened the cravat around Sam's neck.

"No, no, Caroline." Sam hastily pulled her hand away from the neck cloth. "You're choking me to death."

Caroline shrunk back, her lower lip protruding. Loosening the tight loop around his neck, Sam heaved a weary sigh.

"I'm afraid Caroline has been out of sorts ever since she woke up from her nap this afternoon," he said. "She wasn't very happy to find out that she'd missed Aunt Odelphia's party."

"I don't blame her. If I'd slept through a party, I'd be disappointed, too." Kate couldn't resist brushing a hand over the child's wayward curls. "But Caroline can still celebrate Aunt Odie's birthday along with the rest of us in the parlor. I suspect Julia will be ready for Aunt Odelphia to open her presents at any moment now."

"Caroline will probably enjoy all the excitement." A nostalgic expression flickered across Sam's face. "I know I've never forgotten the first time I attended a party at Hopewell House."

"How could anyone forget my seventh birthday?" Kate's laughter rang through the foyer. "Instead of playing games, we chased hogs in the garden. All on account of you, I might add."

"Now, don't go blaming me for spoiling your party, Kate. How could I have known that the damn latch on the hog pen wouldn't hold?"

"Still, you were the one to blame for that dreadful mess. And by the time we got the hogs back into the pen, everyone was covered with mud from head to toe. You even had a big glob of mud in your hair."

"But all that red Georgia clay couldn't have been too noticeable," Sam reasoned. "Back then, my hair was just about the same color as Caroline's."

Kate's eyes twinkled as she gazed down at the little girl. "I bet you didn't know that your daddy's hair used to be the same color as yours, Caroline."

Something akin to understanding flickered across the child's face just before she reached out and grabbed a fistful of her father's hair. Sam gave a yelp, wincing in pain as Caroline yanked on the auburn strands.

"Maybe Caroline knows more than we think," Kate mused, biting her lower lip to keep from laughing aloud.

Struggling to pry the child's fingers from his hair, Sam shot a murderous glance in Kate's direction.

Kate made a quick dash for the stairs, hoping

to escape before Sam could accuse her of instigating Caroline's antics. Laughing, she scurried into her room and retrieved a small package from her dresser.

A smile was still lingering on her lips when she swept into the parlor a few moments later. Just as Kate placed her present for Odelphia on a small table, Sam entered the room with Caroline.

"I appreciate all your help, Kate." The mocking tone in his voice was accompanied by a rueful grin. "Thanks for skipping out on me while my daughter was pulling my hair out by the roots."

"Anytime, Sam." Biting back a smile, Kate settled down on the sofa with Sam and Caroline as rest of the clan trekked into the parlor.

Within a few moments, Odelphia and Dorinda were occupying a settee near the windows, while Tyler and Julia were seated in matching wing chairs beside the fireplace. Standing between the couple was their eldest child, twelve-year-old Rebecca.

Judging by the distraught expression on the girl's face, Kate suspected her niece was torn between maintaining the poise of a young lady or plopping down on the floor beside her younger siblings in a most unladylike fashion.

At the moment, Jeremiah was sprawled across the floor, anxiously waiting to present his gift to Odelphia. Little Emily, seated next to her older brother, was clutching a small parcel to her chest.

"What a wonderful day this has been!" Dorinda affectionately patted her sister's wrinkled hand. "I never dreamed anyone's seventy-fifth birthday party could be so much fun, Odie."

"I never dreamed I would be around long enough to have a seventy-fifth birthday," Odelphia quipped. "But it's been well worth the wait, I must admit. I enjoyed myself so much today that I didn't want the party to end."

"But your birthday isn't over yet, Aunt Odelphia," Julia pointed out.

"We've got lots of gifts for you, Aunt Odie!" Jeremiah leaped to his feet and darted across the room. Grinning impishly, he shoved a package into Odelphia's hand. "I picked this out all by myself."

Emily trailed closely behind her brother. "Open my present first, Aunt Odie!" she pleaded.

"I hope you'll like my gift," Rebecca added, scurrying toward her aunt. "I made it just for you."

Odelphia delved into the gifts, shrieking with delight as she unwrapped each present. She raved over the pendant from Emily, praised Jeremiah for presenting her with a new pair of white gloves, and admired the fine handiwork on the dainty lace collar that Rebecca had crocheted for her.

And a parasol hidden beneath the wrappings of Sam's package brought a smile to Odelphia's lips. "Why, thank you, Sam. And you, too, Caroline. I don't think I've ever seen a parasol as lovely as this one."

At the sound of her name, Caroline drew closer to Sam and burrowed her face into his side. Sam draped a comforting arm around the child's narrow shoulders, acutely aware of her discomfort.

He'd hoped Caroline would sense all the warmth and love that flowed so freely in this room. But it seemed as if the noise and commotion had overwhelmed the child.

Sam scowled, silently cursing himself. He should've realized that Caroline wasn't accustomed to being surrounded by crowds of people. After all, she'd never lived in a home where the sound of laughter was commonplace. Never known the joy of being loved by a large, boisterous family like this one, a family who cherished each other with all of their hearts.

It wasn't that Sam ignored his daughter or withheld his affections for her. On the contrary, he lavished the child with all of his love and attention. But compared to the liveliness of Hopewell House, their home in Macon seemed as dismal and silent as an ancient tomb.

Caroline remained silent while Odelphia opened the rest of her gifts. But as the party continued, Sam noticed that the child's gaze frequently strayed in Kate's direction.

Gauging the expressions on his daughter's face, he sensed that Kate was becoming more and more fascinating to Caroline with each passing moment.

He shifted uneasily. Dozens of grown men had fallen prey to Kate's charms. So what impressionable little girl wouldn't be drawn to a woman whose laughter blew like fresh breezes across the room? Whose smile could steal the most unsuspecting heart? A woman whose alluring scent bore the haunting fragrance of summer roses?

At that moment, the sound of Julia's voice broke into his thoughts. "It's time to get to bed now, children. You've stayed up way past your bedtimes."

Amid groans of protest, the three youngsters bid goodnight to their elders and trekked up the stairs while Sam scooped Caroline into his arms.

"It's time for you to get to bed, too, young lady. You've had a long day."

After tucking Caroline into bed for the night, Sam returned to the parlor. He had just sat down on the sofa when Dorinda glanced over at him.

"I do hope you're planning to stay for more than just a day or so, Sam. We'd like to get to know that dear child of yours."

"I'd like for her to become better acquainted with all of you, too. She's a wonderful little girl." A shadow of concern crossed Sam's face. "But she's been quite defiant since Abigail's death. I'd like to think that she's just growing up, but sometimes I wonder if she's developing a stubborn streak."

Dorinda shook her head in dismay. "The poor little tyke. She must miss her mother terribly." A glimmer of sympathy shone from her eyes as she gazed at Sam. "Of course, I know you're doing all you can to provide a wonderful home for her."

"It's not always easy." Sam raked a hand through his hair. "In fact, I'm looking for someone to take care of Caroline while I'm at work during the day."

Julia leaned forward in her chair, her face awash with dismay. "You don't have anyone to care for Caroline?"

"Not at the moment." He shifted uncomfortably. "My housekeeper—who is also Caroline's nanny—received a wire from her family in Savannah this week. It seems her mother is gravely ill, and she's been called home to care for her. I'm hoping she'll eventually return to Macon. But in the meantime, I need to find a replacement for her."

"But you don't want to hire just anyone to care for Caroline!" Kate shuddered at the thought. "Surely you wouldn't entrust that precious child to a stranger."

"I don't have any choice, Kate." Sam shrugged with resignation. "Besides, I'm certain there are plenty of respectable women who would be willing to care for a child and a house—and be paid handsomely for it."

"Sounds like you need a wife, Sam," Tyler mused, trying to bite back a smile.

"A wife? Hardly." Sam's wry chuckle faded away, and a troubled frown wrinkled his brow. "No, I need someone who doesn't require anything from me except a weekly payment for her services. I need someone who can tend to the routine chores of running a household. A woman who will cook my meals, launder my clothes, clean my house."

"But what about . . . Caroline?" Kate asked.

"Caring for Caroline would be my housekeeper's primary responsibility. My daughter's welfare takes precedence over everything else."

A pensive silence swept through the group. Odelphia gazed at Kate for a long moment, studying her intently. "You know, maybe you could lend a hand to Sam and Caroline for a while, Kate," she finally suggested.

"Me?" Kate's eyes widened in stunned disbelief.

"Why not?" Odelphia challenged. "You could care for Caroline for a few days while Sam is looking for a new housekeeper."

"What a marvelous idea, Odie!" Dorinda exclaimed.

Kate's shock gave way to a spurt of laughter. "I don't think Sam is desperate enough to take me back to Macon with him. Besides, I'm certain he can make arrangements for Caroline's care without any help from me."

"And I believe I need someone with a bit more housekeeping experience," Sam added, grinning meaningfully.

"I may not be as inept at running a household as you think." Bristling at his implication, Kate forced a strained smile onto her lips. "Of course, you'll never have the opportunity to find out what a wonderful housekeeper I could be."

"What a pity." A mocking gleam twinkled from Sam's eyes. "Something tells me it would be an experience that I would never forget."

"You might be surprised, Sam." A hint of smugness appeared on the slight curve of her mouth. "I'm perfectly capable of taking care of household tasks."

"Really, now?" Sam chuckled. "For some reason, I thought you would shy away from any sort of task that might chip one of your nails."

She stiffened. "And how would you know? You haven't lived at Hopewell House for quite some time now."

"But I know you, Kate. You wouldn't enjoy

the mundane tasks of cleaning house every day."

"No one enjoys cleaning house," Kate countered. With each passing moment, she was becoming more and more irritated with Sam's heartless teasing. Did he think she was some mindless little fool who was incapable of lifting a finger around the house?

"And I also need someone with experience in caring for children," Sam continued on. "Someone who has the patience to contend with an inquisitive little girl."

Kate's eyes narrowed with suspicion. "Are you implying that I'm not qualified to care for your daughter?"

He grinned. "You're not exactly the most patient person in the world, Kate."

"I'm well aware of what it takes to raise a child. You're just too blind to see that I could be a wonderful influence on Caroline." Stinging from his offensive remarks, she glared at him. "Of course, I'd never agree to any arrangement that would require me to answer to someone like you."

"Personally, I don't think Odelphia's suggestion should be dismissed so hastily," Tyler interjected. "In fact, I think the arrangement might be beneficial for both of you."

"Beneficial?" Kate echoed. "How?"

"It would solve the problem of your boredom, for one," Tyler explained. "Just this afternoon, you told me you were looking for a meaningful way to spend your time. You said you needed some sort of challenge that would bring fulfillment to your life."

"Scrubbing floors for Sam isn't exactly what I had in mind," Kate mumbled, cringing at the thought.

"But it's a practical solution for everyone," Odelphia reasoned. "Sam, you need someone to look after Caroline. And Kate, you need a sense of purpose in life. Working with each other, both of you could solve all of your problems."

"It sounds perfectly sensible to me," Dorinda chimed in.

"But practicality and sensibility aren't necessarily the most important issues to consider," Sam noted in a strained voice. "It seems to me that everyone is overlooking the most important issue of all."

Julia frowned in confusion. "What's that, Sam?"

"Compatibility." He regarded Kate, wary. "Kate and I can't seem to get along together for more than a few hours without arguing."

"But you haven't spent a great deal of time together since you were children," Julia said. "Now that you're adults, surely you're capable of settling your differences without resorting to heated arguments."

"I doubt it," Kate scoffed. "Sam enjoys tormenting me. He's too stubborn to change."

"And Kate is too accustomed to getting her own way. Her suitors have pampered her for far too long, kissing the hem of her skirts and begging for the chance to cater to her every whim," Sam noted glumly.

"I don't see anything so wrong with that." Kate bristled with defiance. "If a gentleman wants to fetch a glass of lemonade for me, why shouldn't he?"

Sam massaged the nape of his neck and heaved a weary sigh. "You're missing the point, Kate. There isn't anything wrong with someone fetching a glass of lemonade for you. But you can't go through life expecting everyone to treat you like a fairy princess."

Anger flared from Kate's heated gaze, and Sam knew he'd offended her. Anxious to end the discussion, he surged to his feet.

"As much as I appreciate your concern for Caroline and me, I believe it's senseless to pursue the idea of Kate returning to Macon with us. I just don't see any way that the arrangement could work for either Kate or me." Expelling a weary sigh, he forced a strained smile. "It's been a rather long day. If you'll excuse me, I believe I'll turn in for the night."

Without further ado, Sam left the parlor. In the privacy of his room, he shrugged out of his jacket and tossed the garment aside.

He sank onto the edge of the bed, shaking his head in bemused disbelief. Though he adored Odelphia Hopewell, he suspected that the dear soul was becoming a bit daft. Why else would she suggest that Kate return to Macon with him?

The last thing he wanted—or needed—was someone like Kate in his life. Living under the same roof with the woman would be nothing short of disastrous. Kathryn Carey would turn his life upside down within the space of a heartbeat. He was certain of it.

He smiled contentedly, confident there would be no more discussion about the matter. Considering that he hadn't hesitated to voice his opposition to the absurd idea, he felt certain that he'd permanently banished the preposterous notion from everyone's mind.

Eased by those comforting thoughts, he swiftly prepared for bed.

"We missed you at breakfast, Kate." Sitting at the table, leisurely dawdling over a cup of coffee, Julia greeted her sister with a warm smile as she entered the dining room the next morning.

Yawning, Kate sank into a chair beside Julia. "I would've liked eating breakfast with everyone this morning, but I couldn't seem to drag myself out of bed. I suppose I was exhausted from all of the excitement around here yesterday."

"Or maybe you had too much on your mind," Julia suggested. "Were you reconsidering Aunt Odie's suggestion about going to Macon with Sam?"

"There's nothing else to consider, Julia. Sam and I can't stay in the same room together for more than five minutes without clawing each other's eyes out."

"Your discussion with Sam became rather heated at times last night, I noticed." Julia took a sip of her coffee. "But you defended yourself quite nicely."

"It infuriates me to think that Sam doesn't believe I'm capable of taking care of anything—or anyone—other than myself. I'm tempted to go back to Macon with him, if for no other reason than to prove him wrong." Shrugging, she promptly dismissed the matter. "Is there anything here for me to eat? I'm absolutely starving!"

"Aunt Dorinda left one pastry, I see." Julia passed a serving platter to Kate. "And here are some biscuits and a few slices of ham."

Kate filled her plate from the remaining breakfast leftovers. "So where is everybody this morning?"

"Tyler and Sam left for the hotel a few minutes ago. They're planning to stay for lunch at the restaurant. Sam seemed like he was looking forward to seeing the hotel again, but I think he's more anxious to go fishing this afternoon, down by the creek.''

''I should've known Sam wouldn't miss the chance to fish while he's here.'' Kate nibbled on a bite of ham. ''And what about everybody else?''

''The children decided to spend the morning in the playhouse, and Odelphia and Dorinda insisted on taking Caroline for a walk,'' Julia explained. ''But Caroline seemed a little hesitant to join—''

''Wait, Caroline!'' Dorinda's voice sliced through the air just as a pair of tiny footsteps pattered across the foyer.

Odelphia sounded more frantic than her sister. ''Don't be frightened, child!''

At that instant, Caroline stumbled into the dining room. Kate glanced up and froze, stunned by the sight of the little girl.

She looked like a tattered angel. Her gown was ripped, her shoes scuffed, her hair knotted and tangled. A piece of white stocking dangled by a single thread over one chubby leg. Her face was flushed, and her wide, frightened eyes were brimming with unshed tears.

Within the next moment, Caroline was darting across the room as if the devil himself were nipping at her heels. She lunged for Kate, burying her face into her lap with a muffled sob.

"She took an awful tumble in the rose garden," Odelphia explained, gasping for breath as she rushed into the room.

"She tripped over something and fell down." Dorinda scurried behind her sister, dabbing beads of perspiration from her brow with a lace-trimmed hanky.

"And then she took off, running for the house as fast as those little legs would carry her," Odelphia added.

"So you took a tumble, did you?" Kate lifted the frightened child into her arms. "Let me see, sweetheart."

Bravely sniffing back her tears, Caroline held out the palm of her hand. A few dots of crimson oozed from a small, jagged scrape.

"We'll get you doctored up in no time at all, Caroline." Kate swiftly doused a napkin in a glass of water, then dabbed away the droplets of blood. "Are you hurting anywhere else?"

Nodding, Caroline held up her leg.

"Looks like your stockings got snagged on some thorns," Kate surmised. "Is that what happened?"

Caroline nodded again, then leaned her head against Kate's shoulder.

"How sad." Kate rested her chin on the soft crown of the child's head. "It breaks my heart, knowing she doesn't have a mother to kiss away her tears or bandage up her scratches."

"It breaks my heart, too." Julia gazed thoughtfully at her sister. "But maybe there is someone who could do all of those things— and more—for Caroline. Temporarily, of course."

Kate ran a finger across the child's satin-soft cheek, considering the possibilities. "Maybe there is, Julia," she agreed. "Maybe there is."

# Chapter 5

❦

"**R**ebecca and I are having a tea party at the playhouse this afternoon," Emily announced during lunch. Leaning forward in her chair, she reached for a platter of cookies in the center of the dining room table. "Do you think Caroline would like to come, Aunt Kate?"

"What a wonderful idea, Emily!" Kate smiled as she sliced a small portion of ham into bite-size pieces for Caroline. "I imagine she's never been to a tea party, but I'm certain it would be lots of fun for her."

"You could serve lemonade instead of tea, if you'd like," Odelphia suggested. "We have several gallons of lemonade left over from my birthday party. And we should have plenty of birthday cake left, too."

"B-B-Birthday cake?" Dorinda echoed in a tiny voice.

Odelphia cast a stern glance at her sister.

"Don't tell me that you've eaten all of the leftover cake, Dorie."

"Well, not exactly." Dorinda dabbed a napkin over her lips and nervously cleared her throat. "I had a little piece for a midnight snack, but I think there should be enough left for the girls' tea party."

"It's Emily's party, not mine," Rebecca insisted. "I offered to help her, but I'm getting too old to pretend like I'm having a tea party."

"Ladies are never too old for tea parties, Rebecca," Julia said with a smile.

"What about you, Jeremiah?" Emily turned to her brother. "Are you coming to the party, too?"

The boy shuddered. "Are you kidding? I wouldn't be caught dead at a tea party with a bunch of girls." Bolting to his feet, Jeremiah darted out of the room.

Emily rolled her eyes heavenward. "Boys," she muttered in disgust.

Odelphia laughed. "If Jeremiah doesn't come to your party, you'll have lots more cake to eat, you know."

Emily's face brightened. "I hadn't thought about that."

"I suppose I could take the food to the playhouse for you now, Emily," Rebecca offered.

"And I'll set the table and get everything ready for our guests." Emily scrambled down from her chair. "Can you fix a pitcher of lemonade for us, Mother?"

"Of course, dear. I'll bring it to you shortly."

After clearing the table, Odelphia and Dorinda carried the soiled luncheon plates to the kitchen. A few minutes later, Julia left the room to prepare a pitcher of drinks for the tea party.

Suddenly aware of the empty chairs around the table, Kate glanced over at Caroline. The child was still eating her lunch, nibbling on a piece of ham and contentedly licking her fingers.

And no one else was here to watch the child except . . . Kate.

"Looks like we're stuck with each other for the rest of the afternoon, Miss Caroline." Laughing, Kate wiped off the child's face and hands with a napkin, then planted a kiss on the end of her nose. "And we're having dessert in the playhouse. You're going to your first tea party!"

A few moments later, Kate was guiding Caroline across the lawn in the direction of the playhouse. The child meandered through the grass, her short legs wobbling precociously, one tiny hand curled around Kate's outstretched finger.

Approaching the playhouse, Caroline's baby pink lips rounded with awe. Fascinated by the dwarf-size features of the building, she toddled closer, curious.

A white frame structure nestled beneath the shade of a giant maple tree, the playhouse was a one-room, miniature version of Hopewell House. A pair of small Doric columns graced the entrance, and black shutters framed the windows. Though Tyler had built the cottage as a playhouse for Kate and her friends long ago, the little building continued to provide endless hours of delight for Julia's children.

Ushering Caroline into the cottage, Kate noticed that Emily was playing the role of hostess to perfection.

"Would you like to join us for a cup of tea, my dear?" Emily's voice warbled in a high-pitched falsetto.

Rebecca placed a small slice of cake on the table. "We have some wonderful goodies to eat, too," she said, playing along with the game.

Caroline gaped in disbelief at the small table and matching chairs. Eyeing the tiny tea cups and saucers that were just her size, she edged forward.

But after taking one step across the room, she stopped cold. An expression of confusion and fear flickered across her features, and then she whirled around and scampered back to Kate, burying her face in the folds of her skirt.

An ache squeezed Kate's heart. Caroline was pressing up against her legs so tightly that she could feel little ripples of fear coursing through the child's small frame.

"Did I say something wrong?" Distress flooded Emily's voice and face.

"You said just the right things, Emily." Kate brushed her fingers over the mop of carrot-red curls nestled against her gown. "I suspect Caroline doesn't have the chance to play with other children very often. And she doesn't know us very well, I'm afraid. All of us are practically strangers to her."

"Maybe Caroline would feel more comfortable if she sat with you, Kate," Rebecca suggested.

"Maybe so," Kate agreed, sweeping the child into her arms. "Let's give it a try."

The girls resumed their play, offering refreshments to their guests, filling the little cottage with giggles and chatter.

But the merry atmosphere had little effect on Caroline. Much to Kate's surprise and dismay, the child refused to join in the fun.

Though she sipped lemonade from a tiny tea cup and nibbled on a slice of cake, nothing about the party seemed to interest her. Restless and discontent, the child squirmed and twisted in Kate's lap, ignoring her pleas to sit still.

Struggling to appease the fretful toddler, Kate planted a bright smile on her lips. "Would you like to join the girls at the table now, Caroline?"

Defiance glimmered from the little girl's eyes. "No!"

"Then are you ready to go back to the house?"

"No!"

Kate's smile faded away. Obviously, Caroline didn't know what she wanted. Suspecting the child was sorely in need of some rest, Kate rose to her feet. "I'm afraid Caroline and I can't stay any longer, girls," she said in an apologetic tone.

"Don't leave now, Aunt Kate!" Emily pleaded. "We're just getting started."

"I'd like to stay, Emily, truly I would." Kate tightened her hold around the squirming tyke. "But Caroline is getting fretful, and I think it's time for me to put her down for a nap. She needs to get some rest this afternoon."

Hoping to soothe the child's restless spirits, Kate prepared a tub of warm water for Caroline as soon as she returned to the house.

But not even the prospect of bathing appealed to Caroline. As soon as Kate stripped off the child's clothes, Caroline jutted out her chin with defiance.

"No bath," she announced with a shake of her head.

"You'll rest better after you've soaked in the tub for a little while," Kate explained as gently as she could. "And besides, all of us have to do things we don't want to do at times. I'm sure you'll—"

"No bath," Caroline repeated firmly.

"You don't know what you're missing, Caroline," Kate taunted, pouring a few drops of rosewater into the tub.

Just as Kate had hoped, the fragrant rosewater scent attracted the girl's attention. Caroline edged forward and curiously peered into the water. Seizing advantage of the moment, Kate swiftly gathered the child into her arms and set her into the tub.

But within a few minutes, Kate regretted that she'd ever considered bathing the child. Caroline wiggled and squirmed, splashing water onto the floor and drenching Kate's face and blouse. And when Kate attempted to wash her hair, the child shrieked in dismay.

Kate sighed in frustration as she pulled the child from the tub and dried her off with a thick towel. Tending to her nieces and nephew on occasion had been effortless compared to the daunting task of assuming total responsibility for one little girl.

Caroline whined and whimpered as Kate combed the tangles from her hair. But to Kate's astonishment, she readily agreed to wear the blue frock that Kate had chosen for her.

"At least we agree on something, Caroline," Kate teased, slipping the dress over the girl's head.

A few moments later, Kate realized why Caroline hadn't offered any protests against the blue dress. Exhausted and spent, the little girl had been too weary to instigate any further arguments. She'd drifted off to sleep almost as soon as her head had touched the pillow on the bed.

Gazing down at the child, Kate felt an overwhelming sense of satisfaction. Though caring for Caroline had been much more of a challenge than she'd expected, she had no doubts that she possessed the patience and stamina to tend to the child, no matter how cross and fretful the little girl might be. If Sam only knew . . .

But Sam didn't know, Kate realized with a start. Though she'd proven to herself that she was capable of caring for Caroline, Sam had no way of knowing that she'd taken charge of his daughter with the gentle firmness and loving care of an experienced nanny throughout the afternoon. He hadn't been around to see what had transpired between Kate and his daughter.

Judging from Sam's relentless teasing since his arrival at Hopewell House, Kate suspected he still regarded her as the pampered little girl who'd badgered and taunted him in his childhood. And she sensed he always would, unless he was forced to look at her in a new light.

Kate lifted her chin, suddenly determined to avenge Sam's claims about her. God help her, she'd show Sam that she possessed the substance of a mature young woman, a woman who could care for his daughter with far more diligence and devotion than any hired house-keeper or nanny possibly could.

And in the end, it would be such sweet victory. Nothing would give her any more satisfaction than making Samuel Springer eat his own words. Kate smiled, envisioning the joy of hearing Sam's apology, anticipating the delight of hearing him admit he'd been wrong.

Kate dropped a kiss on Caroline's cheek and quietly slipped out of the room. Other than her determination to change Sam's way of thinking about her, she wasn't exactly certain why she'd decided to return to Macon with Sam and take charge of his daughter.

Rationally, it didn't make a lick of sense. She and Sam rarely agreed on anything, and proba-bly never would. Living under the same roof, Kate suspected they'd drive each other insane within a very short time.

But how else could she prove to Sam that she was something more—much more, in fact—than a pampered flirt with a penchant for parties? And what better way to prove him wrong than by showing him what a wonderful influence she could be on his daughter?

Kate swept down the stairs, convinced that she was making the right decision. After all, it wasn't as if the arrangement would be a per-manent one. More than likely, her stay in

Macon wouldn't last for very long. She would be returning to Rome just as soon as Sam found a replacement for his housekeeper.

Suspecting she could find Sam at his favorite fishing hole, Kate pulled back her shoulders and hurled open the door. She was certain she could handle Sam's objections to her plans. It would take a great deal of persuasion, but she was confident she could counter his arguments with some convincing facts of her own.

She picked up her skirts, threading her way through the thicket of trees at the edge of the Hopewell property. Approaching the creek, she saw Sam.

He was sprawled out on a large boulder, his fingers curled around a wooden fishing pole. Dappled sunlight splayed across his hair, highlighting the rich auburn hues. A dark green shirt spanned the width of his broad shoulders, and snug-fitting jeans hugged the length of his long legs.

The rustle of Kate's footsteps captured Sam's attention. He glanced up in surprise and grinned. "Kate!"

"Well, Samuel Springer! Imagine finding you here!"

Chuckling, he bolted to his feet. "Something tells me you're not as surprised as you're pretending to be."

Kate laughed. "Julia told me that you'd planned on fishing this afternoon."

He held out his hand, helping her onto the boulder. "I haven't had the chance to fish in a long time," he said, "and I thought I'd see if the fish were still biting around my old fishing hole."

"Having any luck?" She grasped his hand more tightly to steady her balance and lowered herself to the boulder.

"I'm afraid not." He picked up his fishing pole and sat down beside her. "I must be losing my touch."

She fanned out the hem of her gown around her. "I suppose fishing is a good way to relax. And it gives you a chance to think, too."

"I'm not too keen on the idea of thinking about anything at the moment. In fact, I've been trying to forget about all my troubles."

"You mean . . . finding a nanny for Caroline?"

A shadow of darkness flickered across his face. "It isn't easy to forget that I don't have someone to care for Caroline while I'm at work. One of my neighbors—an older lady who recently lost her husband—has volunteered to sit with Caroline for a few hours at a time. But I need someone who will be available for more than a few hours a day. And I need to find someone soon. The longer it takes for me to locate a new housekeeper, the more my work will mount up."

"I don't think you should be overly concerned about finding someone to care for Caroline." Kate's voice was full of brightness, even to her own ears.

But her optimism evoked a scowl on his face. "It's not as easy as it sounds. I need someone who can be on call, twenty-four hours a day, someone who can—"

"I know exactly what you need." She beamed at him. "You need *me*."

"You? Don't be ridiculous, Kate." Sam threw back his head and laughed, a hearty, boisterous laugh that Kate found unsettling. "We settled the matter last night. For once in our lives, we finally managed to agree on something."

"But that was last night," she reminded him. "I've been looking at the situation from a new perspective this morning, and I—"

"The idea is still preposterous, no matter how you look at it."

"But now that I've had the chance to think about it, the arrangement doesn't seem ridiculous at all. In fact, I've changed my mind about the matter." She inhaled a deep breath, then spilled out the words quickly. "I've decided I'm going to Macon with you and Caroline."

Sam's smile vanished. "Like hell you are," he growled.

She flashed her sweetest smile at him, determined to remain undaunted by his scathing glare. She'd fully expected he would scoff at her proposal, and she planned to present a convincing case. "I intend to be quite useful to you, Sam. After all, I'm quite accomplished at many things."

He snorted. "Such as?"

"I'm a wonderful writer, for one. Everyone in town says my weekly column for the *Rome News-Tribune* is the best part about the entire newspaper. If you need anything written for your work, I could—"

"I don't need anyone writing my legal briefs for me," Sam snapped.

"And I know all about fashion," she rushed on, acting as if he hadn't interrupted her at all. "Everyone insists I have a wonderful sense of style. I'm certain Caroline must need some new dresses from time to time, since she's growing by leaps and bounds. And I know I could help with—"

"I don't need someone to design my daughter's clothes," he interrupted gruffly. "There are plenty of seamstresses in Macon who are capable of making dresses for little girls."

"And I have lots of experience as a hostess," she continued, blithely ignoring his remarks once again. "I planned Aunt Odelphia's birthday party, you know. And it was a smashing success. I could help you entertain your—"

"I don't need a hostess to help me entertain anyone," Sam countered irritably. "I don't give parties."

The natural arch of her brows rose higher.

"You don't socialize with your clients and law partners?"

"Occasionally." He shrugged. "I manage to mingle with them at a dinner or party every now and then. But I don't host any social events."

"Well, maybe you should." She reached out and ran her fingers across the neck of his shirt. "It wouldn't hurt if you loosened up that stiff collar of yours once in a while, Sam. You're getting too stodgy."

"Stodgy?" He glared at her in disbelief. "What makes you think I'm stodgy?"

"You don't laugh as much as you used to." Edging closer, she peered into his face and sighed with dismay. "In fact, I do believe you're getting a permanent crease in your forehead," she pointed out, running an imaginary line along his brow with the tip of her finger, "from frowning so much."

"Well, maybe I have good reasons for frowning," he countered. "This may come as a surprise to you, Kate, but everyone's life doesn't consist of one party after another. Some of us don't have the luxury of devoting all of our time to social obligations and charity balls. Some of us are too busy dealing with other, more important issues."

"I'm well aware that life consists of more than parties and teas, Sam. I'm not as naive as you think." Struggling to hide her annoyance, she attempted to keep her voice on an even keel. "I know you've been contending with more than your fair share of problems lately. Shouldering all the responsibilities of raising a child by yourself couldn't be easy. And I'd like to help, Sam. Truly, I would."

Sam regarded her, wary. What did she know of heartache and worries? Kathryn Carey had lived a charmed life, free of the problems and pain that plagued most everyone else. Why shouldn't she possess a spirit of sunshine? She knew nothing about the cruelties of life. Nothing at all.

Still, her willingness to reach out to him aroused his curiosity. "Why in the hell are you offering to be my housekeeper?"

She lifted one shoulder in a breezy shrug. "I've been longing for a change, Sam. I want my life to count for something. I want more than what I have here in Rome."

"You want *more?*" He gaped at her in disbelief. "Look around you, Kate! Open your eyes! Can't you see that you already have everything you could ever want? You have the whole world at your beck and call. You have a beautiful home, a family who adores you. You have scores of friends who admire you, dozens of suitors vying for your attention."

"But that's precisely my point, Sam! Yes, I have everything—but that doesn't leave room for any challenges in my life. Tending to your house and caring for your daughter would give me the sense of purpose that I've been looking for."

Skepticism flickered across his face. "What's the real reason for wanting to go to Macon with me, Kate?" he probed. "What's behind this sudden, burning desire of yours? Are you expecting to make some new friends? See some new places? Maybe even steal a few kisses from some unsuspecting fools?"

"I've already told you why I want to go to Macon with you. I want to be there for Caroline's sake, to restore some order to your household until you can find a permanent housekeeper. But if I happen to make some new friends, see some new places, or steal a few kisses along the way, what's so wrong with that?"

"Not a damn thing," he snapped, knowing full well she was right. He hedged for a moment, grappling for a new line of defense to keep her at bay. "Still, you wouldn't be satisfied with living in Macon for very long. It might provide you with a nice diversion for a while, but you'd eventually get bored with it all. And it's not as though you've never visited Macon."

"But I haven't had a chance to see much of the town. I toured the campus at Mercer when you graduated from law school, and I visited your church when you and Abigail got married. Of course, last January, I attended the

services at Rose Hill Cemetery, but . . ." She
forced a bright smile on her lips. "I'm certain
there are lots of sites I haven't seen in Macon."

"But I don't have time to entertain you, Kate!
I can't show you all the places you want to see,
introduce you to all the people you want to
meet. My life is too full of meetings and trials
and obligations. It's a daily grind of contending
with clients and judges, attending trials at the
courthouse, filing papers at city hall. I barely
have enough time to sleep and eat!"

"Which is all the more reason why you need
me," she countered.

He raked a hand through his hair in frustration. "I don't deny that I need some help, Kate.
And I truly appreciate what you're trying to do
for me. It's just that—"

"I don't see why we can't give it a try, Sam. If
for no other reason than Caroline's sake, we
could try to make it work for a while. After all,
what harm could it do? Surely we could get
along together for a few weeks. We've known
each other for such a long time, and—"

"It's no use, Kate," he announced abruptly.
He was well aware of what she was trying to
do, and it infuriated him. He'd rather burn in
hell than allow her to manipulate him with the
persuasiveness of her charms.

She blinked in confusion. "What do you
mean?"

"In case you've forgotten, all your tears and

pouts and sweet-sounding words have never worked on me." He yanked on his fishing pole and jerked the line from the water. "As far as I'm concerned, Caroline and I will be leaving for Macon in the morning. You won't be going with us. And nothing you can say or do will change that."

He bolted to his feet. Propping the fishing pole over his shoulder, he turned to leave.

"You don't know what you're turning down, Samuel Springer," Kate warned. "I could be the best nanny for your daughter that you could ever hope to have."

He paused, peering over his shoulder at her. "But if I agreed to take someone like you home with me, I could be the most foolish man in all of Georgia. And that's a risk I'm not willing to take."

Turning on his heel, he stomped up the creek bank and headed back to Hopewell House.

# Chapter 6

**A**s Sam marched up the creek bank and disappeared from sight, Kate seethed with fury.

Samuel Springer was the most stubborn, infuriating, unreasonable man that she'd ever known in her entire life. For heaven's sake, why couldn't he see that she was perfectly capable of taking care of his daughter?

She stilled, seized by a riveting thought. Sam hadn't actually *seen*, firsthand, that she possessed the patience and stamina to care for Caroline. All of his doubts about her abilities stemmed from his preconceived notions about what she could and couldn't do.

But once he saw the way that she and Caroline responded to each other, surely he wouldn't have the heart to deny his daughter of the most devoted nanny she could ever have.

Kate sprang to her feet with renewed determination. Actions spoke louder than words, and she was convinced that Sam's stubborn resistance would crumble before he left for Macon.

That evening, Sam wouldn't have the chance to ignore all the ways that she could relate to Caroline. And how could he refuse her offer to care for his daughter after witnessing a sample of the attentive care that she could give to the child?

A giddy sense of excitement flooded through her. Confident she could obtain Sam's consent to the arrangement before the end of the day, Kate scurried back to Hopewell House.

If Sam intended to leave for Macon in the morning, she had not a moment to spare.

An hour later, standing in front of the mirror in her room, Kate heard the sound of her sister's voice in the hallway. "May I come in, Kate?"

"Of course!" Kate adjusted the brim of her straw hat as Julia entered the room.

"What in heaven's name . . . ?" Julia stopped cold, her mouth agape, her eyes wide and startled.

Following the direction of Julia's stunned gaze, Kate bit back a smile. The room resembled the aftermath of a cyclone.

Corsets dangled from the bedposts. Gowns in every color of the rainbow blanketed the bed. Mismatched pairs of shoes and gloves carpeted the floor. Hats and parasols cluttered the dresser top, and stockings and petticoats covered the chairs.

Bemused that she'd managed to create such a ghastly mess while sorting through her wardrobe, Kate couldn't contain her laughter. "Quite a sight, isn't it?"

Julia shook her head in disbelief. "That's an understatement, Kate."

Kate spun around and peered into the mirror once again. Examining her reflection with a critical eye, she adjusted the straw hat on her head. "Maybe you could give me some sisterly advice, Julia. Do you think I should take this hat to Macon with me?"

"Macon?" Julia gingerly tiptoed around the garments that littered the floor. "You're going to Macon?"

Kate nodded absently. "But I don't know if I have anything to wear with this hat."

"Surely you can find something—somewhere—that would be suitable."

"I hope so. It's hard to decide what to take and what to leave here at home, especially since I don't know how long I'll be gone."

"And it's hard for me to believe that you've actually decided to go." Shoving aside several gowns, Julia lowered herself to the edge of the bed. "As I recall, you and Sam seemed appalled by the idea last night."

"It didn't sound very appealing to me at the time. But, obviously, I've changed my mind." Kate tossed the straw hat into a large steamer trunk that was filled to the brim with an assortment of garments.

"I'm not too surprised, after seeing the look on your face when Caroline latched onto your skirts this morning." A slight frown marred Julia's brow. "But I'm a bit amazed that Sam changed his mind, too. He certainly wasn't shy about voicing his opposition to the idea last night."

Nodding absently, Kate rummaged through an assortment of garments in a large cherry wardrobe. "I'm certain Sam will be coming to his senses soon."

Julia's eyes widened in confusion. "You haven't talked to Sam about this?"

"We discussed the matter this afternoon while he was fishing down by the creek." She retrieved a frilly blouse from the wardrobe. "Of course, he didn't actually agree that I should go with him, but—"

"Sam hasn't given his consent to this arrangement?"

Kate winced. "Not exactly. But I'm sure he'll eventually concede to the idea."

"Aren't you being a bit presumptuous, Kate?" Julia rose, frowning with concern. "On one hand, you admit Sam hasn't agreed that you go to Macon with him. Yet you're already packing for the trip!"

"I'd prefer to think I'm being confident and optimistic rather than presumptuous."

"But why are you so confident that Sam will change his mind?"

"Because I know Sam loves his daughter more than anything else in the world," she answered. "I suspect he rarely denies her of what she wants, and I'm sure he doesn't deny her what she *needs*. And she needs a nanny, Julia. A nanny like me."

"But all of us—including Sam—know that you've never been a nanny, Kate."

"But once Sam sees the way Caroline responds to me, I have no doubts he'll agree that I should be the one who takes care of her for a while. And I'm going to make him admit that he was wrong about me, Julia. In fact, I'd be willing to wager that *he* will be the one who tries to convince *me* to go home with *him*."

Amused disbelief crossed Julia's delicate features. "Honestly, Kate, I do believe you're incorrigible."

Kate resumed packing, unable to suppress an impish grin from sprouting on her lips. "I know."

As the women of Hopewell House gathered in the dining room to serve the evening meal, the enticing aromas of roast beef and freshly baked bread wafted into the parlor.

Sam sank deeper into the sofa and closed his eyes, relishing the mouth-watering scents and the sounds of feminine chatter swirling around him. It almost seemed as if he were a boy again, sitting here in the parlor, waiting for dinner to be served.

And what a wonderful feeling it was. With all of the unsettling changes in his life during the last six months, it was somehow reassuring to know that nothing had changed at Hopewell House. Here, he could still find the same sense of stability and caring he'd known as a boy.

At that instant, Dorinda's voice rang through the house. "Dinner is ready, everyone!"

Emily scampered over to the sofa. "Can I sit next to you at the table, Sam?"

"It would be my pleasure, Miss Emily." Grinning, Sam bounded to his feet.

Emily giggled with delight as Sam tucked her hand into the crook of his arm and escorted her into the dining room. As everyone gathered around the table, Sam slipped into place between Emily and his daughter.

Caught up in the easy flow of conversation and laughter, Sam scarcely noticed that Kate was seating his daughter for dinner, helping the child into the empty chair to his left. And after Tyler had given thanks for the meal, Sam paid little attention to anything other than the serving platters and bowls that were being passed around the table.

But once he'd filled his plate with generous portions of each dish, Sam realized that Kate had been particularly attentive to Caroline's needs. She'd tied a dainty bib around the child's neck, he noticed, and scooped out small servings of each dish onto Caroline's plate.

Even now, her concern for the little girl was apparent. At the moment, Kate was gently prodding Caroline to sample a spoonful of glazed carrots.

Sam wasn't too surprised when his daughter clamped her mouth shut and wrinkled her nose in disdain. Carrots had never been one of Caroline's favorite foods. But he was taken aback when Kate succeeded in convincing the little girl to sample a taste of the vegetable.

He frowned in confusion. Was this the same Kate he'd known for years? The Kate he'd always known had never possessed an ounce of patience.

He finished off the food in his plate, determined to forget what he'd just seen, willing himself to banish the unsettling memory from his mind. He was making far too much out of Kate's efforts to persuade Caroline to eat her vegetables. More than likely, it had been nothing more than a passing fancy to Kate, an amusing way to pass the time.

Sam picked up a spoon and plunged into the

chocolate custard that Dorinda had prepared for dessert. But just as he tasted his first bite, Caroline's dessert dish slipped from her grasp. Chocolate custard splattered over the rim of the glass bowl and dribbled over Caroline's hands and dress.

The dish crashed to the floor and shattered into dozens of tiny pieces. Caroline let out a shriek that bolted Sam out of his chair. Kate sprang to her feet at the same time.

Sam fully intended to sweep the frightened child into his arms and soothe her frantic cries. But just as he reached for his daughter, she swung her outstretched arms and tear-streaked face in Kate's direction.

Kate hastily removed Caroline from the chair and cradled her in her arms. "It's all right, Caroline. We'll get you cleaned up in no time."

Turning, Kate whisked Caroline from the room. Sam trailed behind them, following Kate's lead as she rushed up the stairs.

Sam had just entered Caroline's room when Kate placed the child on the bed. Distracting her with smiles and giggles and silly, nonsensical phrases, Kate wiped away her tears and cleaned the splotches of chocolate from her face. Caroline's cries faded into mere whimpers, then disappeared into nothing at all.

"I don't understand any of this, Kate," Sam mumbled, genuinely perplexed. "When Caroline gets frightened or upset, she always turns to me. I would've never dreamed that she would turn to someone else—especially someone she doesn't know very well."

"But I'm not a stranger to your daughter anymore, Sam. I've been taking care of her for most of the day."

"You've been taking care of . . . Caroline?" As Kate nodded, Sam couldn't suppress his surprise. "I assumed that Julia was watching Caroline today. During breakfast, she said she'd keep a close eye on her for me."

"And she probably had every intention of doing so. But after Caroline fell down in the rose garden this morning, she—"

"I didn't know about this." Alarm raced through Sam. "Did she get hurt?"

"Just a scrape or two," Kate assured him. She grasped Caroline's hand, pointing out the tiny scratches on the child's outstretched palm. "Some thorns from the rosebush snagged her stockings, and she ripped the hem of her gown."

"Poor kid." Sam planted a kiss on his daughter's scratches. "Falling into a rosebush could not have been any fun."

"It scared her more than anything, I think. When she came running into the house, she seemed terribly distraught. And for some reason, she decided she wanted me to kiss away her tears." Subdued amusement sparkled from Kate's eyes as she gazed down at the red-haired tyke. "After lunch, though, I suspect she was wishing she'd latched onto Julia instead of me."

"What happened after lunch?"

"Emily and Rebecca wanted us to attend a tea party at the playhouse. I thought Caroline would enjoy playing with the girls, but she was so fretful that we didn't stay for very long."

"Did you bring her back to the house?"

Kate nodded. "I was hoping that a nice, warm bath would make her feel better. But things only got worse. She splashed most of the water out of the tub, and she pitched a fit when I washed her hair."

Sam couldn't help but laugh. "She always does that."

"I wish you'd warned me," Kate returned with a playful moan. "Both of us were exhausted after I'd dried her off and brushed the tangles from her hair. In fact, Caroline fell asleep almost as soon as I tucked her into bed."

"So she actually took a nap this afternoon?"

"Fortunately." Something akin to pride flickered across her delicate features.

"That's good," Sam mumbled halfheartedly, wondering if there was more to Kathryn Carey than he'd thought. Perhaps a maternal instinct or two was lurking beneath that dazzling smile and flirtatious manner of hers after all.

"Caroline and I managed to agree on one thing today, though. When I picked out this blue dress for her to wear, she didn't argue with me at all."

As Kate fingered the collar of Caroline's dress, the child pointed out the chocolate stains on her gown. "Ugh," Caroline murmured, wrinkling her nose in dismay.

"We'll find another dress for you, Caroline." Kate quickly retrieved a smocked gown from the girl's traveling bag. "I like this pretty green one, don't you?"

Red curls bobbed around Caroline's face as she nodded with approval. Kate hastily removed her soiled dress and slipped the clean one over her head. "I do believe we have the same taste in clothes, Miss Caroline."

"God help me if you do." Sam shook his head, feigning despair. "Now she'll be wanting every dress in sight. She'll be pleading with me to buy her a new dress every day."

"There's nothing wrong with wanting pretty clothes to wear." Amusement glimmered from Kate's eyes. "Besides, a woman can never have too many dresses."

"If anyone would know, it would be you. Even when you wore your hair in braids, you were always insisting on having more dresses than anyone else in town." His heart warmed at the memory of Kate as a little girl, the precocious lass who was constantly preening over her ruffles and petticoats.

Kate fluttered her thick, dark lashes with exaggeration. "What can I say? I'm not the only woman in the world with an affinity for beautiful clothes. Some women collect figurines. I collect dresses." Her smile faded away. "But I suppose I do get carried away with my passion for dresses at times."

Sam clutched his chest in mock horror. "You mean you're admitting you're not flawless?"

"I've never claimed I was perfect." Kate brushed a hand through Caroline's mop of red curls, her expression suddenly turning serious. "In fact, I know I'm far from perfect. I talk a bit too much when I get excited. I tend to pout when things don't go my way. I know I'm not a great cook like Aunt Dorinda or a wonderful gardener like Aunt Odelphia. And I'm not as patient and kind as Julia."

"Well said, Kate." He grinned. "You won't get an argument from me on any of those points."

Her grim expression told him that she didn't appreciate his teasing. "I'm not trying to start an argument, Sam. I'm perfectly aware of my strengths and weaknesses. But I'm deeply offended when someone assumes that I'm incapable of doing something when I haven't even had the chance to prove myself."

Sam heaved a troubled sigh, knowing where all of this was leading. "Both your faults and your charms are admirable, Kate. But I don't need someone like you in my life right now."

"Maybe you don't." She fingered the ribbons in Caroline's hair. "But maybe Caroline does."

Sam reeled. Those four little words had the effect of a knife ripping into his soul. In essence, Kate had stabbed straight into the most vulnerable part of him, the part that he treasured above all else . . . Caroline. There was nothing he wouldn't do for his daughter, nothing he would deny her.

He sucked in a deep, shuddering breath, reminding himself that Kate wasn't the only woman in the world who could make his daughter happy. "I'm sure I can manage to find someone in Macon who can give Caroline what she needs."

"I'm sure you can, too. But do you really want a stranger to care for your daughter? Wouldn't you rather have someone who knows Caroline? Someone who can make her laugh and smile again? Someone who is sensitive to her needs?"

She sounded so reasonable that he wanted to wring her neck. If only she were acting like a spoiled child instead of a compassionate woman. If only . . .

He steeled himself. How could he invite this woman into his home? He didn't want her invading his life. Didn't even want to think about the fusses and squabbles that would be certain to ensue. "It'll never work, Kate. We might get along with each other for a day or two, but we couldn't be decent to each other for very long."

"But I wouldn't be staying long enough for us to murder each other, Sam! As soon as you find a new housekeeper, I'll be on my way."

Clenching his jaw, he gave his head a stern shake. "We can't avoid fussing, arguing, grating on each other's nerves. And Caroline doesn't need to be exposed to that kind of atmosphere. God knows, the child has been subjected to enough ranting and raving—thanks to her mother's surly disposition—to last a lifetime or two. I don't want her to be surrounded by any more conflicts or heated debates."

"I don't blame you. Every child needs to live in a home filled with love, free from tension and strife." Compassion glowed from her eyes. "All I want to do is love Caroline, Sam. Love her with all the affection and attention that a little girl deserves. Surely you wouldn't deny her of that."

Sam felt something tight and restricting grip his chest. No woman had ever loved Caroline as she should be loved. Abigail had never given a damn about their daughter. Kate held more compassion for the child in her little pinky than Abigail's cold heart had ever possessed.

"I realize we've always had a tendency to squabble when we're together, Sam," Kate continued on. "But can't we make an effort to set aside our differences for a while . . . for Caroline's sake?"

Hearing the hopefulness in her voice, Sam felt a rush of certainty in his heart. Caroline would have someone to tie satin ribbons in her hair, kiss away her tears, buy her frilly dresses. Someone who could tend to her needs in a way that only a woman could.

Surely he possessed the stamina to contend with Kathryn Carey for a week or so. After all, it wouldn't be a permanent arrangement. As soon as he hired a suitable housekeeper, she would be on her way back to Rome.

He clenched his jaw with resolve. He would take what Kate was offering. He would use her for this small space in time. For Caroline's sake.

Without warning, he leaned forward and took Caroline from Kate's lap. "You'd better get moving, Kate. If you're planning to catch the ten-fifty to Macon with me in the morning, you don't have a lot of time to waste."

She gaped at him. "I'm leaving . . . in the morning . . . for Macon?"

"At ten-fifty sharp."

"Did you hear that, Caroline? I'm going home with you and your daddy in the morning!" She surged to her feet, squealing with delight. "And I've got so many things to do that

I don't know where to start! I'm so glad I've already packed a few things to take with—"

"Hold on, Kate." Sam grasped her arm. "You've already started packing?"

She managed a tiny smile. "Just a little bit. Just in case you changed your mind."

Sam grinned, even though he was sorely tempted to wring that pretty little neck of hers. "You're incorrigible, Kathryn Carey."

"So I've heard." Laughing, she scurried toward the door.

Halfway across the room, Kate stopped cold. Peering over her shoulder, she flashed one of her most dazzling smiles in Sam's direction.

"I'm going to take care of your daughter as if she were my very own, Sam. And you won't be sorry for taking me back to Macon with you. I promise you won't regret it at all."

# Chapter 7

**"I**t's good to know that you young folks finally came to your senses." Odelphia's eyes twinkled with delight as she bid farewell to Kate and Sam at the train depot the next morning. "Of course, I always knew you would."

"And I'm certain everything will work out nicely for both of you in Macon," Dorinda insisted.

"And I'm glad you managed to reach a mutual agreement," Julia chimed in.

Tyler clapped Sam on the shoulder. "Just don't forget that working together is much easier than working against each other. Believe me, it's the only way to—"

The clatter of wheels rumbling across the wooden platform cut off the rest of Tyler's sentence. In the next instant, Sam noticed that a large cart of baggage was being pushed across the platform by some railroad employees.

As the workers loaded an assortment of bags and trunks through the open door of a cargo car, Kate's brow knitted with worry. "I do hope those baggage handlers take good care of my trunks. I don't know what I would do if anything happened to all of my clothes."

"Look on the bright side, Kate." Tyler chuckled. "You'd have a legitimate excuse to buy a whole new wardrobe."

"Couldn't you have just packed the basic necessities?" Sam asked. "You probably won't be gone for more than a few days."

"But my basic necessities are my clothes, Sam!" Kate rolled her eyes heavenward. "For goodness sake, I'm only taking two trunks with me."

Sam shook his head in bemused disbelief. "I shudder to think how much more you might have packed if you were planning on a longer visit."

At that moment, the conductor's voice sliced through the air. "All aboard!"

Kate scrambled to bid farewell to her family for a final time. After a flurry of hugs and kisses, she picked up her skirts and boarded the train with Sam and Caroline.

Sam was sitting opposite from Kate in the half-filled passenger car, bouncing Caroline on his knee, when the shriek of the train's whistle pierced through the air. Startled, Caroline nearly jumped out of her skin.

"It's nothing to worry about, Caroline," Sam assured the child. "The whistle just means we're getting ready to leave."

Within a few moments, the train was chugging along the tracks, sending billows of black smoke through the summer sky. Caroline pressed her face and hands against the window, watching in amazement as the depot disappeared from sight.

A matronly woman seated across the aisle flashed a warm smile in Sam's direction. "Your daughter is simply adorable," the woman said. "She has the most beautiful red hair that I've ever seen. And she's so full of life and energy!"

"She loves to ride on a train," Sam revealed.

"And she's always full of life," Kate added.

"Both of you must be very proud of her," the woman remarked. "By the way, my name is Perlina Gordon."

"I'm Kathryn Carey," Kate returned. "This is my dear friend, Samuel Springer, and his daughter, Caroline. I'm Caroline's nanny."

The woman's eyes widened. "You don't say! I would've never dreamed you were a nanny, my dear."

"It's a new position for me," Kate admitted. "In fact, this is my very first day on the job. We're traveling to Macon, and . . ."

As Kate rambled on, Sam shook his head in

bemusement. He couldn't begrudge Kate for her friendliness. But something told him she would know everyone in the passenger car on a first-name basis before their journey was over.

Most people—men, in particular—couldn't resist Kathryn Carey's charms. Yet, she was much too gregarious, too vivacious, for the likes of Sam. He'd much rather be traveling with a demure, shy woman, someone who was quiet and reserved. Someone who would sit quietly at his side instead of striking up a conversation with every stranger who came passing by.

Sam was still musing over these thoughts when he felt something small and warm wiggling over him. He looked down at his daughter and grinned. "You're getting too fidgety to sit on my lap, Caroline." He set the child on the floor, holding onto her hand until she steadied her balance.

Just as he released his hold on Caroline, Kate glanced over at him and smiled. "If you'd like to stretch your legs for a while, I can watch Caroline for you."

"Not a bad idea." Sam pulled himself up from the seat. "I think I'll head over to the dining car and have a cup of coffee. I shouldn't be gone too long."

Relieved for the chance to escape the confines of the small seating area, Sam turned to leave. Taking his time, he ambled down the center aisle, then crossed the platform that led to the dining car.

He ordered a cup of coffee, browsed through a morning newspaper, and made some small talk with several businessmen before returning to the passenger car. When he returned to his seat, he discovered that Kate and her new friend were still chatting away, acting as if they'd known each other for years.

"You two must have a great deal in common," he observed with a wry grin.

"Perlina has been telling me all about Macon, Sam! She's lived there for most of her life, and she knows everyone in town. Now I know where I can find a seamstress for Caroline, and—"

"Caroline?" Sam glanced at the empty seat next to Kate, and his heart gave a crazy lurch. "Where is Caroline, Kate?"

"Caroline?" Kate looked down at her feet. "Why, she was here just a few seconds ago. She was playing in the floor right here beside me, and—"

"She's not here now."

"But she couldn't have gone very far." Kate sprang to her feet. Bending from the waist, she peered beneath several rows of seats. "Caroline, where are you?"

"Dammit, Kate! How in the hell could you have lost Caroline?"

She straightened, bristling with defiance. "I

haven't lost her, Sam. She's just gotten away from me."

"For God's sake, what's the difference?" He scowled. "As I recall, you promised me that you'd care for Caroline as if she were your very own. Is this how you'd care for your own daughter?"

Before Kate could respond, something resembling a red mop emerged from beneath one of the empty seats. Caroline lifted her head, peering up at her father, her face awash with innocence and surprise.

Sam didn't know whether to smother her with kisses or reprimand her with a harsh lecture. He was still trying decide what to do when the sound of muffled laughter snared his attention.

He glanced over at Kate. She clamped a hand over her mouth, attempting to hold her laughter at bay in front of Caroline. Torn between wringing her neck or laughing along with her, Sam scowled in frustration.

Stalking back to his seat, Sam heaved a weary sigh. "Women," he muttered in disgust, wondering how long he could survive in the same household with both of them.


"I'm truly glad we've had the chance to get to know each other, Perlina." Kate flashed a warm smile at the matronly woman as she stepped down from the train.

"Perhaps we can get together while you're here in Macon," Perlina suggested. "Would you like to meet for lunch one day this week?"

"What a wonderful idea! But . . ." Kate's smile suddenly vanished. "But I'm not very familiar with Macon. Meeting you at a certain place might be rather difficult for me, I'm afraid."

A shadow of disappointment flickered across Perlina's face. "I was hoping I could introduce you to my daughter Harriet. You're about the same age, and I think you'd truly like each other."

"Then perhaps you and Harriet could drop by to see me. We could have some tea and spend the afternoon together. I'll be staying at Sam's house, and I'm sure it won't be difficult to find." Kate peered up at Sam. "It's not hard to find, is it?"

"Not at all," he answered smoothly. "I live on College Street, Perlina."

The woman's eyes widened in surprise. "College Street? Why, that's one of the most beautiful streets in town."

"I think so, too." Sam quickly recited the street number to Perlina. "And like Kate said, it isn't hard to find."

"Then Harriet and I will be seeing you soon, Kate. Take care, my dear."

As Perlina disappeared into the crowd, Sam

chuckled under his breath. "I should've known you wouldn't waste any time."

She whirled around to face him. "What do you mean?"

"You arrived in Macon less than five minutes ago. You haven't even left the terminal station. And you're already filling up your social calendar!"

She lifted her chin a notch. "You're exaggerating this whole thing, Sam. One little engagement does not mean that I'm vying for a spot in the most popular social circle in Macon."

"You could have fooled me," he grumbled.

"I don't see anything wrong with wanting to be friends with Perlina Gordon. She seems like a very nice lady. And I'd like to meet her daughter, too."

"But you don't even know how long you'll be staying here! Why would you want to initiate new friendships when you don't know how long you'll be around?"

She dismissed the question with a careless shrug. "You worry too much, Sam. If I don't get to see Perlina again this week, maybe our paths will cross again another time."

Sam scowled and tightened his hold around Caroline.

Kate regarded him for a long moment, then lifted her hand to his face. "Your frown line is showing again, I'm afraid," she observed, running an outstretched finger over his forehead.

He jerked away from her, acting as though the touch of her hand had scorched his brow. "Hell's bells, Kate! I don't need you pointing out that again."

"I think maybe you do. You're so much more handsome without that worrisome frown, Sam."

His scowl faded away, replaced with an expression of disbelief. "You think I'm . . . handsome?"

Kate stilled. She hadn't expected that Sam would take her flippant remark so seriously.

But why couldn't she give him an honest answer? After all, she knew a handsome man when she saw one.

She inhaled a deep, steadying breath, determined to look at Sam as if she were peering through a stranger's eyes, seeing him for the very first time.

Summoning up her courage, she lifted her gaze to his face. And what she saw stunned her beyond words.

Somewhere in the recesses of her mind, Kate had always known that Sam was an attractive man. But seeing him now, she found herself struggling to catch her breath. She raked her gaze over the chiseled lines and grooves of his face, liking everything she saw.

But heaven help her, she couldn't tell him what she really thought. Not in a serious way. If she admitted that she was enchanted by the deep green of his eyes and the sensuous line of his lips, he'd never let her hear the end of it.

She planted a saucy smirk on her lips. "In all honesty, I have to admit that you've cleaned up quite nicely since your childhood days, Samuel Springer."

"But I'm not chasing hogs in the garden anymore, either." His lips twitched with amusement. "Of course, if you don't—"

"Springer!" a deep bass voice rumbled through the terminal.

Sam glanced up and groaned. "Just what I need," he mumbled.

Kate followed the direction of Sam's gaze. Stalking toward them was a distinguished-looking man with a white mustache and neatly trimmed beard. At his side was a tall, slender woman with dark hair and a formidable scowl on her face.

Kate immediately recognized the couple. She'd met Judge Vance and his wife when Sam had married their daughter. Six months ago, she'd crossed paths with them again at Abigail's funeral.

But now, as the couple approached Sam, Kate sensed they weren't overjoyed to see their son-in-law and granddaughter.

"You should've told us that you were going out of town, son." Judge Vance frowned with disapproval. "Estelle and I have dropped by your house several times in the last few days to see Caroline. Of course, you weren't there, and we've been frantic with worry."

"You could have contacted my office, Judge. They could've told you that I was visiting my family back in Rome."

"I see." The judge glanced over at Kate. "And is this young lady a friend of yours?"

"We met at your daughter's wedding," Kate offered. "I'm Kathryn Carey."

"Kate and I grew up together," Sam added. "She'll be staying here in Macon for a few days."

Estelle Vance lifted one eyebrow. "This woman will be staying with . . . you?"

The line of Sam's jaw tightened. "Kate has generously offered to take care of Caroline for me until I can find a new housekeeper."

"You don't have a housekeeper?" Estelle's eyes widened in surprise.

"Not at the moment," Sam admitted. "Hopefully, I'll be hiring someone by the end of the week."

"I see." Promptly dismissing Sam, Estelle shifted her gaze toward her husband. "Shall we meet that friend of yours now, dear? His train should be arriving at any moment, I believe."

"We should be on our way," the judge agreed. "We'll be contacting you in a few days, Sam. Estelle and I would like to spend some time with our granddaughter this week."

Without waiting for a response, the couple

turned to leave. Appalled by their haughty behavior, Kate frowned in dismay.

"Why in the hell don't they just mind their own business?" Sam muttered.

Kate glanced over at Sam, surprised by the intensity of his anger. His jaw was clenched, his shoulders were stiff, and his eyes were cold and hard.

"If they truly cared about their granddaughter, I could understand why they were concerned about not being able to locate us," he continued on. "But they don't give a damn about anyone other than themselves."

"I couldn't help but notice that they didn't even speak to Caroline." Kate reached out and brushed a hand through the little girl's hair. "Do they always act this way?"

"You saw them at their best," he scoffed. "They're always ranting and raving about something. Usually, it's much worse than today."

"But surely they wouldn't be holding some sort of grudge against you, Sam. After all, you were married to their daughter."

"But for some ungodly reason, the Vances have decided that I'm the one to blame for their daughter's death. In the last six months, they've done nothing but make my life a living hell."

Kate's heart sank. "Oh, Sam. I never realized . . ."

"Let's just forget about it for now." Sam expelled a weary sigh. "It's been a long day, and I'm anxious to get home."

Trying to shrug aside the disturbing encounter with the Vances, Kate fell into step beside Sam. When they reached the front of the terminal, Sam quickly procured a hack and driver for the ride home.

As the buggy pulled away from the station, Sam instructed the driver to head for College Street. "Let's go by way of Mulberry," he added.

Within a few moments, the driver turned onto a wide avenue. Brick office buildings and shops lined both sides of the street. The center of the thoroughfare contained a multitude of small parks with neatly trimmed shrubs, flowering trees, and wooden benches.

When they reached the third block, Sam motioned to a three-story building. "My law firm is located here, Kate. If you use the church on the corner as a landmark, you shouldn't have any problems finding it."

The resplendent church and its towering steeple were familiar to Kate, and she knew the reason why. The First Presbyterian Church had been the site of Sam's wedding ceremony to Abigail.

Kate was wondering why Sam hadn't bothered to mention anything about his wedding site when a magnificent spire came into view.

Rising above the heart of the city, the spire was the crowning glory of Mercer University. The towering steeple capped the university's main building, stretching high above the hill-top campus.

Though Kate had caught a glimpse of the spire during her previous visits to Macon, she hadn't appreciated its beauty until now. Framed by the golden glow of the setting sun, the spire seemed to be standing watch over the city like a protective guardian, providing a sense of security and serenity with its constant presence.

Kate smiled contentedly, tightening her arms around the little girl nestled against her breast. Something told her she was going to like it here.

As they left the heart of the business district and entered a residential area, Kate admired the gracious homes and gardens along the way. She was especially impressed with the immense mansions on College Street. An abundance of homes were adorned with white columns and wide porticos, reminiscent of the South's plantation era.

And she was pleasantly surprised when Sam instructed the hack driver to stop in front of a charming white cottage.

"We're home," Sam announced, leaping down from the buggy. He swung Caroline to the ground, then offered a steadying hand to

Kate. Gathering up her skirts, she stepped down from the vehicle.

While Sam helped the driver unload their baggage, Kate strolled alongside the white picket fence that bordered the property, admiring the trail of climbing roses woven through the slats. Caroline wobbled along beside her, contentedly stretching her legs after the long train ride.

Approaching the cottage, Kate liked what she saw. The roof line was steep and sloping, jutting over a wide verandah that spanned the front and the sides of the cottage. White columns graced the verandah, and cut glass panels adorned the front door.

Flanking the entrance were two pairs of long narrow windows, trimmed with black shutters. Neatly pruned shrubs and rows of blossoming flowers skirted the stone foundation, and a massive magnolia tree towered over the lawn.

Swinging open the front gate, Kate ushered Caroline into the front yard. They ambled over the stone walkway, then paused on the verandah while Sam and the hack driver traipsed past them. After lugging Kate's trunks into the house, the driver pocketed Sam's payment for his services and quickly sped away.

Sam was lighting the wick of an oil lantern when Kate entered the cottage with Caroline. "I thought we could use a bit of light in here," he said.

The lantern glow cast a golden hue over the room, permitting Kate to view her surroundings more clearly. She edged forward, suddenly curious about Sam's home.

But as she gazed around the front parlor, a snippet of disappointment surged through her. Judging by the charm of the cottage's exterior, she never expected the inside of the house to be so bland. The walls were bare, the furniture scant, and the colors tepid.

Kate struggled to find something nice thing to say about the room. "Why, what a-a-a large parlor!" she finally blurted out.

"It's not Hopewell House, mind you, but I'm proud to say it's all mine. Would you like the grand tour?"

"Certainly, Sam. You lead the way."

The kitchen held an icebox, a cookstove, two storage cabinets, and a breakfast table with four chairs. In the dining room, an assortment of fine china filled the shelves of a corner cupboard, and the table was large enough to accommodate eight guests. White wicker furniture graced the large sun porch that stretched across the back of the house.

Exploring each room, Kate became vividly aware of Sam's pride in his home. She could tell by the tone of his voice, the swell of his shoulders, the gleam in his eyes.

But when they came to the hallway, Kate detected a slight hesitation in Sam. Though he nodded toward the closed door directly to Kate's left, he made no attempt to open it.

"This room is yours, Kate. It's not too fancy, but I believe you'll find everything you need. When my housekeeper was still working for me, she cleaned it every week. I know it's not what you're used to at Hopewell House, but—"

"I'm sure it will be fine, Sam." She motioned toward the room across the hall. "What's over here?"

"This is Caroline's room," he said, opening the door. Caroline darted past her father, scurrying into the room. Plopping on the floor, she pulled a small doll from a miniature cradle.

Kate lingered in the doorway, standing beside Sam. "So how long have you lived here?"

"About six months, more or less. We moved in right after Christmas last year."

An uneasy feeling rolled through Kate. Sam had moved into this house with his wife, the woman he'd expected to share his life with.

But Abigail never had the chance to turn this house into a home for her family. She'd lived here only a few weeks before she'd been killed in that horrible train accident.

And the wretched timing of Abigail's death explained why the cottage was sorely in need of a woman's touch, Kate realized with a start. "You know, I would be glad to help out with some decorating while I'm here," she offered.

To her surprise, Sam's eyes glimmered with a hint of belligerence. "It may not be much to you, Kate, but this is the only home I've ever had."

"I'm not criticizing your home, Sam! It's a wonderful house. But if you'd like to add a splash of color or hang a picture or two, I'd be glad to lend a hand."

"I suppose it does need some work." He kneaded the nape of his neck and sighed. "I've tried to turn this house into a home for Caroline and me, a home in the true sense of the word. It's all I've ever wanted from life, I suppose."

He gave his head a shake, as if he regretted saying too much. "I'll be back in a moment, Kate. I'd like to unpack a few things while I can. I've got an early meeting at the office in the morning, and I—"

"Go right ahead," Kate insisted. "While you're unpacking, I'll get Caroline ready for bed. She didn't have a nap this afternoon, and I suspect it won't be long before she'll be ready to get to sleep."

Kate rummaged through a small dresser until she located a nightgown. "Here you go, Miss Caroline," she crooned softly, removing the girl's dress and slipping the nightgown over her head. "Tonight, you'll be sleeping in your own bed again. Won't that be nice? After I've been away from home for a few days, it's always nice to sleep in my own room again."

After planting a kiss on the child's forehead, Kate gently placed her on the bed. To her surprise, Caroline tightened her arms around Kate's neck. "No bed," she proclaimed.

"Then let's try something else. I'd wager you'd like to be rocked to sleep, Miss Caroline."

When the girl offered no response, Kate sank into a rocking chair beside the bed and gathered Caroline close to her breast. "When I was a little girl, I loved to be rocked to sleep. My mother died when I was just a baby, too, but I had a wonderful sister and two loving aunts who took care of me. They rocked me to sleep almost every night, just the way I'm rocking you now."

Between the rhythmic creak of the rocker and the soothing tone of Kate's voice, Caroline's eyes grew heavy. Humming a lullaby, Kate patiently waited for the child to drift off to sleep.

Little did she realize that Sam was standing at the door of Caroline's room, stunned by the intensity of the wrenching sensation in his chest.

He'd returned to the room to give Caroline a goodnight kiss just as Kate had slipped into the rocking chair with Caroline. He'd heard every word that had crossed her lips. And he'd realized, with a start, that Kate was giving his daughter something he hadn't even known she'd needed, something he couldn't give her, something she'd been denied.

The warmth of a woman's touch.

The child was starving for it. God knows, Abigail hadn't bothered to give the babe anything other than a few careless caresses. She had been much more concerned with meeting her own needs than tending to the needs of her daughter.

He would've never dreamed that Kate would be the one to nurture Caroline. Never would've fathomed that she'd evoke emotions within him that he never knew he had.

But standing there, watching her, Sam felt something tight and restricting grip his chest. God help him, he had the insane urge to kiss the blasted woman.

Not for show, of course. And not for pretend. But for himself.

He was moistening his parched lips with his tongue when Kate rose and gently lowered Caroline to the bed. After brushing her lips across the child's cheek, she quietly slipped out of the room.

Kate was a bit surprised to find Sam standing by the door. She hadn't realized he'd been watching her.

"Caroline seems glad to be back in her own

room, her own bed," she said. Gazing up at Sam, she discerned the fine lines of fatigue etched into his handsome features, the shadows of discontent beneath his eyes. "And what about you, Sam? Are you glad to be home, too?"

He shrugged. "I suppose so."

The lack of enthusiasm in his reply made Kate realize just how little she knew about Sam's life, especially since his wife's funeral. She'd always assumed he was satisfied with his life here in Macon, but now she wondered if her assumption had been wrong.

The few days they'd spent together in Rome had passed so quickly that they hadn't had the chance to share much of anything with each other. There were so many things she wanted to know, so many questions she wanted to ask.

"I've thought about you a lot in recent months, Sam," she admitted. "I've been wondering how you've been coping since . . . since the funeral."

"I've been fine." His eyes evaded hers. "My work keeps me busy."

"But have you given yourself time to . . . grieve?"

"Of course I've grieved." The line of his jaw clenched tightly. "But that part of my life is over now, and I have other things to consider."

He refused to say anything more, but Kate sensed there was much more to the story than he was willing to admit. And his silence roused her curiosity all the more. Was he angry with Abigail for dying? Leaving him to raise their daughter alone? She couldn't be certain until he told her.

"It's Abigail, isn't it?" she pressed on. "You miss her, don't you?"

"No." His eyes hardened. "I don't miss Abigail at all."

His denial shocked her, but some inner instinct warned Kate not to press the matter further. She suspected Sam was not in the mood to discuss anything about his late wife.

"Then what's bothering you? Is it something about Caroline . . . or me? Have I said or done something with Caroline that you don't—"

"The child's own mother didn't dote on her the way you do, Kate. Abigail spent as little time as possible with Caroline."

Kate reeled from the startling revelation. Why would Abigail avoid spending time with her own child? Hadn't she been a loving, caring mother?

And what was bothering Sam? "Is it your work, then? Or perhaps—"

"It's everything, Kate." Expelling a frustrated sigh, he dragged a hand through his hair. "And nothing at all."

"Well, now I understand," she mumbled in annoyance. "You've made everything perfectly clear to me now."

"It's just that . . . it's complicated, Kate. So complicated that even I don't understand what's going on."

She frantically groped for another reason that might be causing his dismay. "If you're concerned about the gossip our living arrangements might cause, I don't think you have anything to worry about, Sam. Once everyone knows we were raised together in the same household like brother and sister, they'll realize that everything is legitimate between us."

"I'm not too concerned about the proprieties," Sam said. "It's just that . . ."

His voice faded away, and Kate became vividly aware that his gaze was roaming over her face, studying each feature with alarming intensity. Then he lifted his hand to her cheek, brushing his knuckles across her skin with a caress so warm and tender that she melted inside.

Her heart thundered in her chest as he edged forward ever so slowly, bending his head. She saw the passion in his eyes, sensed the longing in his gaze. She even felt the warmth of his breath whispering across her lips as his mouth edged closer to hers.

But just as she tilted back her head, lifting her lips to his, he pulled away without warning. Abruptly edging back from her, he closed his eyes and inhaled a deep, shuddering breath.

"It's been a long day, Kate." His voice was

strained and low. Turning, he headed for the room at the end of the hall. "I'll see you in the morning."

# Chapter 8

Kate lingered in the hallway long after Sam had retreated into the privacy of his room, bewildered and shaken by what had just transpired between them.

Sam had wanted to kiss her. And God help her, she'd wanted the same thing. It was as simple—and as complicated—as that.

She'd sensed his intentions in that heart-stopping moment when he'd edged forward, bending his head toward hers. His lips had been slightly parted, his gaze focused on her mouth, his eyes dark with longing.

But as she'd waited in breathless anticipation, it seemed as if some inner instinct had flashed a warning signal to him, holding him at bay. And when he'd pulled away from her, Kate had been besieged by a sharp stab of disappointment.

Even now, she was still reeling from the shock of it all. Dear heavens, what had gotten into her? Never before had she ever considered kissing Sam—except for the sole purpose of discouraging Augustus Moulton's advances.

And she was astounded by Sam's shocking claim that he didn't miss his dearly departed wife. She'd always assumed that Sam's marriage had been blissfully happy. But now she realized that she'd known very little about his marriage.

With a troubled sigh, Kate slipped into her room. She retrieved a nightgown from her trunk, not bothering to unpack the rest of her belongings. There would be plenty of time to get settled tomorrow.

She stepped out of her dress and shrugged into her nightgown. In spite of this evening's unsettling events, she couldn't afford to forget why she was here.

Before she returned to Rome, she had every intention of proving to Sam that she could tend to his house and care for his daughter.

She tumbled into bed. First thing in the morning, she'd launch her plan with a breakfast that would prove her worth beyond all doubt.

As soon as Sam stepped out of his room the next morning, he stopped cold.

A smoky haze was filling the hallway, and a harsh, acrid scent was drifting through the air. What in the hell was burning?

Heart pounding and pulse racing, he bolted down the hall and flung open the door to Caroline's room. Relieved the child was still sleeping peacefully, he quickly closed the door and raced through the house.

When he reached the kitchen, Sam halted, stunned by what he saw. Smoke was streaming from the cookstove, and the foul odor of scorched food hung heavily in the air. Kate was struggling to open the window, grunting and moaning beneath the strain of her unsuccessful efforts.

"I'll take care of the window, Kate." Sam lunged across the room, shoving her aside.

Kate darted toward the cookstove and opened the oven door, coughing as the smoke billowed around her. Just as she pulled a black-ened tray from the oven, Sam hurled open the window and spun around. "What in the hell is going on here?" he demanded.

A brave little smile appeared on her lips. "I was just fixing breakfast for us."

He glowered at the charred remains on the tray. "Looks more like you're burning break-fast," he grumbled.

"It didn't go as well as I'd hoped." Her smile began to waver. "But I'm sure I'll do better tomorrow."

"I'm sure you will, too." He grimaced. "You couldn't do any worse, I suppose."

"That's only because I ran into a few problems this morning." She set the tray on top of the cookstove. "You see, I had planned to make a wonderful breakfast for all of us. When I found some yams and flour in the pantry, I knew I had all the ingredients to make Aunt Dorinda's sweet potato biscuits." She wrinkled her nose in dismay. "But I didn't realize that I wasn't familiar with your cookstove."

"Or any cookstove, no doubt."

"I know what a cookstove is supposed to do, Sam." She bristled with defiance. "It's just that . . . well, your cookstove isn't like the one we have at Hopewell House."

"Something tells me that the cookstove isn't the real problem here, Kate." He narrowed his eyes. "For some reason, I suspect the cook is at fault."

She lifted her chin. "I always helped with the meals at Hopewell House until Tyler hired a cook for us. Why, I've done all sorts of things in the kitchen! I've snapped green beans, capped strawberries, scrubbed potatoes. And I've even shucked corn from Julia's garden, too."

"But you've never cooked an entire meal by yourself in your life," Sam surmised, irritated that she'd conveniently forgotten to tell him that her culinary talents were limited to boiling water.

She concocted another tiny smile. "I just
need a little practice, that's all."

He groaned. "I don't particularly relish the
idea of being a guinea pig, Kate."

"It won't be that bad, Sam. The sweet potato
biscuits may be ruined, but our breakfast isn't a
total loss. I found a jar of applesauce in the
pantry that I'd planned to serve. And I even
made some fried potatoes and coffee for us,
too."

She picked up a skillet of potatoes from the
cookstove. After scraping the fried food onto a
serving platter, she set the plate on the table
and motioned for Sam to sit down.

"I really don't have the time to eat breakfast
this morning," he said, eyeing askance the
strange concoction on the platter. About half of
the potato slices had been burned to a crisp,
and the remaining half looked raw.

Her chin gave a little quiver. There was a
smudge of flour on her cheek, Sam noticed, and
a spot of black soot dotting the tip of her nose.

"I know it's not the tastiest breakfast in the
world, Sam. If you don't want it . . . well, I
won't shove it down your throat. But I made it
especially for you, and I-I-I tr-tr-tried s-s-so h-
h-hard . . ."

The bravado in her voice crumbled, shatter-
ing all of Sam's resolve. Good God, how could
he refuse? It wasn't as if she'd purposely set out
to make a mess of things. Obviously, she'd

awakened before the crack of dawn, intent on preparing a scrumptious morning meal until her plans had gone awry.

He sat down at the table. Beaming with delight, Kate poured coffee into his cup, then dished out generous helpings of applesauce and potatoes onto his plate.

Summoning up his courage, Sam drew in a deep breath and put a forkful of potatoes into his mouth. Unfortunately, the taste was just as revolting as he thought it would be.

He reached for his coffee, hoping a hefty gulp would wash away the awful taste in his mouth. But drinking the foul brew only made matters worse. The coffee was as thick as molasses, bitter and black, without a snippet of sugar or cream for flavoring.

The applesauce was the only thing he could manage to swallow without launching into a choking spasm. As he finished the last spoonful, he glanced over at Kate, wishing she would say or do something that would spare him the torture of eating anything else. But when he saw the expression of pure delight on her face, he almost asked for more.

"I suppose I should stock up on some supplies today, but I'm not certain where I should go." Kate took a sip of coffee, though Sam didn't know how she could keep from gagging. "Do you have any recommendations?"

"I have an account at Bell's Market. You

shouldn't have any problems finding the place. It's located about four blocks from here. Just be sure to tell the clerk where to deliver the order."

He retrieved a watch from his vest pocket and checked the time. "It's getting late. I need to get to the office, Kate."

Seizing the chance to escape before she asked him to eat anything more, he rose from the chair and left the room.

When he reached the front door, Kate called out to him. "Have a wonderful day, Sam. And don't you worry about anything here."

Stifling a groan, Sam jammed a hat over his head and stepped outside. Judging by the bitter taste still lingering in his mouth, he had more reason to worry than he'd ever suspected.

As soon as he arrived at the office, he knew what he had to do. Composing an advertisement for a housekeeper—one with plenty of culinary skills—would be his top priority of the day.

"Come on, Caroline." Kate grasped the child's hand, leading her across the sun porch. "Let's go outside and get some fresh air. Maybe that terrible stench in the kitchen will be gone by the time we go back into the house."

Ambling through the small lawn that stretched behind the cottage toward a garden that bordered the back edge of the property,

Kate tried to enjoy the beauty of the summer morning. Not a cloud appeared in the sky, and soft breezes were stirring through the air.

But no matter how hard she tried, Kate couldn't forget the chaos of the early-morning hours. She was vividly aware that her efforts to prepare breakfast had been a dismal failure.

Only her stubborn pride had prevented her from expressing her dismay in front of Sam. She didn't care for him to know that her botched attempts at cooking were both embarrassing and humiliating to her.

Worse yet, Kate had no idea how she would ever manage to cook a complete dinner all by herself. Until this morning, she'd never realized that cooking was an art, a skill that required practice and mastery. Always before, she'd assumed that preparing meals wasn't a difficult task. After all, it had never been a problem for Julia and her aunts.

Wishing she had been more attentive to her family's culinary skills, Kate heaved a troubled sigh. What was she going to do about dinner?

She tried to set aside the disturbing thought for a moment, admiring the yellow marigolds and red impatiens that skirted an assortment of shrubbery in the garden, the stone benches and matching urns that had been placed amid the lush green foliage.

As Caroline squatted beside the flowers, fingering the bright blossoms, Kate glanced to her right. A neat row of hedges and a high iron fence bordered one side of the property, separating the lawn from a narrow lane that led to a brick carriage house.

She was absently gazing across the neatly trimmed lawn that bordered the left side of Sam's property when she spotted a slender woman in the yard.

By Kate's assessment, the woman appeared to be in her late fifties or early sixties. At the moment, she was gathering fresh flowers from her garden and placing the cut stems into a wicker basket.

Catching Kate's curious gaze, the woman offered a friendly smile. "Good morning," she called out, crossing the lawn. "I'm not trying to be a nosy neighbor, mind you, but I thought I noticed some smoke coming from the direction of Sam's house earlier this morning. I do hope nothing is wrong."

"We had a slight problem with the cookstove." Kate felt a heated flush rise to her cheeks. "Actually, I was the problem," she admitted sheepishly. "I burned the sweet potato biscuits to a crisp."

"It happens to all of us, every once in a while." Laughing, the woman offered her hand. "I'm Ida Mae Walker, Sam's neighbor. And you're . . . ?"

"Kate Carey from Rome, Georgia. I'm helping out Sam until he can find a new housekeeper." She managed a weak smile. "But I'm afraid I'm not getting off to a very good start."

"It's no sin to burn a batch of biscuits, dear. In fact, it's easy for anyone to do."

"Maybe so, but cooking is a lot harder than I thought it would be." Kate's gazed drifted toward the little girl with red curls tumbling about her shoulders. "When I volunteered to take care of Caroline for a while, I didn't have any doubts that I could take care of running a household, too. But I never realized that my cooking skills were so inadequate until this morning."

"It will come naturally to you, after you've practiced for a while."

"But I'm afraid I don't have any time to practice." Kate sighed with dismay. "Maybe I should find a restaurant in town that would be willing to cater our dinner for this evening."

"You don't have to resort to ordering dinner from a restaurant, dear," Ida Mae insisted. "I don't have much of a chance to cook for anyone since my dear Herbert died last year. But I love to cook, and I would like nothing more than to prepare dinner for you and Sam this evening."

Kate's eyes widened in disbelief. "You would do that . . . for me? Why, we don't even know each other! And you would be going to so much trouble—"

"It's not a bother at all, Kate. In fact, it will be my way of welcoming you to Macon." Ida Mae grinned. "And you wouldn't want to deny me of that, would you?"

"No, but . . ." Kate floundered, struggling to find the right words. "I wasn't spouting off my troubles in the hopes that you would fix a meal for us."

"Of course you weren't, dear." Ida Mae patted Kate's shoulder affectionately. "I've been wanting to be a good neighbor to Sam for a long time, but I didn't exactly know what to do for him. I'm always volunteering to watch Caroline, but I'm too old to be running after a three-year-old for more than a few hours at a time. Fixing dinner for the three of you is the least I can do."

"Thanks, Ida Mae."

Turning, the woman smiled. "I'll bring the food over about six o'clock, dear."

Watching Ida Mae return to her flower garden, Kate breathed a sigh of relief. She'd been given a reprieve until tomorrow. Until then, she would have to find another way to prove herself to Sam.

WANTED: EXPERIENCED HOUSEKEEPER.
PLEASANT WORKING CONDITIONS, EXCELLENT PAY.
CULINARY SKILLS REQUIRED,

EXPERIENCE WITH CHILDREN PREFERRED.
MUST BE ABLE TO START IMMEDIATELY.
CONTACT SAMUEL SPRINGER,
GENTRY, SPRINGER, AND PIERCE,
MULBERRY STREET.


Sam scanned the wording for a final time, satisfied with what he'd written. Just as he placed the paper into the pocket of his jacket, Verna Dunbar appeared at the door of his office.

Though grim-faced and somber, Verna was the best legal assistant in town. Now, she addressed Sam in her customary, businesslike tone.

"Mr. Peyton Ransom has arrived for his ten-thirty appointment with you, Mr. Springer."

"Send him in, please."

Sam rose as a stocky, muscular man with dark blond hair entered the room. The finely tailored lines of his clothes and the confidence in his stride suggested that Peyton Ransom was a wealthy, successful man.

Exchanging a firm handshake with his new client, Sam surmised the man was in his early thirties. "Please make yourself comfortable, Mr. Ransom. What can I do for you this morning?"

"A great deal, I believe." Peyton settled

down in the chair, seeming at ease with himself. "I've just purchased a business here in Macon, and I would like for you to be my legal representative. Professor Holcomb highly recommended you to me."

Holcomb had been one of Sam's favorite professors in law school, and Sam was pleased to know that the man had recommended his legal services. He'd always held a high regard for the professor. "So you're a friend of Holcomb's?" Sam asked.

"He and my father have been friends for years," the man explained. "As a matter of fact, when Professor Holcomb discovered that I was looking to make an investment here in Macon, he told me that the widow of your finest jeweler, Douglas Norwood, was looking for a buyer for Norwood Jewelry."

"The establishment has been for sale for quite some time," Sam acknowledged.

"Mrs. Norwood verbally accepted my offer last week, and now I would like to proceed with legal ownership of the business. Mrs. Norwood's son has agreed to manage the store for a percentage of the profits. I will be an absentee owner."

"So you're not planning to become a permanent resident of Macon?"

Peyton chuckled. "I've never settled down in one place for more than a few weeks at time. There are far too many interesting places in the world to explore. But I'll be visiting here occasionally, of course, to check on the business."

"I see." Sam jotted down a few notes. "This is strictly an investment for you."

"But the store has to be successful." The man grinned. "I like the good life, Mr. Springer, and I have no intention of changing my lifestyle. I plan to upgrade the merchandise by stocking the store with goods that I intend to purchase on my buying trips overseas. Jewels are quite—"

"Pardon me, gentlemen."

Sam swung his gaze toward the door, startled by what he saw. Kate was standing in the doorway, looking every inch the fashionable young woman that she was. A mauve hat trimmed with a white plume was perched on the top of her head, and she was wearing a stylish mauve gown that emphasized the lush dips and swells of her petite frame.

"I know it's terribly rude of me to interrupt such a very important meeting," she continued on, sauntering into the room. "Normally, I wouldn't consider barging into anyone's office, but—"

"Excuse me one moment, Mr. Ransom." Sam snapped up from his chair and stalked toward Kate. Clasping a firm hand around her elbow, he guided her into the hall. "I'm in the middle of a very important meeting with a very important client, Kate."

"I realize that," she began, "but I thought—"

"And you'd better have a good reason for interrupting me," he warned, wishing she didn't look so beautiful in that fetching shade of pink. "Couldn't you have waited?"

"Not for very long. You see, after you left for the office this morning, I started feeling just awful about the horrible food that I served you for breakfast and I—"

"But barging into my office—and disrupting a meeting with a new client—isn't exactly the best way to make things better between us, Kate."

"For heaven's sake, Sam, don't get into such a tizzy!" She rolled her eyes heavenward. "It's not the end of the world. Your client can wait a moment or two."

"I'm trying to conduct business here, Kate. This isn't the place for socializing or discussing personal matters." He gritted his teeth. "God only knows how you managed to slip by Miss Dunbar. She never allows anyone to get past the front door without an interrogation."

"She didn't interrogate me." A sparkle of delight twinkled from her eyes. "In fact, she even offered to take Caroline for a little stroll down the hall so I could have a moment of privacy with you."

"There must be some mistake here. We must not be talking about the same person." Sam shook his head in disbelief. "Miss Dunbar is well aware that Lawrence Gentry and I don't encourage visits from friends or family members during business hours. The interruptions are disruptive to our schedules, and—"

"That's odd." A puzzled expression flickered over Kate's delicate features. "I was just talking to that nice Mr. Gentry, and he said I was welcome to drop by the office anytime I wanted to see you. He even encouraged me to make myself at home here."

At that moment, Peyton Ransom stepped into the hall. "Mr. Springer, I really can't wait much longer."

"This is all my fault, I'm afraid." Kate's voice was warm and apologetic. "I'm terribly sorry that I interrupted your meeting. Considering the high demand for Mr. Springer's legal services, I know it must be difficult to schedule an appointment with him. And I'm certain a busy man like yourself doesn't have any time to waste." Her thick, dark lashes fluttered with concern. "Can you ever forgive me for being such an imposition for you this morning?"

"There's nothing to forgive, ma'am. No harm has been done."

"But something tells me you're too much of a gentleman to complain." Kate sighed. "What a nuisance I've been! There you were, trying to discuss an important legal matter with Mr.

Springer, and I barge into the middle of your meeting and—"

"Don't give it another thought, ma'am." Peyton shifted his gaze to Sam. "Just who is this enchanting creature, Mr. Springer?"

Sam introduced Kate to his new client. "Miss Carey is visiting here from Rome, Georgia," he added.

Peyton grasped her hand and brushed his lips across her fingers. "Ah, Miss Carey. It's truly a pleasure to meet such a beautiful lady."

"Why, thank you, Mr. Ransom."

"It's Peyton to you, my dear."

"Then please call me Kate."

Sam grimaced, slightly nauseated by the sugary sweetness in the air. "Peyton is purchasing a jewelry store here in Macon, Kate. He plans to purchase the inventory for the store in Europe."

"I'm always on the lookout for unusual pieces of jewelry," Peyton revealed.

"So you must spend a great deal of time traveling," Kate surmised.

"I tend to get bored after I've stayed in one place for a while," he admitted. "I'm always looking for a new adventure, I suppose. Have you ever been to Europe, Kate?"

"I'm afraid not, but I've always dreamed of going there someday."

"There are many beautiful places to visit and

explore in the Old World." He paused. "I'll only be in town for a few days, but I've purchased a pair of tickets to a concert at the Academy of Music for later this week. Would you do me the honor of being my guest?"

"Why, how very thoughtful of you, Peyton. I would be delighted to accompany you."

Sam drew in a sharp breath. Apparently, Peyton Ransom wasn't as sharp as he'd suspected. But then, had he ever seen a man who could resist Kathryn Carey's charms?

Of course, Sam knew better than to fall prey to the woman's beguiling ways. He was no stranger to that little knot of worry creasing her brow, the slight protrusion of her lower lip, the tiny quiver in her chin. Each of her enchanting tactics—practiced to perfection and perfectly timed to achieve the most effective results—had been etched permanently into his mind. He could read her like an open book, and he knew all of the lines by heart.

"Well, this has certainly been a delightful morning," Peyton said. "Mr. Springer, I would be grateful if you would file all of the appropriate business licenses with the city for my new business. And I would also like for you to draw up a legally binding agreement between Mrs. Norwood's son and myself."

"I can have those items prepared for you within a few days," Sam promised. "Are there any other legal matters you would like to address this morning?"

"I believe that takes care of everything for now." Peyton exchanged a handshake with Sam before turning to Kate. "I'm looking forward to our engagement later this week, Kate."

As Peyton left the office, Kate sighed contentedly. "What a delightful gentleman," she murmured.

Sam glowered at her. "You don't even know the man, Kate."

Her lashes fluttered with confusion. "Should I have consulted with you before I accepted his invitation?"

"Of course not. You don't have to answer to me," he snapped. "You're a grown woman. You can see whoever you'd like to see. Why in the hell should I care?"

"For heaven's sake, Sam! You don't have to get so testy about this."

"I think I have every reason in the world to get testy, Kate. Apparently, you've forgotten something very important."

"I have?" She glanced up at him, surprise flickering across her delicate features. "What have I forgotten?"

"Everything we discussed in Rome." He pursed his lips together in a thin line. "I thought you understood that socializing wasn't supposed to be the primary reason for your visit here."

"It's only one little engagement, Sam. And it's not as if I forced him to ask me to accompany him."

"Still, you don't have any business accepting invitations from total strangers—especially since you don't even know how long you'll be here."

Sam clamped his lips into a tight line, infuriated beyond words. Most women wouldn't think of waltzing into a man's office and disrupting his morning. Most women wouldn't dream of accepting an invitation from a stranger. Most women were shy and demure, too submissive to even consider barging into a man's life and turning it upside down.

But, then, most women weren't like Kate.

She couldn't have been here for more than half an hour. But in that brief span of time, her beguiling ways had charmed everyone who'd crossed her path.

And Sam still didn't know why she was here. He regarded her, wary. "Did you have some reason for paying me a visit today?"

"I just came by to apologize for ruining your breakfast. But now I wish I hadn't even bothered." She absently patted her hair. "I suppose Caroline and I should be getting back to the house now. I haven't even unpacked my trunks yet, and I suppose that's something a good housekeeper would do before she officially starts keeping house."

"That reminds me," Sam mumbled, retrieving a crumbled piece of paper from the pocket of his vest. "I'd like to run an ad for a new housekeeper in the *Macon Telegraph,* and today is the deadline for submitting copy. Would you mind taking this ad to the newspaper office for me? If you're going straight home, it shouldn't be out of your way."

"I suppose I could do that." She carefully placed the paper into the pocket of her dress. "When will the ad hit the streets?"

"On Sunday morning. An advertisement in the Sunday paper will get more coverage than any other day of the week. Everyone in Macon always reads the Sunday edition of the newspaper."

"But today is Wednesday, Sam. If your advertisement doesn't appear in the newspaper until Sunday, you can't expect to hire a new housekeeper before then." She paused. "And you know what that means, don't you?"

Sam paled. "I'll be eating your cooking for another four days?"

"At least!" Kate laughed at the thought.

But the situation was no laughing matter to Sam. He shifted uncomfortably, his stomach churning at the dreadful prospect.

# Chapter 9

Kate swept into the reception area with Sam, startled to find that Caroline was sitting atop Verna's desk. The child was twisting and squirming, and Verna was wringing her hands in dismay.

"I've done everything I can to entertain Caroline," the woman said in an apologetic tone, "but I'm afraid she's getting a tad bored."

"You've done a remarkable job, Miss Dunbar, considering the circumstances." Sam snatched Caroline away from the desk with ease. "Caroline tends to get tired of things rather easily."

"Thanks for everything, Miss Dunbar." Kate turned to leave. "I don't know what I would've done without you today."

As Sam swung open the door, Kate paused, admiring the brass name plate at the entrance to the law firm. "Gentry, Springer, and Pierce, Attorneys-At-Law," she read aloud.

"Looks nice, doesn't it?" Sam halted beside her, shifting his daughter's weight from one arm to the other. "Sometimes it's hard for me to believe that I'm actually a partner in this firm."

"You should be very proud of yourself for being where you are, Samuel Springer." With an outstretched finger, Kate traced the outline of his name on the door. "Earning a law degree, setting up your own practice—none of it could have been easy for you."

"I can't take all of the credit. If it hadn't been for Tyler's help, I couldn't have gotten through law school. I didn't have enough money to pay for my education and support myself, too."

"But Tyler says you insisted on paying him back every cent."

"It was the least I could do." He shrugged. "Besides, after all Tyler and Julia have done for me, I couldn't allow them to foot the bill for my schooling, too."

"But you—and only you—were the one who graduated near the top of your class. And Tyler didn't have anything to do with you becoming a partner in the most prestigious law firm in Macon." She glanced at the names on the door once again, pointing to the last of the three. "Is this Nathan Pierce? The same Nathan Pierce who was the best man at your wedding?"

Sam nodded. "The one and the same."

"I remember him well." Images of a dark-haired man floated through her memories, and Kate couldn't suppress a smile. "I danced with him at your wedding reception. He was very charming, as I recall. And quite handsome, too. Tall with dark hair and the most vivid blue eyes . . ."

Noticing the rigid set of Sam's shoulders, the sudden hardness in his eyes, she paused. "Wasn't Nathan your best friend, Sam?"

"At one time. We roomed together during law school, worked side by side as law clerks before we graduated. Then we became full-fledged partners of the same law firm. We shared a lot of the same dreams."

"And . . . now?"

"Things have changed." Sam clamped his jaw into a tight line. "Nathan is no longer associated with our firm, Kate. Lawrence and I have taken over all of his cases. And we've been so busy that we haven't had the time to remove his name from the door."

The rough edge in Sam's voice, the pinched lines of his mouth, told Kate far more than words could say. "Not a friendly parting of ways, I take it."

"Let's just say I'd like to forget everything I ever knew about Nathan Pierce, and leave it at that." Forcing a bleak smile, he planted a kiss on his daughter's forehead before relinquishing the child to Kate. "See you this evening. I'll be in court for most of the afternoon, but I shouldn't be too late getting home."

A few moments later, Kate was sauntering past the shops on Mulberry Street, idly gazing at the window displays, and thinking about . . . Sam.

A troubled frown creased her brow. The depths of Sam's losses in recent months had been much greater than she'd realized. While coping with the death of his wife, he'd also been struggling to deal with the loss of a close friendship. And even though he and Nathan had parted on unfriendly terms, Sam must be feeling some remorse over the loss. After all, good friends are hard to find.

Still, Kate couldn't personally identify with Sam's feelings, even though she sensed he was hurting very badly. She couldn't imagine how she would feel if she had parted ways with Maggie O'Neill. Though she and Maggie occasionally disagreed on issues, nothing had ever threatened to destroy their lifelong friendship.

And though Kate vaguely remembered the profound sense of sadness that had suffused her at the time of her father's death, the memories were too distant, too hazy, to recall with much clarity. She'd only been six years old when the Reverend Jeremiah Carey had died from pneumonia, and she had no way of comparing the loss of a parent with the death of a spouse.

Still, Kate wondered if she knew Samuel Springer as well as she thought. What else had happened in his life in recent months? If she hadn't known about the rift in his friendship with Nathan, there must be other events in Sam's life that she wasn't aware of.

Kate was still mulling over the situation when she noticed the sweet aroma of freshly baked bread wafting through the open door of a bakery.

She paused for a moment. As she admired the attractive display of baked goods in the window, a scrumptious-looking assortment of breakfast pastries caught her eye. Some were sugar-coated, and others were filled with jam . . .

Seized by sudden inspiration, Kate scurried into the shop. Why couldn't she serve pastries for tomorrow's breakfast?

After selecting a half-dozen pastries from the display, Kate purchased a loaf of bread, some yeast rolls for dinner, and two oatmeal cookies for Caroline. Immensely pleased with her ingenuity, Kate made note of the bakery's location when she emerged from the store.

Until she improved her cooking skills, Kate suspected she would become one of the bakery's most loyal customers.

* * *

After lunch, Kate rolled up her sleeves to her elbows, donned a bibbed apron, and set to work. Unpacking her clothes and getting settled in her room were her most pressing priorities for the afternoon.

She delved into the first of two steamer trunks that she'd brought from Hopewell House. As Caroline played contentedly on the floor, trying on Kate's hats and shoes, Kate transferred an assortment of gloves, nightgowns, drawers, stockings, and corsets into an oak dresser.

After hurling open the double doors to a matching oak wardrobe, Kate removed her gowns, blouses, and skirts from the second steamer trunk. Though the wardrobe contained a great deal of storage space, she soon discovered that it wasn't large enough to hold all of her clothing.

Heaving a sigh of dismay, Kate peered around the room. Where could she store the rest of her clothes?

She spied a hump-backed trunk at the foot of the bed, a trunk much smaller and more accessible than her enormous steamers. It was the perfect size for storing hats and other small items.

Assuming the trunk would be empty, Kate pried open the lid. To her surprise, she discovered the container was filled to the brim with an assortment of gowns.

Curious, she knelt beside the trunk. None of the gowns had been folded neatly. It almost seemed as if they'd been tossed aside and stashed away from sight with careless disregard.

The first gown was an exquisite garment, embellished with lace and tiny mother-of-pearl buttons. The next gown was lovely, too, a fetching dress in a deep shade of blue.

Gingerly pulling the blue gown from the trunk, Kate rose and held the garment to her chest. Though the size seemed right, it was far too long for her. It had been designed for a slender, tall woman . . .

*Abigail.*

With a troubled sigh, Kate returned the dress to the trunk. She felt very much like a fool for not realizing that she was riffling through Abigail's personal effects. The instant she'd seen the garments, she should have known that they had once belonged to Abigail. But she'd been too busy admiring the clothing to think about anything other than their beauty.

Closing the trunk lid, Kate wondered why the garments had been stored away so haphazardly. If these were Sam's treasured mementoes of his wife, why would he have tossed them aside with such negligence?

Setting aside the unsettling thoughts, Kate removed several small items from the steamer trunk. She was tucking the garments into the drawers when she noticed a lovely hand mirror on the dresser.

The backing of the mirror was sterling silver, exquisitely detailed with elaborate flourishes. Grasping the handle, Kate gingerly fingered the finely crafted details. But her fingers glided to a halt when she saw the initials etched into the silver. *AVS.*

Kate set down the mirror, acutely aware that she was admiring something that had once belonged to Abigail Vance Springer. And she felt as though she were intruding upon another woman's privacy.

She knew she shouldn't be surprised to find some of Abigail's belongings here. After all, this house had once been the woman's home, and it was only reasonable that she should find some of her personal possessions.

And it was only logical that Sam could have stored some of Abigail's belongings in this room. It was an extra bedroom, after all.

But had this been Abigail's room for the brief time that she'd lived here?

Surely not. Surely Abigail and Sam had shared the same room, the same . . . bed.

A heated flush rose to her cheeks. "It's none of your business," she scolded herself.

Willing herself to banish the wayward

thoughts from her mind, Kate gave her head a shake. She shouldn't be wasting her time thinking about things that were none of her concern. She should be focusing her thoughts on the reason why she was here.

She pulled back her shoulders and lifted her chin. "Just think about how happy you'll be when Sam admits he was wrong about you."

She sighed, wishing she could find more comfort from the thought.

By the time Kate had finished unpacking, Caroline had fallen asleep on the floor. After Kate hastily tucked the child into bed, she set to work, vowing to spend the rest of the afternoon brightening up the cottage.

She sped through the house at a frantic pace, rearranging furniture, adding touches of color in every room, arranging fresh flowers, setting the table for dinner. She had just placed the last fork on the table when Ida Mae arrived with their evening meal.

Kate hastily ushered the woman into the kitchen. Removing the dishes from Ida Mae's basket, she was delighted to find a fresh pork roast, fried apples, broccoli with cheese sauce, several ears of corn, and a peach pie for dessert.

"Won't you stay and join us for dinner, Ida Mae? You've gone to so much trouble, and—"

"It wasn't any trouble, dear. I truly enjoyed making dinner for you. And I appreciate the invitation, but I saved a portion of everything for my own dinner. I have a plate waiting for me at home."

"I envy you, Ida Mae. You make it sound as though cooking were effortless." Kate sighed in dismay.

"If you're still feeling uneasy about cooking dinner by yourself, I wouldn't mind preparing a few more meals for you. And along the way, I'd be happy to give you a few tips about cooking."

"Oh, would you, Ida Mae? All day long, I've been thinking about asking for your help. But I didn't have the courage to ask you for anything else, knowing how much you've already done."

"I'm more than happy to help, dear, especially since you seem so eager to please Sam. It couldn't be easy for him, trying to raise a child by himself. He deserves a helping hand every now and then." A pensive frown crossed her brow. "Frankly, I don't know how he managed when his wife was alive. I don't think she had too much to do with their daughter."

"What do you mean?" Kate asked, curious.

Her frown deepened. "I never saw the woman give any affection—or attention, for that matter—to Caroline. She didn't live here for long, mind you, before she was killed in that horrid train accident. But I got the feeling that she didn't want to be bothered with the child."

An ache swelled in Kate's chest. "I suspected something was wrong, but I never realized . . ."

Ida Mae's face reddened with embarrassment. "Forgive me for upsetting you, Kate. I don't know what got into me. I'm usually not prone to gossiping about anyone." Planting a bright smile on her lips, she turned to leave. "Enjoy your dinner, dear. I hope you have a wonderful evening."

"Thanks, Ida Mae," Kate said, escorting her to the door. "I hope we have a wonderful evening, too."

Returning home for the evening, Sam loosened his cravat as he crossed the verandah and approached the front door.

God only knew what sort of concoction was waiting for him on the dinner table. Considering the ghastly mess that Kate had created during breakfast this morning, he expected nothing less for the evening meal.

Bracing himself for the worst, Sam hurled open the door and stepped into the house. As soon as he entered the parlor, he promptly tripped over the leg of a small table.

And it was a table that had never stood near the entrance to the room, he realized with a jolt. Steadying his balance, he gazed around the parlor in stunned disbelief.

Nothing was where it used to be. Every stick of furniture had been moved somewhere else. His favorite parlor chair, the one he'd purposely placed by the window to take advantage of the light for reading, now stood by the fireplace. And the table near the door—the one he'd stumbled over—had once been located next to the sofa.

Worse yet, the entire cottage reeked of a flowery scent. Wandering aimlessly through the house, he noticed vases of fresh flowers in every room.

And there was more. A crocheted doily here, a little figurine there. A lace pillow on a chair, a framed painting on a wall.

Making his way through the cottage, Sam supposed he should feel grateful to Kate. Had he been in a better humor, the changes might have appealed to him. He might have even complimented or thanked her for brightening up his home.

But gratitude was not the emotion coursing through Sam as he stalked through the house. Annoyance was flooding through his veins.

God help him, his worst nightmares were coming true. Everything about his life was changing since Kate had waltzed into it. She was affecting his work, his home, everything in his entire world. Nothing was untouched by her presence.

As he stormed back into the parlor, Kate emerged from the kitchen. "Have you noticed anything different about the house, Sam?"

"Oh, I've noticed." He grimaced. "I knew something was different as soon as I walked through the door and tripped over a damn table."

"Oh, dear." Her smile vanished. "I didn't realize . . ."

"Apparently, you don't realize what you're doing at all," he muttered irritably.

"I beg your pardon?" Bristling, she compressed her lips into a tight line. "I'll have you to know that I'm acutely aware of what I'm doing, Sam. And if you had a lick of sense about you, you'd know what I'm doing, too. Your home was dreadfully dull and bland before I arrived. And in case you haven't noticed, it's much more appealing and comfortable since I've—"

"But you haven't consulted me on anything, Kate! Dammit, this is my house. My home. I should have the last word here."

"For heaven's sake, Sam! I was just trying to brighten up your life a little bit. Was I supposed to ask your permission to place a doily on a table?"

"It wouldn't have done any good, even if you had. You always do as you damn well please, regardless of anyone else's opinion," he scoffed. "But I can't contend with it, Kate. I have no intention of letting you walk all over me. If I did, you'd soon hold as little regard for me as you do for those sniveling idiots who are constantly sniffing around your skirts and begging for your attention."

"And since when did you become an expert on my feelings?" she shot back. A heated flame burned in the depths of her eyes. "You're presuming too much, Sam. You couldn't possibly know how I might feel."

"But can't you see what you're doing here?" He dragged a hand through his hair in frustration. "You're making too many changes in my life much too quickly."

"Well, maybe you need some changes in your life. Maybe you need to relax and enjoy yourself more, get away from your daily routine every once in a while." She wrinkled her nose. "You're not any fun, Sam. You're getting as stodgy and grumpy as an old man."

That was the final straw. Sam glowered at her, seething with fury. "You don't know what you're talking about, Kate. And to prove my point, I'm not going to the office tomorrow. I'm going to take the day off, and we're going to spend the day on the river. And I'm going to show you just how much damn fun I can be."

# Chapter 10

When Sam sat down at the dinner table later that evening, he was stunned by what he saw.

The linen-draped table was set for three. Each place setting was neatly arranged with china, crystal, and silver. A vase of fresh roses and a pair of tapered candles adorned the center of the table. The glow of the candles cast a soft golden light over the elegant setting.

And he was flabbergasted by the meal. The pork roast was tender and juicy, the corn tasty and sweet, the apples and broccoli cooked to perfection.

He glanced up, wary. "Did you cook this meal, Kate?"

"I'm afraid not." She boldly met his gaze. "When I met Ida Mae Walker this morning, she offered to fix dinner for us. She said it was her way of welcoming me to Macon."

"And it's a very nice gesture on her part." He

174

finished off his last bite of pork roast. "Quite convenient for you, too, I would think."

Sam knew he was being a bastard, but he couldn't seem to help himself. He couldn't bring himself to compliment her on the table setting or offer to help clear the table when the meal was over. He was much too disconcerted from the tumultuous emotions ripping through him to do anything other than mumble a brief thanks for the meal and stalk out to the verandah.

He slumped into a wicker settee and heaved a troubled sigh. Damn her, she was driving him out of his mind. A strange, pulsing restlessness had possessed him, and he had no idea how to purge himself of the chaotic emotions swirling through him. The only thing he knew for certain was that Kathryn Carey was the root cause of it all.

He was still thinking about the situation when he heard the front door creak open. Startled to find that the waning twilight had given way to darkness, he gave his head a shake, trying to clear his troubled thoughts. He hadn't even noticed how late it was until now.

Kate stepped out of the house, inhaling a deep breath, drinking in the evening air. The hazy light spilling through the windows cast a golden glow around her, and Sam thought she'd never looked more enchanting.

"Caroline has already fallen asleep," she said, sauntering across the verandah. She tilted back her head, gazing up at the sky. "Beautiful evening, isn't it?"

"I suppose so," he mumbled, too distracted by her beauty to say anything more.

She sank beside him in the settee. "I finished unpacking my things this afternoon," she announced.

"All settled in?"

"Just about." A frown creased her brow. "But while I was unpacking, I stumbled across some things that belonged to Abigail. They were stored away in a trunk."

"I didn't realize there was anything left of hers around here. Most of her belongings were destroyed in the crash." He shifted uncomfortably. "Her parents took a few items— mementoes of sorts, I suppose—after the funeral, but I told my housekeeper to get rid of the rest. She must have packed them away into the trunk and forgotten about them."

"I thought maybe you had saved some of her things," Kate said. "I thought maybe you wanted to keep—"

"I don't want to keep anything that belonged to Abigail." He gave a careless shrug. "Whatever is left can be burned, for all I care. I never want to see anything of hers again."

She gasped, stunned by his words. "You

sound as if you hated her, Sam. Surely you must have cared for your wife!"

"Cared about Abigail? Oh, I was quite besotted over her in the beginning. So smitten that I was too blind to see that she was batting her lashes at half the men in town. Too much of a fool to realize why she wanted to take a little trip right after Christmas last year." He gave a choked laugh. "She was leaving me, Kate. Leaving me and Caroline."

"Oh, Sam." Her heart wrenched. "I'm so sorry. I never realized . . ."

"Don't feel sorry for me. I don't want your damn pity, or anyone else's. I stopped loving Abigail during the first month of our marriage. As soon as she found out she was pregnant, everything changed. She never wanted Caroline, never wanted any child. And she hated me for getting her pregnant." He raked a hand through his hair. "I suspect she probably bedded half the men in Macon after that. But I didn't realize that one of her conquests was Nathan Pierce . . . until the day of the accident."

"Nathan and . . . Abigail?" Kate whispered in stunned disbelief.

Sam gave a curt nod. "Abigail was leaving town with Nathan. Quite a pair, they were. Everyone thought Nathan possessed the morals of a priest, the integrity of a saint. But he had everyone fooled, including me. And I was supposed to be the bastard's best friend."

His voice was laced with the bitterness of betrayal."Both of them made a damn fool out of me," he continued on. "And I didn't even know how much a fool I had been until it was all over. Until both Abigail and Nathan were dead."

"Oh, Sam." Aching for him, Kate curled a hand around his arm. She hoped the simple gesture would show him just how much she cared.

"Abigail's parents only made matters worse. They refused to believe me when I told them that Abigail was leaving Caroline and me. They implied that I must have been a terrible husband. They insisted I must have made life miserable for their daughter. What other possible reason would she have for leaving me? In their eyes, Abigail Vance Springer could do no wrong."

"So you never told them about . . . Nathan?"

"I didn't see any point to it. It wouldn't have changed anything. Besides, I was having a difficult time coming to terms with it all myself. When I learned about Nathan's death in the accident, I didn't know why he'd been traveling on the same train as Abigail . . . until I found the note that Abigail had left for me in her room."

*"Her* . . . room?" Kate echoed, sensing her suspicions had been correct.

He nodded. "We hadn't shared a room since the first month of our marriage, Kate. Even though we moved to the cottage right after Christmas, hoping to start afresh for the new year, we never shared the same room in this house." He gave his head a shake. "But that's all in the past now, and there isn't any use rehashing it. Besides, it doesn't make any difference now."

"But it's hard for me to believe that the Vances are still blaming you for Abigail's death."

"And they're bent on convincing everyone else of it, too. They're the type of people who place a great deal of importance on social proprieties. Mrs. Vance is the nervous sort who always worries about what other people will think or say, and the judge has a very stubborn disposition."

"I wish I had known about all of this, Sam. I wish you'd come back to Rome, let us know what was going on in your life. Maybe we could have comforted you, helped you deal with this nightmare somehow."

"But I didn't want you—or anyone at Hopewell House—to know anything about my mockery of a marriage. Coming back for a visit was out of the question. Until my visit last weekend, I didn't believe enough time had passed, enough wounds had healed." A shadow of darkness crossed his face. "And I was ashamed, Kate, too damn ashamed. I've always been determined to make something of myself, to prove to Tyler and Julia that they hadn't been wrong to take a kid like me under their wing."

"None of us at Hopewell House would have thought less of you, Sam. We can't be responsible for someone else's actions or behavior."

"I suppose you're right." He heaved a disgruntled sigh. "I didn't mean to get carried away, you know. Talking about Abigail—and Nathan—dredged up some bad memories that I've been trying to forget."

"But if you keep all those bad feelings and memories inside you, they won't go away. Talking about your troubles should ease some of your pain."

"Maybe you're right, Kate." His lips twitched with the hint of a smile. "Do you realize I've just agreed with you—twice, nonetheless—within the last minute?"

"Odd." She lifted her hand to his face, pressing her fingers across his brow. "You don't feel like you're running a fever."

He chuckled. "Maybe I'm getting a mental disorder."

Her gaze drifted across his face, then lingered on his lips. "I like it much better when you smile, Sam." She sighed contentedly. "I suppose I should be turning in for the night," she finally said. Leaning forward, she brushed her lips across his. "Goodnight, Sam. I'll see you in—"

"You shouldn't be kissing me, Kate." His arm tightened around her shoulders.

"It was just a little a goodnight kiss, Sam. It wasn't meant to be anything more."

"My mind understands that. But my body doesn't comprehend a word that you're saying."

She felt a heated blush rise to her cheeks. "You mean . . . your body likes it when I kiss you?"

"Very much so, Kate. Too much, in fact."

"And what about your mind? Does your mind like it, too?"

"Part of my mind says I shouldn't like being kissed by someone who makes me furious. But the other part reminds me that we're not kids anymore, insists I should enjoy what you're doing to me." His voice became husky and low. "And demands I should be enjoying more of your kisses."

"Oh, my." She forced a tremulous smile. "I think that part of your brain is making far too much out of one goodnight kiss."

"But it's not the goodnight kiss that's causing my brain so much turmoil, Kate." His fingers skittered across her cheek. "The turmoil comes from knowing that you want more than just a goodnight kiss, too."

She gazed up at him, intending to voice a reply. But as his mouth came down on hers, she couldn't remember what she wanted to say. The instant she felt the heat of the kiss sizzling through her, everything else became very distant and far away.

Everything but her feelings. A torrent of emotions was spinning through her, a torrent as strong and powerful as the man who was holding her in his arms.

This kiss was different from the one they'd shared in the rose garden, different from any kiss Kate had ever known. The touch of Sam's mouth awakened emotions she never knew she had, aroused feelings she never knew she possessed.

Sam was kissing her with such reverence, such tenderness, that she ached inside. His lips were moving across hers in a slow, exacting way, as if he were savoring, sampling, exploring the taste of her.

It was sweet torture, the feel of his mouth stroking and gliding, lingering and hovering, over hers. Reveling in the strange new sensations pulsing through her, Kate drew closer, wanting more. Losing herself in the feel of him, the taste of him, she glided her hands across the broad expanse of his shoulders, then slipped her arms around his neck.

A groan of desire rumbled from his throat.

"You don't know what you're doing to me, Kate," he murmured, his voice rough and low.

His mouth pressed down on hers again with more urgency, more pressure. His tongue, hot and wet and demanding, surged into her mouth, and he crushed her more tightly against him.

Trembling, Kate tightened her arms around his shoulders. Her breasts were aching and swollen, her heart was thundering in her chest, and a slow, simmering warmth was seeping through every pore of her body.

"I never knew kissing could be like this," she admitted in a hoarse whisper. She threaded her fingers through his hair, feeling it slip like silk against her skin. "I never knew anything could be like this."

"This is only the beginning, Kate." His breath was warm against her mouth. "There's so much more to feel . . . to taste . . . to explore . . ."

Kate couldn't imagine anything more glorious than the kiss that Sam had just bestowed upon her. But she became vividly aware that she'd merely been sampling a taste of something much more potent and powerful when his mouth clamped down over hers again.

Sam was sweeping her away into a world she'd never known existed, a world of passion and heat and desire. And when he cupped her breasts in his hands, running his fingers over the hardened tips of her nipples, she thought she would die from the sudden surge of heat coursing through her.

Just when she was certain she could endure no more of the blissful agony, Sam dragged his mouth away from hers. "This is what I've been wanting to do ever since I kissed you in the rose garden, Kate," he said, his breathing ragged and deep.

"I thought for certain you were going to kiss me last night . . . until something caused you to change your mind."

His eyes clouded with a mixture of regret and sorrow. "I was trying to convince myself that I shouldn't *want* to be kissing you." He lifted his hand to her face, brushing his knuckles across the curve of her jaw, then threading his fingers through the golden curls that tumbled around her temples, her cheeks. "Shouldn't want to be touching you . . . feeling the softness of your skin . . . the silkiness of your hair . . ."

Everything about him—the low, husky timbre of his voice, the touch of his hands, the depth of emotion shimmering from his gaze— mesmerized her. "And . . . now?" she whispered.

"And now . . ." His fingers stilled in her hair, and she felt his muscles tighten. "And now I know I shouldn't be feeling this way about you, Kate. It's not right for you—or for me."

A pained expression flickered across his ruggedly handsome face as he pulled away from her and eased up from the settee. "Emotions aren't always trustworthy, and feelings aren't always logical, you know."

He shook his head in frustration, turning to retreat into the house. "And God knows, there's nothing logical about my feelings for you."

Sam slept little that night. Visions of a golden-haired beauty kept intruding into his dreams.

When he awakened the next morning, he tried to disregard the images of Kate dancing through his mind. But the haunting images lingered in his thoughts, no matter how hard he tried to ignore them.

And it was impossible to forget the memory of their kiss on the verandah. He'd never intended to draw her into his arms, but it had seemed as if he couldn't help himself. The instant his mouth had brushed across hers, all reason had deserted him. Feeling the receptiveness of her lips, sensing her eagerness for more, he'd been consumed by flames of desire raging through him.

Now, recalling the kiss with vivid clarity, Sam cursed himself soundly. Good God, didn't he have an ounce of self-control around the woman? Hadn't he sworn to resist the temptation of kissing those sweet, sweet lips? Hadn't he vowed never to touch her?

But how much torture could a man endure? He was a man, for God's sake, not a damn saint. Though his heart and mind understood the grim reality that there could never be anything between Kate and him, his body was tormenting him with an insatiable desire for her. And the battle between his mind and his body was raging out of control.

He stalked out of his room, his mood darkening with every step. Living under the same roof with Kathryn Carey, trying to restrain himself from pulling her into his arms, was far more torturous than he'd imagined.

But he was going to have a damn good time with her on the river today. Even if it killed him in the process.

Over breakfast, he told her about their plans. "It looks like it's going to be a scorcher of a day, but we'll be much cooler on the water. I'm intending to rent a paddle boat for us, so bring along a parasol to shade Caroline from the sun. With her fair complexion, I wouldn't want her to get burned this afternoon."

"We'll be ready in just a few minutes, then."

When she emerged from her room a few moments later, dressed for the day, Sam had no idea how he was going to keep his eyes off her while he was paddling the boat.

She was wearing a white poplin dress with a carter's frock and an underskirt of green and white striped sateen. A straw skimmer was perched on her head, and a few wisps of golden hair dangled along her temples and cheeks. And never had she looked so ravishing.

An hour later, Kate was picking up her skirts and climbing into the paddle boat that Sam had rented for the day. After getting Caroline settled inside the small craft, Sam launched the boat into the water.

The river was filled with an assortment of vessels, ranging from elaborate yachts to simple paddle boats. Sam paddled at a steady pace, alternately dipping the oar on one side of the boat, then the other, until they reached a secluded area near the shoreline.

Leaning back in the boat, Sam set the oars aside and enjoyed the gentle lapping sounds of the water and the cool breezes that were easing the stifling heat of the July afternoon.

But Kate could hardly contain her excitement, peering from side to side, drinking in the sights as though she'd never viewed anything from the water. Her cheeks were tinted with a rosy hue, and elation shone from her eyes.

Caroline, too, seemed fascinated by her new surroundings. The child's wide, innocent eyes peered curiously at the other boats drifting over the river as she sat quietly in Kate's lap.

Enjoying the peacefulness of the setting and the lulling motions of the boat drifting along the water, Sam was tempted to close his eyes. But at that instant, Kate pointed toward the shoreline.

"Look, Caroline!" Kate motioned toward a flock of geese. "Look over there!"

Overwhelmed by excitement, Kate set Caroline on the bench beside her and sprang to her feet. The sudden jarring motion tipped the boat to one side, throwing Kate off balance. Her feet slid out from beneath her, and she landed on the bottom of the boat with a splat.

Sam glowered at her. "For God's sake, Kate! You could have dumped us all in the river! Don't you know better than to stand up in a little boat like this one? Caroline is only three years old, and she's behaving more appropriately than you are."

Kate struggled to pull herself upright. "For heaven's sake, Sam! Don't be such a fuddy-duddy. You should know I had no intention of tipping the boat over. I don't know why you're always so worried about everything. You're always thinking that something awful is going to happen. Can't you just relax and have fun?"

"I was having fun, until you nearly drowned us," he growled, grasping her hand and pulling her to her feet. "Why can't you be like every other woman in the world, Kate? Why can't you be shy and demure, unassuming and timid?"

She plopped down on the bench. "Is that what you truly want, Sam?"

"Of course it is. Isn't that what every man wants?"

"But is that the kind of woman that you want for yourself? If you could have your choice of any woman in the world, what kind of woman would that be?"

He heaved a disgruntled sigh. "I've never been good at games of pretend, Kate. You know that."

"But it wouldn't hurt you to dream a little, Sam," she urged.

"I don't particularly relish the thought of dreaming about something I don't want, Kate. I have no intentions of getting involved with another woman anytime soon. I've never given the matter a great deal of thought. And, quite frankly, I don't care to."

She opened the parasol and propped it behind her, allowing the shade to cover herself and Caroline. "But maybe you should think about what you want, what you could have, in a woman. If the world was perfect and you could have your heart's desire, what kind of woman would you want for yourself?"

Kate was so tempting, so convincing, he thought. Her urgings reminded him of the time when they were children. Kate had persuaded

Sam to sprawl out on the grassy lawn of Hopewell House and peer up into the heavens, coaxing him to tell her what he saw in the clouds drifting through the summer sky.

Initially, Sam had balked at the idea. Gazing up into the sky was nothing but a silly waste of time, he'd thought, nothing but one of Kate's little games of pretend.

But to his astonishment, he'd never enjoyed anything more. Seeing all those hidden faces, all those dreamy formations written in the clouds, Sam had discovered that there was much more to Kate's silly games of pretend than he'd thought.

"Come on, Sam," Kate urged once again. "What would it hurt to dream a little? Don't you think it would be kind of fun to create the woman of your dreams?"

"Sounds like you've done this sort of thing before," he said in an accusing tone. "You've been giving this issue some thought yourself, haven't you?"

A smile blossomed on her lips. "I've been thinking about the man of my dreams for years. And I guess that's why every man I've ever known has never been able to catch my eye. I'm always comparing every man I meet to the elusive man of my dreams."

"Even Augustus Moulton?" Sam couldn't resist teasing.

"Even Augustus," she confirmed with another grin. "Most of the suitors who have called on me I've known since childhood. Since I know everything about them, there's nothing about them that interests me, nothing new to discover about them."

"But they're always quite willing to please you," Sam noted.

"They're much too willing to please me," Kate admitted. "Actually, it's almost nauseating at times. Most of them act like I don't have a brain in my head. They're always trying to prove that I need their protection from the cruelties of life." She rolled her eyes heavenward. "And Lord knows, I don't want to be protected or treated like some mindless fool."

"Heaven forbid if any man should treat you as less than his equal," Sam chimed in.

"I suppose I'm waiting for someone exciting to sweep me off my feet, like a dashing prince or a knight in shining armor." A dreamy expression clouded her delicate features, and her eyes took on a wistful glow. "I want someone who will whisk me away to places I've never been. Someone who will show me all the things the world has to offer, who can take me to parties and balls, who can introduce me to people across the globe. Ah, what a wonderful life that would be. Every day would be a new, exciting adventure."

"So you're not thinking of settling down?"

Sam probed. "You're wanting someone who moves from place to place all of the time?"

"I want someone who will never settle for anything less than a new adventure each day. If that means moving from place to place, I could accept that. But I suspect the man of my dreams will probably be a risk taker, a gambler of sorts."

"I see," Sam mumbled, acutely aware that he met few, if any, of the qualities and traits she'd just described. If he ever had any inkling of being the man of Kate Carey's dreams, she had just shattered the notion. By far, Samuel Springer wasn't the type of man with whom Kate Carey wanted to spend the rest of her life.

"And what about you, Sam? It's your turn, now."

He narrowed his eyes, gazing into the distance, deciding to play along with the game. After all, what harm could it do?

"The perfect woman for me? Ah, let's see . . ." Leaning back, Sam crossed his arms over his chest. "I suppose she would have to be the sort of woman who likes spending quiet evenings at home. Someone who likes good books, good conversation, a few close friends."

He continued on, deciding this was more fun than he thought it would be. "She would have to be domesticated, of course. A meek, mild woman. Someone who is patient and thoughtful, quiet and kind. The sort of person who thinks of others' needs before she thinks about her own. She would have to be polite, of course, and possess a touch of shyness about her."

"And what about looks?" Kate probed.

"It really doesn't matter to me," Sam confessed. "In fact, she doesn't necessarily have to be beautiful. But she has to possess a special inner beauty, a quiet peace. And she can't be bossy or controlling or demanding. I want someone who will adore my daughter as if she were her very own. Someone who will be content to live in the same place with one man for the rest of her life."

Sam lapsed into silence, and a bittersweet sadness engulfed Kate. She gazed off into the distance, suddenly wondering why some things were never meant to be.

# Chapter 11

It was mid-afternoon by the time they returned to the cottage. As Sam's buggy pulled up to the house, Kate was delighted to see that two visitors were standing on the verandah.

"Perlina!" Kate scrambled down from the buggy and rushed across the front lawn to greet the guests. "It's so nice to see you!"

"It's wonderful to see you again, too, dear. Have you been enjoying your visit to Macon?"

"I certainly have." Kate glanced at the young woman with light brown hair who was standing beside Perlina. Though she wasn't an exquisite beauty, her face bore a sweet expression. "You must be Harriet."

"My mother has spoken very highly of you, Miss Carey," Harriet said politely. "It's a privilege to meet you."

"And we have a little housewarming gift for you, dear," Perlina said, presenting an apple pie to Kate. "Harriet made it just this morning."

At that moment, Sam stepped up on the verandah, holding Caroline by the hand.

"Look, Sam!" Kate held up the apple pie. "Perlina's daughter made a pie for us."

"How very thoughtful of you, ma'am." Sam flashed a friendly smile in Harriet's direction. "I don't believe we've met, have we?"

Her face blossomed with color. "No, we haven't, Mr. Springer. I'm Harriet Gordon."

"Why don't we all sit down and treat ourselves to a slice of Harriet's pie?" Kate suggested. "We can use the wicker table here on the verandah. I'll fetch some knives and forks and a pitcher of iced tea for all of us."

Within a few moments, the little group was gathered around the table. After tasting his first bite of the pie, Sam glanced over at Harriet and grinned. "I must say, it's pure pleasure to meet a woman who knows how to bake an apple pie the way you do, Miss Gordon."

Harriet blushed to the roots of her hair. Dropping her gaze to her plate, she mumbled, "Thank you, Mr. Springer."

"Harriet does all the baking at our house." Motherly pride glimmered from Perlina's eyes. "And she contributes much of her time to charitable work, too. Her favorite organization is the library."

"Right now, our library is housed in the Knights of Columbus building on Mulberry Street," Harriet revealed. "But all of us in the library association dream of having our own building someday."

"We're holding our biggest fund-raising event of the year next week," Perlina added. "We've been working on it for months. It's a dinner and dance at the Johnsons' home."

"And it should be the most elaborate affair of the year," Harriet rushed on. "The Johnsons' home is like a palace, from what I hear. It has closets in the bedrooms and rooms just for bathing. And I've heard it even has hot and cold running water from the pipes!"

"The picture gallery is supposed to be marvelous, too. It's large enough to serve as a ballroom, so we'll be holding the dance there," Perlina noted.

"It all sounds very exciting. Are you planning to go, Harriet?" Kate asked.

She nodded. "Mother and I have been planning to attend for months."

Perlina and Harriet lingered on the verandah with Kate and Sam for more than an hour, discussing other upcoming events in town.

Though Kate thoroughly enjoyed the conversation, she couldn't help but notice Harriet's awkwardness around Sam. Every time he addressed her, she stammered and blushed, fumbling over her words and refusing to meet his gaze.

"Well, I suppose we should be leaving now," Perlina finally said. "We've had such an enjoyable visit, haven't we, Harriet?"

"The afternoon has passed very quickly," the young woman agreed.

"You'll have to drop by again very soon," Kate said.

"With another one of your pies," Sam added with a charming grin. "I don't think I've ever tasted an apple pie that was any better than yours, Harriet."

"Thank you," she returned, her voice scarcely above a whisper.

"And I do hope we'll be seeing you at the library fund-raiser," Perlina added, turning to leave.

As the women left the verandah, Sam reached for another slice of pie. Kate glanced at him across the table. "The dinner and dance at the Johnsons' home sounds like a fabulous gala, Sam. Do you plan to attend?"

"Those black-tie affairs don't appeal to me very much. I'll probably send a donation to the library association instead of attending the fund-raiser." His eyes narrowed. "Why do you ask?"

"I was just wondering. I thought you might be thinking about asking Harriet to attend the ball with you."

"And why would you think that?"

She shrugged. "You seemed rather interested in her."

"Interested in Harriet?" A bewildered expression crossed Sam's face. "What gave you that impression?"

"You were flirting with her, Sam. And you can't tell me that you weren't. A blind man could have seen what you were doing!"

"I don't know how in the hell you conjure up all of this rubbish, Kate. I never had any intention of asking Harriet to some damn ball."

"Then you shouldn't have been flirting with her," Kate admonished. "You should have had some compassion for the poor woman. Couldn't you see how painfully shy she was? Why, every time you looked at her, she was blushing and stammering."

"Well, at least she knows how to blush. Some women don't have enough grace about them to feel embarrassed about anything." He gave a wistful sigh. "And she sure as hell knows how to cook, too."

Kate forced a strained smile. "Well, if you like Harriet Gordon's cooking so much, why don't you ask her to be your housekeeper?"

"Not a bad idea, Kate," he mused, chuckling at the thought. "Maybe I will."

Still chortling, he rose and retreated into the

house. Kate remained in her seat, glaring at him until he disappeared from sight.

The cottage was quiet when Kate awakened the next morning. She slipped a wrapper over her cotton nightgown and padded into the kitchen.

The coffee was still warm, and she suspected Sam hadn't been gone for very long. Still, she wished she'd awakened early enough to share breakfast with him.

She poured a cup of coffee for herself and sank into a chair at the table. Maybe it was just as well that Sam had left before she'd awakened.

Truth was, she felt terribly confused. She'd always cared for Sam, but her feelings for him were changing into something more, something that reached beyond friendship and fondness, and she wasn't certain how to deal with the unfamiliar emotions soaring through her.

And no matter how she felt about Sam, Kate was determined not to forget that she was responsible for running his household and caring for his daughter while she was here.

Vowing to set aside her disconcerting thoughts, Kate rose from the chair. At some point, she had to muster up the courage to hone her skills in the kitchen. She couldn't depend on purchased goods and Ida Mae's generosity for every meal. And she needed to stock the pantry with some basic supplies without delay.

An hour later, she was meandering down the street, pushing Caroline in her stroller. In her arms were several garments from Sam's wardrobe. A quick survey of his clothing had revealed that numerous pieces were in dire need of a good cleaning, and Kate had wasted no time in obtaining the name of a laundress from Ida Mae.

A good housekeeper, after all, would make sure that the man of the house was properly dressed for all occasions.

Kate dropped off the garments at the home of the laundress. Then she inhaled a deep breath and headed straight for Bell's Market.

But as she browsed through the merchandise for sale in the market, Kate became painfully aware that someone—Julia or Aunt Odelphia or Aunt Dorinda—had always supplied her with a list of goods to purchase at the store. Kate had never been solely responsible for planning menus, purchasing supplies for an entire household . . . or even cooking a complete meal.

But if she requested delivery of her purchases for the next morning, she could devote all day to preparing the evening meal.

And surely she could manage one simple meal. Surely she could bake a potato, toss a salad, string some green beans. And with a little luck, maybe she could even fry a chicken without burning it.

With renewed determination, she marched up to the counter and placed her order, then charged the purchase to Sam's account.

"When would you like this order to be delivered?" the clerk asked.

"Tomorrow morning. And the earlier, the better."

Leaving the market, Kate vowed that she would cook a wonderful meal for tomorrow night's dinner. And along the way, she'd make certain that Samuel Springer knew who cooked every bite.


Sam retrieved a stack of documents from his desk as he prepared to the office for the evening. Stashing the papers into his briefcase, he expelled a disgruntled sigh.

He had no choice except to finish his work at home this evening. Throughout the course of the day, he'd accomplished little of what he had to do. Thoughts of Kate had kept intruding upon his work, wrecking havoc on his concentration.

As soon as he returned home for the evening, he retreated into the privacy of his room. Shrugging out of his jacket, he hurled open the door to his wardrobe and stopped cold.

To his astonishment, all of his clothes were missing.

Sam stared at the empty wardrobe in disbelief. Where in the hell were his clothes?

He stormed to the door. "Kate, I need to see you," he bellowed. "Right now."

She swept down the hall, a flurry of petticoats and skirts swishing around her legs. "Is something wrong, Sam?"

"You're damn right there's something wrong." Grasping her arm, he pulled her into the room. Then he placed his hands on her shoulders and spun her around, forcing her to gaze into the empty wardrobe. "My clothes are missing, Kate. Can you tell me anything about this?"

"What would you like to know?"

He clenched his jaw. "I'd like to know what you've done with my clothes."

"For heaven's sakes, Sam! There's no reason for you to get so upset. There's a simple reason why your clothes aren't here. I'm having them cleaned for you."

He didn't know whether to be relieved or mortified. "Who's cleaning my clothes?"

"A lady who works next door to your tailor's shop. She has a little business there, laundering and pressing clothes. And she promised she would have your clothes ready by tomorrow."

"And what am I supposed to wear in the meantime?"

"The suit you wore today, of course. What else would you wear?"

"Wait just a minute, Kate." Sam frowned in confusion. "You said this lady works next door to my tailor. But how do you know my tailor?"

"Because I went to see him today."

"Do I dare ask why?" he growled.

She shot him a scathing glare. "There's no need for you to get so upset with me, Sam. In fact, I'm the one who should be upset, not you. You've spoiled my surprise."

"Your . . . surprise?" He gripped the bedpost, bracing himself for the answer.

"If you must know, I found the name of your tailor on a little tag inside one of your jackets. And I thought it would be nice if you had a new suit to wear."

"So . . . you ordered a new suit for me . . . from my tailor?" he surmised.

She nodded brightly. "That's my surprise. And I know you'll like the fabric, Sam. It's a beautiful tweed, with touches of blue and—"

"Did it ever occur to you that I might prefer to pick out my own clothes, Kate? Did you ever stop to think that you might be overstepping your bounds?"

Dismay shadowed her delicate features. "I didn't think you'd mind, Sam. Actually, I thought that's what I was supposed to do."

"What do you mean?"

"I thought a good housekeeper would take

care of your wardrobe, just like she's supposed to take care of your house. Isn't that what a housekeeper would do?''

"Making sure my clothes are cleaned and neatly pressed is a housekeeper's job, Kate," he conceded. "But that doesn't include buying new clothes for me. That's not something you should be doing . . . unless you're my wife."

"I see." Her smile was tepid, her gaze unusually cool. "Well, I don't really have the time to be purchasing clothes for you, anyway. Tending to my own wardrobe takes up a great deal of my time." She picked up her skirts. "Now, if you'll excuse me, I need to get moving. Peyton should be arriving soon, and I—"

"Peyton?"

"Yes, Sam. Peyton Ransom, your new client. Does the name sound familiar?"

"Of course it does," he snapped. "I'd just forgotten this is the night that Peyton is escorting you to some music house."

"You forgot?" Kate's gaze was full of skepticism and doubt. "After the way you fussed and fumed when I accepted Peyton's invitation, I'm surprised you didn't remember."

"Maybe I had other things on my mind," he muttered. "Maybe I had better things to do than to keep up with your social calendar. Maybe I—"

"Honestly, Sam, I can't stand here squabbling with you all night. I want to be ready when Peyton arrives." Promptly ending the discussion, she picked up her skirts and scurried into her room.

Sam was sitting in the parlor, reading a book to Caroline, when Kate's voice rang through the house. "Has Peyton arrived yet, Sam?"

"Haven't seen any sign of him," Sam answered.

He had just turned to the next page of the book, intending to resume the story, when he heard the soft rustle of a woman's skirts sweeping across the floor.

Sam glanced up and froze, stunned by what he saw.

Kate was wearing a heart-stopping evening gown of silk taffeta, an off-the-shoulder creation trimmed with silk roses. White opera-length gloves accentuated the gown, and she was carrying a white clipped ostrich fan. As an added touch of elegance, she'd swept her hair off her neck and placed some silk roses into the soft mounds of golden hair swirling over her head.

The sight of her ripped the breath from Sam's lungs. But it was the plunging neckline of the gown that prompted a scowl on his face.

"Don't you think your dress is a bit daring, Kate?" Sam pointedly fixed his gaze on the enticing line of cleavage that protruded above the daring bodice of her gown.

"Low necklines have become fashionable of late, Sam. Everyone has an evening gown like this."

"But I dare say no one else looks the way you do in that gown," he mumbled. "For God's sake, Kate, you're practically indecent."

"And what if I am?" she countered. "What I choose to wear shouldn't be of any concern to you. Besides, you're not my escort for the evening."

"But you can't wear that gown in public, Kate! You'll have every man in this town panting after you." He raked his gaze over her once again, frowning. "Can't you wear a wrapper or shawl and cover yourself up?"

At that moment, Caroline wiggled across Sam's lap. "Pretty, pretty," she said, pointing to Kate.

"Thank you, Caroline." Kate smiled at the child. "It's nice to know someone appreciates my dress."

"She shouldn't even be looking at you," Sam grumbled, placing his hand over Caroline's eyes. "She's too young to be exposed to such lewdness."

Caroline let out a shriek, yanking Sam's hand away from her face, just as a knock sounded at the door.

"Would you mind answering the door, Sam? Since this is your home, I believe it would be most appropriate if you greeted Peyton." Kate absently fingered one of the silk roses in her hair. "Besides, I don't want to act like I'm too eager to see him."

"And God forbid, we shouldn't behave in an inappropriate manner," Sam muttered.

Clenching his teeth, he begrudgingly complied with Kate's request. But as soon as he opened the door, he sorely wished he hadn't. The instant he saw Peyton Ransom, he was seized by an overwhelming urge to knock the man's smile off his face.

"Good evening, Mr. Springer," Peyton said. "I do hope Kate hasn't forgotten our engagement this evening."

"How could I possibly forget, Peyton?" Sweeping across the room, Kate greeted her escort with a dazzling smile. "I've been looking forward to this for days."

Peyton entered the house, sidestepping Sam, never once removing his gaze from Kate. Clearly enchanted by the sight of her, he reached for her hand.

"Something tells me that I shall be the envy of every man in town this evening." He pressed his lips across her gloved hand. "You look absolutely ravishing, Kate."

"Why, thank you, Peyton." Her thick, dark lashes fluttered beguilingly. "How nice of you to notice."

"How could I not?" His gaze raked over the length of her with brazen approval. "You're the most exquisite creature I've ever seen."

"And I feel very fortunate to have such a charming escort for the evening," Kate returned smoothly.

Standing at the door, witnessing the exchange, Sam felt something akin to nausea surging through him. Not only was he repulsed by the sight of Peyton drooling over Kate, but he was sickened by Kate's responses to the man. Dammit, she was practically fawning over him!

Sam was still fuming when Peyton tucked Kate's hand into the crook of his arm. "We really should be leaving now, Kate," Peyton said. "Are you ready to go?"

She tipped her head. "I wouldn't want us to be late."

Sam gallantly opened the door and stepped aside. As the couple swept past him, arm in arm, he forced a bleak smile. "Have a wonderful evening," he muttered, then slammed the door behind them.

"I must say, I'm surprised by the size of the crowd this evening," Peyton said, perusing the throng of fashionably dressed ladies and gentlemen who were milling through the foyer of the music hall. "Macon must have a strong contingency of residents who appreciate fine music."

"I heard someone say that tonight's performance has been sold out." Kate glanced across the crowd. "And judging by the number of people here, I suspect it's true."

"Perhaps the musicians who are performing this evening have a strong following in Georgia." A hint of a smile touched his lips. "What did you think about the first half of the concert?"

"I don't think I've ever been to a performance that I've enjoyed more thoroughly than this one," she admitted in all honesty.

"I have to agree with you." Warmth and admiration shimmered from his eyes as he gazed down at her. "I've attended concerts all over the world, but nothing can compare to this."

Kate's eyes widened incredulously. "But all the great masters—Bach, Beethoven, Mozart— hailed from Europe. Surely their native countries have produced masterful musicians over the years. I would think you could attend performances in Europe that surpass any of the concerts held here."

"Skillful and talented musicians can be found everywhere, Kate. But I've discovered one noticeable difference between this concert and all the rest."

"And what sets this one apart from the others?" she asked, genuinely curious.

His voice became husky and low. "It's the only one I've ever attended with you."

Kate's breath lodged in her throat. Scores of besotted admirers were constantly extolling her virtues, lavishing her with more flowery phrases and words of adulation than she cared to remember. Accustomed to the cajolery, Kate had practically become immune to the frivolous remarks, tossing them aside without a second thought.

But Peyton's comment rattled her beyond all reason, and she wasn't certain why.

Struggling to catch her breath, she noticed that the crowd was streaming back into the music hall.

"Apparently, the intermission is coming to a close, Peyton."

He nodded in agreement. "We should be getting back to our seats now."

Kate slipped a gloved hand around his outstretched arm. But just as she fell into step beside Peyton, Kate heard the rumble of a deep bass voice behind her.

"Well, Miss Carey. What a pleasant surprise to find you here."

Kate froze, tightening her grip around Peyton's arm. Then she slowly turned and peered up into the face of Judge Vance.

"Good evening, Judge," she said with a gracious smile. Taking note of the woman standing next to him, she tipped her head. "And you, too, Mrs. Vance."

Stunned by the sight of Kate's plunging neckline, the Vances offered no reply. The judge's white, bushy brows narrowed with disapproval, and Estelle clamped a hand over her mouth to stifle her gasp.

After Kate hastily introduced Peyton to the couple, however, Judge Vance recovered his voice with amazing speed. "Is Sam attending the concert this evening, too?"

"I'm afraid not, Judge," Kate replied. "He remained at home tonight with Caroline."

"I thought you were supposed to be taking care of Caroline while you were here, Miss Carey." An accusatory glare shone from Estelle's eyes.

"I am caring for her, I can assure you, Mrs. Vance. But even the most dedicated nanny in the world deserves to have some time to herself on occasion." Kate nodded cordially, then turned to leave. "Good evening, Judge, Mrs. Vance."

Heading into the music hall, Peyton squeezed Kate's hand. "I hope that couple's audacious behavior hasn't been too disconcerting for you, Kate."

She smiled up at him. "The Vances couldn't

possibly spoil my evening. From what I understand, they look at everything in life with scowls on their faces."

Kate slipped into her seat beside Peyton, setting aside all thoughts of her encounter with the judge and his wife. Within a few moments, she was thoroughly engrossed in the second half of the concert.

All too soon, the performance came to a close. As soon as they left the building, Peyton inhaled a deep breath and smiled. "Ah, what a beautiful evening. Do you mind if we take a stroll and enjoy the fresh air?"

"That sounds like a wonderful idea, Peyton."

Kate sauntered along beside him, enjoying the full moon and the evening breezes. "Where will you be going when you leave Macon?"

"I plan to spend a few days in New Orleans," he explained. "Then I'll head to New York. And from there, I'll be going to Paris."

"Paris?" Kate sighed. "I've always dreamed of going to Paris."

"It's an enchanting city. As a matter of fact, it's one of my favorite places."

Kate lost track of the time, enthralled with Peyton's descriptions of the places he had visited. And somewhere along the way, she became enchanted with the man himself, captivated by his sense of humor, his winning smile, his engaging ways.

As they ambled through a small park, Peyton reached out and captured Kate in his arms. Whirling her around, he flashed a disarming smile. "I suddenly feel like dancing. Would you care to dance with me this evening, Miss Carey?"

She laughed. "I'd like nothing more, Mr. Ransom."

He whisked her through the park until she was breathless and dizzy and shrieking with delight. And then, without warning, he bent his head and kissed her.

Kate eagerly accepted his kiss, curious about the feel of his mouth on hers. All of her life, she'd dreamed about meeting a man like Peyton Ransom. He was lively and adventurous, fascinating and intriguing, even a tad bit reckless in an irresistible sort of way. He was everything she'd ever dreamed of, everything a man could be.

His lips were soft and compelling, his kiss warm and sweet. "Ah, Kate," he whispered, slowly dragging his mouth away from hers. "I wish I'd met you long before this."

Kate gazed up into Peyton's ruggedly handsome face, desperately wishing she felt something stirring deep inside her.

His smile was disarming in a dashing sort of way, but it didn't make her feel warm and giddy and wonderful inside. His eyes were a beautiful shade of blue, but not an enticing hue of green. And his hair was dark blond, but not a rich, deep shade of auburn.

Though Peyton made her laugh, he didn't infuriate her like another man she knew. He didn't look at her as if he were torn between strangling her or kissing her senseless. He didn't have a worry frown creasing his forehead, and he didn't make her heart thunder in her chest.

"It's getting late, Peyton," she finally whispered. "I suppose I should be getting home now."

His smile was warm and understanding. "As you wish, Kate," he agreed.

She fell into step beside him, a bittersweet ache filling her heart.

# Chapter 12

Sam paced the length of the verandah, his movements stiff and rigid, his body taut with tension. Where in the hell was Kate?

It was nearly midnight, and the concert couldn't have lasted for more than an hour or two. She should've been home long before now.

"Dammit," he muttered, clenching his fists into tight balls. No decent, self-respecting woman should be roaming the town at this hour of the night, cavorting with a man she barely knew.

Why hadn't she come straight home after the concert? Where in the hell had Peyton Ransom taken her?

And why in the hell should it matter to him?

Sam stormed back into the house. It was none of his business what Kate and Peyton were doing. None of his business at all.

He snatched up the documents he'd brought home from the office, determined to banish all thoughts of Kathryn Carey from his mind. But as soon as he collapsed into a parlor chair, intent on devoting full attention to his work, he found himself listening for the shuffle of footsteps on the verandah.

He tossed the paperwork aside, cursing under his breath. From the instant Kate had entered the parlor, wearing that indecent dress, something had snapped inside him.

He'd been tempted to lock her away in her room, forbidding her to leave the premises until she agreed to cover up that enticing cleavage of hers. And once he'd witnessed Peyton's approving appraisal of her, he sorely wished that he had. It had taken every ounce of discipline Sam possessed to keep his balled fists away from the man's nose.

By the time they'd left for the concert, Sam had been glad to see them go. He'd been certain that the turmoil ripping through him would cease as soon as Kate disappeared from sight.

But the evening had been far more torturous than he could have ever imagined. Caroline had whined for most of the night, roaming through the cottage, peering into every room, her eyes searching for someone, someone who wasn't there.

Worse yet, after Sam had tucked his daughter

into bed for the night, he caught himself doing the same thing. Muttering a string of oaths, he'd stalked into the parlor and promptly resolved to gain control of his wayward behavior.

But all night long, Sam found himself listening for the sound of Kate's chatter, straining to hear the breezy lilt of her laughter.

His house seemed empty, barren, without her. But God help him, he didn't want to admit that he missed her, missed the warmth of her presence in his home. Didn't even want to think about how bleak his life would be without her, what an important part of his life she had become in so short a time.

He was still struggling with the disconcerting thoughts when the sound of voices drifted through the open parlor window.

"Oh, Peyton, you're such a tease. You don't really mean that . . . do you?"

"I wouldn't mislead you, my dear. I'm deadly serious. If I knew that I could turn your head, I could be tempted to give up my wandering ways."

"Settling down in one place might be rather difficult for you, Peyton. Something tells me that traveling is in your blood."

"But that doesn't make me immune to your charms, Kate. Already, you're infecting my bloodstream."

"You're much too kind, Peyton." Kate stretched up on her toes and lightly pressed her lips against his. "Thank you for a wonderful evening. I can't remember the last time I've enjoyed myself so much."

"I hope it's only the first of many more delightful evenings for us," Peyton said, turning to leave.

Kate quietly slipped into the cottage. Standing in the foyer, she sagged against the closed door and heaved a heavy sigh. Just as her lashes fluttered to a close, Sam's voice shattered the silence.

"So you had a wonderful evening?" he goaded. "Can't remember the last time you've enjoyed yourself more?"

Her eyes shot open. "Samuel Springer! You were eavesdropping on me!"

"I wasn't eavesdropping," he insisted. "I just happened to overhear a conversation between you and your besotted suitor."

"And what's the difference?" She crossed her arms over her chest and glared at him. "Were you peeking through the window, too?"

"For God's sake, Kate!" His face reddened with fury. "I was sitting in the parlor, minding my own business, when you came home with Peyton. It's not hard to hear someone on the verandah when the windows are wide open. And the two of you weren't exactly whispering. How could I not listen?"

"But you could have given us a moment of privacy, Sam. You could have had the decency to remove yourself from the parlor when you heard us at the door."

"You think I should have abandoned the comfort of my own parlor so you could have some privacy with your suitor?" he scoffed, glowering at her in disbelief. "I believe you're forgetting that this is my home, Kate. Not yours."

"But that doesn't give you the right to be so inconsiderate!" Kate snapped.

"You shouldn't have been discussing anything that you didn't want anyone else to hear," he countered. "Besides, I didn't learn anything new from listening to your conversation on the verandah. Earlier this evening, I noticed the two of you were quite smitten with each other."

"Peyton Ransom is a very intriguing man. I don't think I've ever met anyone who leads such an adventurous life. He's always whisking off to new places, exploring the unknown."

"How fascinating," Sam remarked, his tone flat and dry.

"There's a dashing, reckless appeal about him," Kate continued on. "Why, we even danced together under the stars tonight! We may not have had any music, but it didn't seem to matter to him."

Some of the color drained from Sam's face. "You . . . danced together?" he echoed in a strangled voice.

"Do you find that disturbing?" she taunted.

"No," he snapped. "I find that ridiculous. Whoever heard of dancing without music?"

"Actually, it's very romantic. There's something wonderful about getting caught up in the magic of the moment and being swept off your feet by a man who takes you into his arms and—"

"Don't, Kate." Sam's eyes hardened. "Spare me the details. We may have known each other since we were kids, and we may have shared a lot of things in our lives, but I don't care to hear about Peyton Ransom sweeping you off your feet."

"I just thought you'd like to know that I enjoyed myself this evening." She frowned. "But you don't seem very pleased. In fact, you're acting like you're downright angry about it."

"I am not angry, dammit!" His fists knotted into tight balls. "Why should I even care?"

She edged closer to him, studying the wrinkles in his brow. "You're frowning again, Sam," she warned.

"I've got a right to be frowning," he snapped. "I've spent the whole damn night worrying about you, wondering if Peyton Ransom was behaving himself." He paused, gazing around the room. "And this house was so damn empty without you."

"You . . . missed me?"

He stilled. "I should have known better than to get accustomed to having you around here. I've always sworn that no woman would find a place for herself in my home. I don't like the idea of giving any female the chance to wreck havoc on the only place I've ever been able to call my own." He forced a strained laugh. "For some reason, the women in my life have never cared to stay around for very long."

Kate's throat tightened with emotion. "You mean your . . . mother?"

"What mother?" he chided, his eyes becoming cold and hard. "I never had a mother in the true sense of the word. What kind of woman would toss aside a ten-year-old kid without a second thought? Leave him to fend for himself so she could take off with some sweet-talker who probably promised her a few trinkets in exchange for her services?"

Kate felt a knot swell her throat, remembering how the kids at school had taunted Sam about his ragged clothes and his mother's loose morals.

Yet, in all the years that they'd known each other, Sam had rarely mentioned anything about his life before moving to Hopewell House. And he'd never discussed the pain and heartache he must have felt when he'd been struggling to make his way in the world as a frightened, abandoned boy.

"When we were children, I don't think anyone really knew what you were going through," she mused. "All I knew for certain was that I wanted to be friends with you more than anything else in the world. In the beginning, you were a bit of a mystery to me, I suppose. But after you came to Hopewell House, I couldn't help but admire your determination to forget about your past and make a better life for yourself."

"You . . . admired me?" he echoed in disbelief.

Kate nodded. "You defied the odds against you, Sam. You escaped from the past you'd inherited and never looked back. I respected you for that, even when we were kids. And now . . ."

"And . . . now?"

"I don't think I fully understood the depths of your strength and determination until now. Who would've ever dreamed a starving, abandoned boy could accomplish what you have? You've carved out a new life for yourself, Sam. You have an honorable profession, a beautiful daughter, a home of your own."

"But you've neglected to mention that I made the blunder of my life when I married Abigail. I was a damn fool not to see that the woman was just like my mother. She abandoned Caroline just like my mother abandoned me, seeking refuge in the arms of another man."

Kate's heart ached. "Your mother and Abigail were the losers, Sam. Not you." She paused. "If you could only see yourself through my eyes, see the man who I see . . ."

"I can just imagine what you see," he mumbled in disgust.

"I don't think you do." She peered up at him, liking everything she saw. "I see a man who should be very proud of himself for what he's accomplished in his life, for having the courage to raise a precious little girl all by himself."

His eyebrows rose in surprise. "I didn't realize that you thought—"

She silenced him by placing an outstretched finger over his lips. "I'm not finished yet, Sam. Let me tell you what else I see."

She brushed her hand across his forehead. "I see someone who has frowned so much that he has a permanent crease in his brow." Her fingers trailed over the intriguing line of his jaw, then skittered over the sensuous line of his lips. "And I see a man who is so handsome that my heart nearly jumps out of my chest when he smiles at me."

Skepticism and doubt glimmered from his gaze. "Don't hand me that, Kate. I'm not one of your besotted admirers who dotes on your every word."

"I'm well aware of who you are, Samuel Springer. And I'm well aware of what I see when I look at you. And I'm just trying to tell you what I see, truthfully and honestly." Her heartbeat quickened beneath the intensity of his gaze. "And whether or not you believe me, everything I'm saying is true."

Sam swallowed hard. "Sometimes we need someone in our lives to help us look at ourselves from a different perspective, I suppose."

"With my tendencies toward getting carried away with things, I know I need someone in my life who is a calming voice of reason . . . someone like you, who makes me see life from a different point of view."

The tiniest hint of a smile curved on his lips. "We can usually count on each other for an opposing viewpoint."

"But it's nice to know I can be myself around you. You know the real me, Sam. I'm the woman who can burn water and has a penchant for pretty dresses. But no matter what I say or think or do, I know you won't banish me from your life forever."

"But I have been tempted to strangle you a few times," he reminded her, his grin broadening. To illustrate his point, he placed his hands around her bare neck and gave a playful squeeze.

But the instant he felt the satiny smooth touch of her skin beneath his fingers, the light-heartedness of the moment vanished. Sam's smile faded away, and his heart thundered in his chest.

She must have sensed the electricity surging between them, too. Peering up at him, she whispered, "Have you ever stopped to think that we need each other, Sam? Need each other . . . badly?"

Wrought with emotion, Sam couldn't utter a sound. Why was it so hard for him to acknowledge that he needed Kate? Why couldn't he admit that he needed her in ways he'd never dared to fathom?

Surrendering to the turmoil that had been gnawing away at him for days, he gave up trying to understand the reasons for the emotions flooding through him. Logic played no part in this obsessive, pulsing need to claim the woman as his own.

"Come here, Kate," he whispered, his voice low and strained.

She took a step forward, and that was all she needed to do. No longer able to control the desire surging through him, he crushed her against him and lowered his mouth to hers.

He kissed her with all the passion and fervor that had been building inside of him, kissed her with the urgency of a man who had been denied his dreams for far too long.

By the time he finally tore his mouth away from hers, his hands were trembling, his heart was thundering, and his breathing was shallow and ragged. Peering down into her face, he swallowed thickly.

"It isn't easy for me to admit I need anyone, Kate." His throat tightened with emotion. "But I can't deny it any longer. I've never needed anyone in my life as much as I need you."

Without a moment's hesitation, he grasped her by the hand, guiding her down the hall and into his room.

Kate hesitated at the door. "Sam, I've never . . . I haven't . . . I'm not sure if . . ."

"It's only me, Kate," he whispered, lifting his hand to her face, brushing back a few tousled strands of hair from her cheek.

"Only you," she whispered back, as if to find some assurance in those simple words.

But her voice was shaking, her body trembling. Sam struggled to do something, say something, that would ease her fears. "I would never do anything to hurt you, Kate. You know that, don't you?"

She nodded weakly.

He planted his hands around her waist, feeling the shudders rippling through her. "Don't tie yourself up in knots. There's no reason to be nervous. I won't do anything you don't want me to do."

"That's the problem, Sam." She managed a tremulous smile. "I can't think of anything I don't want you to do. I want . . . everything. Everything you have to give. I want all of you."

Shaken to the core, Sam drew her closer her to him. "God, do you realize how much I've wanted to hear you say that? How long I've denied feeling the same way about you?"

"Too long," she whispered back.

"But I know what I want now, Kate. I know what I need. I want to make love to you. All night long. In every way you can imagine . . . and ways you've never dreamed possible."

He crushed her against him. Shudders were still rippling through her, but Sam knew that fear wasn't causing her to tremble. Desire—for him—was the reason for the tremors quaking her body. And it made him want her all the more.

When his mouth claimed hers again, Kate felt as if she were drowning in a sea of sensations and feelings. The touch of his mouth, wet and open and hot against hers, ignited a wave of heat that consumed every part of her body and soul and mind.

Eager for the feel of him, Kate moved her hands across his back, savoring the play of muscles beneath his smooth skin. Her fingers trailed downward, gliding over the small of his back, coming to rest on his taut derriere, pulling forward until she could feel his arousal nudging the gentle swell of her belly.

She moaned against his mouth, pressing closer, as his hands glided down to the neckline of her dress. Edging away from her, he tugged at the garment, dragging it down the length of her body until it slithered to the floor and puddled around her feet.

As soon as he'd stripped away her undergarments, Sam raked his gaze over the length of her bare body, admiring her hardened nipples and swell of her breasts, the indentation of her waist, the gentle flare of her hips.

"You're more beautiful than I could have ever imagined, Kate," he rasped.

His words of approval and the desire glimmering from the heat of his gaze gave Kate the courage to reach out and run her fingers along the waistband of his trousers.

In some small way, she hoped the gesture would show him that she was becoming as impatient as he. Every nerve in her body was on fire, throbbing with a need far greater than any she'd ever known.

He trembled at the touch of her hand gliding across his belly. "You're driving me insane, Kate," he said with a moan of desire.

He released the button on his trousers, and the garment dropped to the floor. The sight of his arousal sent another surge of heat coursing through her, a surge so powerful that her legs quivered from the intensity of it.

He edged her toward the bed and eased her

down onto the sheets. And then his hands and mouth were everywhere, touching, exploring, feeling. Beneath his hands, her breasts budded, tightened with passion, ached with pain. Beneath his mouth, her skin burned from the heat of his touch.

Gasping, she arched her back. His kisses drifted down her neck and came to rest on her breasts. First one, then the other. As his tongue flickered lazily across the hardened tips, Kate thought she would die from the glorious sensations coursing through her.

While she struggled with those feelings, his hand dipped lower, across her stomach, then moved lower still. Feeling the pressure of his fingers gliding across the warm, moist juncture between her thighs, Kate trembled with longing.

But it was the feel of his fingers inside of her that brought a moan to her lips. "Oh, Sam," she groaned, rasping for breath. "I never knew . . ."

The sound he made was strangled, somewhere between a sigh and curse. "It's only the beginning, Kate. Only the beginning . . ."

He moved like lightning, planting his knees on either side of her, entering the place that no man had ever been, taking her as gently as his raging passion would allow.

A cry of pleasure rose from her throat. She was hot and wet, moist and pliant, ready for him. Feeling the warmth of her melting around him, Sam rocked his hips in a rhythm as old as time.

He wanted it to last forever, this union of their minds and bodies. He would have given anything to wait, just to watch her face as she skimmed from peak to peak and back again.

But he had already waited a lifetime for her, and he couldn't find the strength to wait a moment more.

With one, final thrust, with her name tearing from his lips, Sam shuddered as he spilled his seed inside of her. Sated with passion, he dropped his head to her breast.

"I wish I could have given you more," he said, regret tainting his voice. "I wish I could have taken you with me, showed you what heaven could be. But I couldn't wait, Kate. I couldn't—"

She placed an outstretched finger over his lips, silencing him. "I've already had a glimpse of heaven in your arms, Sam," she whispered. "How much more glorious could anything be?"

"More glorious than you ever dreamed, my sweet Kate. And I promise I'll take you there. Just you wait and see."

She didn't have to wait for long.

Time and time again throughout the night, Sam made love to her. He showed her just how wondrous the love of two people could be. He took her to places she'd never been, never even known existed. And brought her back to earth with kisses so tender and loving that she ached from the beauty of them.

When the first light of dawn shimmered through the open window, Kate quietly pulled away from the warmth of Sam's embrace, gathered up her clothes, and slipped out of the room. Caroline would be awakening soon, and Kate wanted to be dressed and ready to greet the new day by the time the child awoke.

But as she went through the motions of preparing herself for the day, Kate couldn't shake the erotic memories of the passion-drenched night she'd shared with Sam. She'd loved him with total abandon, allowing him complete possession of her body and mind and soul, giving him everything she could offer in return.

Even now, every pore of her body was still tingling from the aftermath of their lovemaking. Her lips were swollen and red from his kisses, her cheeks pink from the scrape of his beard. And her most private parts were still tender and aching from the newness of his gentle invasion.

Without a doubt, Kate knew that the physical marks of their lovemaking would soon fade away. But she wasn't so certain that the emotional effects would disappear so easily.

Yes, he'd said he'd needed her, wanted her.

But he'd never made any mention of love. Though she knew he cared for her, cared for her deeply, Kate wasn't certain about the extent of Sam's feelings. Did he love her enough to marry her? Share the rest of his life with her at his side?

She thought not. If something had driven him to the point of confessing his need for her, surely that something would have urged him further, convinced him to do the right thing and ask her to marry him before taking her to his bed.

She suspected his claim of needing her had stemmed from the same reason that had brought her here in the first place. Sam needed a mother for his daughter, didn't he? He'd never claimed he needed her in any other way, other than to satisfy the physical needs that were coursing through him.

"You fool," she whispered, ashamed of herself for her wanton behavior.

What did the future hold for her now? No one could ever take Sam's place in her life. Not after she'd given herself to him so completely.

Hearing Caroline stirring, Kate slipped into the child's room. But as she cradled the child in her arms, a heavy weight filled her chest.

How could she stay here, after what she'd done?

But how could she bear to go?

# Chapter 13

❝**I**❞'m running behind schedule this morning, Kate." Sam hurried into the kitchen, adjusting a silk cravat around his wing-tipped collar. "I'll just grab a pastry and eat it on the way to the office."

Seated at the table with Caroline, Kate glanced up in surprise. "You don't have the time to eat breakfast with us?"

"I'm afraid not. But this is all your fault, you know. I wouldn't be running late if I hadn't overslept." He reached out and brushed back a wayward curl from her forehead. "And I wouldn't have overslept if you hadn't kept me up half the night."

"You must have been dreaming, Sam." Kate blinked with mock innocence, but she couldn't hide the smile that was blossoming on her lips. "I would never disturb you while you're sleeping."

He leaned over and nuzzled his chin against the soft curve of her neck. "I wish you'd disturbed me before you slipped out of bed this morning. I was disappointed when I woke up without you."

She motioned toward his daughter, who was contentedly sitting at the table, nibbling on a breakfast pastry. "Caroline was already stirring when I awakened. I couldn't ignore her, Sam. I just couldn't."

"I wouldn't have wanted you to," he assured her.

With reluctance, he prepared to leave for the office. After grabbing a pastry and bidding goodbye to Kate and Caroline, he headed for the door.

But as soon as Sam stepped outside, he noticed that everything seemed different to him. Colors appeared brighter, noises sounded crisper, smells seemed stronger.

He even felt different. There was a noticeable spring in his step, and his heart was thundering in his chest. He'd never felt so alive, so wonderful, so spirited.

And he knew the reason why. She was sitting in his kitchen, caring for his daughter.

He'd never known anything as wondrous as their night of wanton passion. In spite of her innocence, Kate had been a willing, eager lover, more passionate than he'd ever fathomed.

He was still thinking about Kate when he

entered the courthouse later that morning, smiling at the memory of their heated night of lovemaking. But the smile on his lips vanished when he encountered Judge Vance in the hallway.

"You're just the man I wanted to see, Springer." The judge's face bore a stern, disapproving expression. "I'd like to talk with you about an important matter. And the sooner, the better."

Sam narrowed his eyes, suspicious. "What kind of important matter?"

"One that concerns you, son. And I—"

Judge Vance halted abruptly as several men emerged from a nearby room. He twisted his mouth into a frown, refraining from saying anything more until the men had shuffled past them. "I'd prefer not to hold a private discussion in a public hallway, Springer. I'd rather prefer the privacy of my chambers. Are you free to join me there?"

"I can spare a few moments," Sam conceded. "I'm not due in court until eleven."

Following Judge Vance into his chambers, Sam sank into a chair in front of the man's desk. As soon as the judge was seated, he cast a scathing glare in Sam's direction.

"I won't waste any words, Springer. I want to talk about this woman who is living with you."

Sam went rigid. "Then we have nothing to discuss, as far as I'm concerned."

Judge Vance's eyes grew cold and hard.

"Need I remind you that I am Caroline's grandfather? If Miss Carey is supposedly taking care of my granddaughter, I believe I have every right to voice my reservations about the woman.'"

"You're entitled to your opinion, Judge. But Caroline's welfare is my responsibility. I'm the one who decides what's best for my daughter. And I'm the one who decides who should care for her."

"But Miss Carey wasn't taking care of Caroline last night," the judge noted. "Estelle and I saw her at the Academy of Music."

"I'm perfectly aware that Kate attended the concert," Sam returned smoothly. "You're not telling me anything that I don't already know."

"But I don't think you're aware of what happened at the music hall. Your Miss Carey is the talk of the town this morning, Springer."

Sam narrowed his eyes. "What do you mean?"

"Everyone was appalled by that decadent gown of hers. The woman caused quite a ruckus. Half the town attended the concert, and she flaunted herself in front of everyone in that scandalous dress." The line of his jaw hardened. "I don't want a woman like that caring for my granddaughter, Springer. I don't want Caroline to be exposed to someone like her."

"Kate's dress might have attracted some attention last night, but that doesn't mean she isn't capable of caring for my daughter."

"But her choice of attire raises serious doubts about her character. People are already speculating about the situation between the two of you, knowing that you're living together under the same roof. And I'm distressed by what they are saying. It doesn't reflect well on either you or me, Springer."

"And that's your real problem, isn't it?" Sam countered hotly. "Caroline's welfare isn't the issue here. You don't really give a damn about who takes care of Caroline."

The judge's face reddened with fury. "I'll have you know that my granddaughter's well-being is of utmost concern to me."

"But I suspect it's not your primary concern at the moment. Something tells me that you're more concerned that people might associate you with a woman who happened to stir up some talk by exposing her generous cleavage at a public function last evening. You're more worried about what people are saying about you than the care of your granddaughter."

"It's a wonder my daughter hasn't risen from her grave to haunt you, Springer. Abigail would've been chagrined to know that Miss Carey is Caroline's nanny."

"Abigail wouldn't have given a damn. When

she was alive, she never cared a snippet about our child." Seething with fury, Sam bolted to his feet.

"How dare you speak so disrespectfully about my daughter! Abigail would have never—"

"I don't believe Abigail has anything to do with the issue at hand, Judge Vance. And it's perfectly clear to me what you're trying to say. But I suspect that you wouldn't approve of anyone who takes care of Caroline, no matter who she might be."

He wheeled and stormed toward the door. But he'd taken only two steps across the room when Judge Vance called out to him.

"If you know what's best for you and Caroline, you'll get rid of the woman, Springer."

Sam stopped cold. Turning, he glowered at the judge. "And if I don't?"

"Most likely, you'll regret that you didn't listen to me."

Every muscle in Sam's body went whipcord taut. "Is this a threat, Judge?"

"You can interpret my warning any way you wish. But mark my words, if you don't find another nanny for Caroline, I'll make certain that you'll rue the day you were born."

Kate had just finished dressing Caroline for the day when she heard a knock at the front door.

She scurried into the foyer, pleased to find

that a young boy was standing on the verandah, carrying a wooden crate packed with an assortment of food.

"You must be from Bell's Market," she surmised. "I've been expecting you."

"Where would you like your order, ma'am?" he asked.

"Just follow me," she instructed, leading him into the kitchen.

The boy quickly placed the crate on the table, then turned to leave. Kate escorted him to the door, then returned to the kitchen to check her order. But just as she began to sort through the goods, another knock sounded at the door.

"Maybe the delivery boy forgot something," she mumbled, heading back to the foyer.

Kate hurled open the door, startled by the sight of the unexpected caller standing on the verandah.

"Good morning, Miss Carey," Estelle Vance said coldly.

"What a surprise to see you, Mrs. Vance." Kate motioned for the woman to step inside the house. "Would you like to come in?"

"Only for a moment." The woman entered the foyer, appraising the interior of the cottage with a critical eye. "Is Caroline here?"

Kate nodded. "She's in her room, playing at the moment."

"I see." Estelle pursed her lips into a tight line. "And is she ready to leave?"

Kate frowned in confusion. "What do you mean?"

"Sam must have forgotten to tell you," the woman said in a short, clipped tone. "I'm taking care of Caroline today. She's spending the day with me."

"That's odd." Kate nibbled on her lower lip. "Perhaps there has been some sort of misunderstanding. I can't understand why Sam wouldn't have told me about your plans with Caroline. Are you certain he knows about this?"

Estelle bristled with defiance. "Are you accusing me of trying to deceive you?"

"Not at all, Mrs. Vance." Kate lifted her chin. "I'm merely wondering why Sam failed to inform me about the arrangement."

"Perhaps he told you, and you simply don't remember it." The woman's eyes glimmered with a contemptuous gleam. "After all, you've been quite busy of late. Judging from what I saw of you last evening, I would suspect that you've had other, more pressing concerns on your mind."

"What do you mean, Mrs. Vance?"

"It's quite evident that you're much more concerned about finding a suitable husband for yourself than caring for my granddaughter," she said crisply.

Kate's eyes widened in stunned disbelief. "Whatever gave you that impression?"

"Why, it was perfectly obvious last night when you were parading through the music hall, calling attention to yourself with that outlandish dress of yours."

"That outlandish dress of mine is quite fashionable, Mrs. Vance," Kate retorted through gritted teeth.

"Still, everyone knew what you were trying to do. And I was personally mortified to see that you were flaunting yourself in front of every man in town, knowing that you are responsible for tending to my granddaughter." She rolled her eyes heavenward. "I shudder to think what kind of influence you are on Caroline."

"I am a wonderful influence on Caroline," Kate countered in a cool tone. She pulled back her shoulders and glared at the woman, outraged by her audacity. "You're being quite unreasonable, Mrs. Vance. My dress may not have met with your approval, but you can't judge my abilities to care for Caroline on the basis of my choice of attire."

"Your abilities?" she scoffed, laughing scornfully. "You're far too young to possess the experience of a skillful nanny, my dear. It's quite obvious that you're merely masquerading as a housekeeper and nanny. You've merely agreed to this absurd arrangement so you could come here to Macon and find a husband for yourself."

"Don't you think you're being a bit presumptuous, Mrs. Vance?"

"Not in the least. Of course, at first, I suspected that you had pegged Sam as your future husband. But after last night, I'm convinced that you're still shopping around, trying to find the best value in town."

Kate summoned up every ounce of willpower she possessed to keep from yanking the woman's hair out by the roots. She couldn't remember the last time that anyone had infuriated her this much. Unwilling to contend with any more of the woman's insulting remarks, she motioned toward the door.

"I must ask you to leave, Mrs. Vance, before I do or say something that I might regret."

"Just as soon as you fetch Caroline for me, I'll be on my way."

"I don't think it would be wise for you to care for Caroline today, Mrs. Vance. Perhaps another time might be better."

"Don't try to deny me of my right to see my own granddaughter, Miss Carey." She crossed her arms over her chest and frowned. "I am Caroline's grandmother, and I have no intention of leaving here without her this morning."

Kate floundered for a moment, not certain what to do. She couldn't bear the thought of releasing the child into the hands of this wretched woman. Yet, Estelle Vance was Caroline's grandmother. What right did Kate have to withhold her granddaughter from her?

Heaving a frustrated sigh, Kate made her decision. "I'll get Caroline ready for you, Mrs. Vance."

Caroline was not at all pleased at the prospect of spending the day with her grandmother. Fussing and whining, she wrinkled her nose in dismay as Estelle grasped her hand and guided her through the door.

"I'll be returning with Caroline around dinnertime," Estelle announced stiffly as she turned to leave.

Kate quietly shut the door behind them, praying she wouldn't regret her decision to relinquish Caroline into the care of Estelle Vance for the day.

"Please send the bill to Mr. Samuel Springer," Kate informed the shopkeeper. "His office is located on Mulberry Street."

"I'll get this over to him right away," the shopkeeper agreed. "And I hope your little girl enjoys her new dresses."

Emerging from the shop, Kate smiled with satisfaction. After her disturbing encounter with Estelle Vance, she'd decided that a shopping spree would be the best remedy for boosting her dismal spirits.

And she'd been right. Immensely pleased

with the dresses that she'd purchased for Caroline, Kate could hardly wait to present the child with her new wardrobe. To Kate's astonishment, the shop had carried a large of selection of ready-made dresses for little girls, and Kate had eagerly selected a half dozen new garments in Caroline's size.

Merrily humming under her breath as she returned to the cottage, Kate placed her purchases in Caroline's room. But as soon as she entered the kitchen, the lilting tune on her lips faded away.

"Oh, for heaven's sake," she grumbled, dismayed to discover the crate of goods on the kitchen table. Caught up in the frenzy of the morning, she'd totally forgotten about unpacking the supplies that she'd ordered from the market.

Sorting through the goods, Kate was pleased to find that nothing had been omitted from the order. And she was satisfied with the freshness and quality of the food, too.

She hastily placed the chicken into the icebox, vaguely aware that the poultry felt a bit warm. Dismissing the matter without a second thought, she turned her attention to preparing a simple lunch of ham and cheese for herself.

Deliveries from the laundress and tailor consumed some of Kate's time after lunch. By mid-afternoon, she was ready to face the challenge of preparing dinner. Donning a bibbed apron, she lifted her chin with determination and set to work.

After she'd scrubbed the potatoes, stringed the green beans, and sliced the chicken, Kate set a pot of water on the cookstove. She had just pulled an iron skillet from the cupboard when the sound of Ida Mae's voice drifted through the air.

"Ready for that cooking lesson now, Kate?"

Kate scampered to the door, delighted to see Sam's neighbor. "As ready as I'll ever be, I suppose," she returned with a grin.

Grateful for Ida Mae's help, Kate sought the woman's advice on how to season the beans and prepare a coating for the chicken. Following Ida Mae's instructions, step by step, Kate was delighted with the results of her efforts. By late afternoon, the green beans were simmering on the cookstove, the chicken was browning in the skillet, and the potatoes were roasting in the oven.

"You're doing just fine, Kate," Ida Mae praised. "Just remember to keep an eye on the skillet, dear. After all your hard work, you wouldn't want the chicken to burn."

"I'll remember, Ida Mae," Kate promised, escorting her neighbor to the door. "I wouldn't dare forget."

\* \* \*

"This just arrived for you, Mr. Springer," Verna announced, dropping an envelope on Sam's desk.

"Thanks, Miss Dunbar."

As Verna retreated from the room, Sam ripped into the envelope, curious about its contents. Unfolding the enclosed paper, he froze in stark disbelief, stunned by what he saw.

The paper was an invoice, a bill of sale for a half dozen dresses. And the total sum for the garments was beyond anything Sam would have ever considered reasonable for even one dress.

"This is all Kate's doing," he mumbled in disgust, jamming the bill into his pocket. The woman obviously had no inkling about the value of a dollar.

He heaved a frustrated sigh, wishing he could recapture the sense of optimism that had brightened his morning. But his unsettling conversation with Judge Vance had considerably dampened his spirits, and his foul mood had intensified throughout the day. Receiving an unexpected bill for a preposterous sum was all he needed at the moment.

As soon as he arrived home for the evening, Sam drew in a deep, steadying breath and silently resolved to remain calm about the matter. "Can I speak with you for a moment, Kate?" he called out.

She emerged from the kitchen, wearing a bibbed apron over her dress. "Is something wrong, Sam?"

"I'm afraid so." He retrieved the invoice from his pocket and presented it to her. "What can you tell me about this?"

She hastily scanned the document. "Why, I do believe it's a bill for some dresses."

"And what do you know about these dresses?" he demanded, struggling to hold on to his patience.

"I purchased them today for Caroline. And I can't wait for you to see them, Sam. They're absolutely delightful, perfect for—"

"They should be more than delightful," he grumbled. "At these prices, they should be trimmed in gold."

"Considering the quality, I really didn't think the prices were too bad," Kate began. "They're one-of-a-kind dresses, you know. Caroline will be the only little girl in Macon with—"

"For God's sake, Kate!" Sam roared. "She's only three years old! She's not vying for a place in society. What made you think I would agree to spend such an outlandish sum on six measly dresses?"

"I didn't think you'd mind, Sam. Honestly, I didn't. I didn't think you would—"

"That's the problem, Kate. You don't think at

all. You don't bother to stop and consider the consequences of what you're doing."

Fury blazed from her eyes. "I was thinking about Caroline, Sam. She needed some new clothes, and I don't see any harm in—"

"Forget it, Kate," Sam snapped. "Just forget I ever mentioned it to you."

He stormed into his room and slammed the door behind him, trying to calm his frazzled nerves. But after shrugging out of his frock coat and cravat, Sam decided he was sorely in need of a breath of fresh air.

Heading for the verandah, he sensed a faint whiff of something unpleasant wafting from the kitchen, something that resembled the smell of scorched food.

But he chose to ignore it. He'd already wounded Kate with his scathing remarks, and she didn't need the additional humiliation of having him gawk at the charred remains of dinner. And if something other than food were in danger of catching fire, he was certain she'd seek out his help.

He remained on the verandah, staring out into space, purposely avoiding any contact with Kate until she quietly announced that dinner was ready to be served.

When he stepped into the dining room, he was surprised to find that the meal looked edible. But as soon as he sat down at the table, he frowned in confusion. Where was Caroline?

"Has Caroline already eaten dinner?" he asked.

Kate shifted uneasily in her chair. "Caroline isn't here, Sam. But she should be returning home shortly. Mrs. Vance promised she would bring her back around dinnertime."

Sam stilled. "You allowed Estelle Vance to take Caroline for the day?"

"She said you'd agreed to the arrangement," Kate explained. "She said—"

"You should've known better than to believe that woman, Kate!" Sam trembled with fury. "For God's sake, you should have known that I don't want Caroline spending any time with her!"

"What was I supposed to do, Sam?" Kate retorted. "Estelle is Caroline's grandmother, after all. When she barged into the house, demanding to see her granddaughter, what right did I have to refuse her?"

Sam clamped his mouth shut, knowing he couldn't argue with her. After a long moment of silence, he conceded, "It's all said and done now, I suppose."

Vowing to remain civil for the duration of the meal, Sam said nothing more until Kate passed the serving dishes to him. Startled to see that the serving platter held only one piece of chicken—a thick breast, fried golden brown— he glanced up at her in confusion.

"Aren't you having any chicken tonight?" he asked.

"Don't worry about me, Sam," she assured him, evading his startled gaze. "I'm not very hungry. I snacked on some pastries this afternoon. Between the potatoes and green beans, I have plenty to eat for dinner."

He scowled. "You'll have to come up with a better excuse than that, Kate. I'm not a damn fool. What's going on here?"

"It's just that . . ." Dismay clouded her eyes and her voice. "I don't enjoy admitting my mistakes, Sam. And I'm getting tired of confessing that I'm a miserable failure in the kitchen." She heaved a frustrated sigh. "Why can't I cook something without burning it to a crisp?"

"You haven't burned everything." He stabbed some beans and potatoes with his fork. "You didn't burn the potatoes, or the beans."

"That's only because Ida Mae dropped by this afternoon and stood over me while I cooked them. And she warned me to keep an eye on the skillet so I wouldn't burn the chicken. But when you came home and called me into the parlor . . ."

Sudden understanding assaulted him. "The chicken burned while you were talking to me," he surmised, grimacing.

"Except for one piece that I couldn't fit into

the skillet," she explained. "I cooked it by itself, after I burned the rest."

He took a bite of the chicken and nodded with approval. "It's very good, Kate. But I think it might taste even better if I added something spicy to it. You wouldn't take offense if I sprinkled a little hot sauce over my chicken, would you?"

She shrugged. "It won't hurt my feelings at all."

Sam retreated into the kitchen and grabbed a bottle of hot sauce from the pantry shelf. There was an odd flavoring in the chicken, something he couldn't identify. He suspected some sort of strange spice had been mixed into the coating, something he wasn't used to.

He returned to the table and smothered the chicken with a generous helping of hot sauce. Just as he finished the last bite, a rap sounded at the door.

Kate leaped up from her chair. "That must be Mrs. Vance with Caroline."

Sam followed Kate to the door, startled by the haggard look on Estelle Vance's face, chagrined by the condescending tone in her voice.

"You're ruining this child, Samuel Springer," she declared. "Caroline used to possess my lovely daughter's sweet spirit. But she's picked up some horrible mannerisms and habits since this woman has come to live with you."

Sam snatched his daughter away from the woman's grasp. "You don't know what you're talking about, Estelle. You've never spent enough time with Caroline to know what she's really like."

The woman tossed back her head. "I spent enough time with her today to see what she's becoming. And I don't like what I see at all."

"Maybe the problem isn't Caroline," Kate interjected. "Maybe the problem is you, Mrs. Vance."

The woman's eyes widened in stunned disbelief. "I shall make certain that my husband hears about this, Miss Carey."

Snapping around, Estelle marched across the verandah. Sam quietly closed the door behind her, shaking his head in dismay. "I could wring that woman's neck," he muttered.

Wrestling with his tumultuous emotions, Sam avoided Kate for the remainder of the evening. The reasonable, rational part of him knew that he shouldn't be angry with her for granting Estelle permission to take Caroline for the day. Just as Kate had pointed out, what right did she have to deny Estelle's request?

But the other half of him, the emotional part, wouldn't let him forget that Kate had only added more fuel to the fire simmering between the Vances and him. Allowing Estelle access to Caroline had given the woman added ammunition against him, and he'd never hear the end of the woman's complaints.

He had just slumped into a wicker chair on the verandah, mulling over the situation, when Kate came out of the house. "Caroline must have been exhausted," she said. "She's already asleep."

"Estelle probably made her march in place all afternoon, barking orders at her like some blasted general," Sam grumbled. "Of course, none of this would have ever happened if you hadn't let that wretched woman take Caroline for the day."

Kate stiffened. "We've already discussed this, Sam. It wasn't my place to refuse her demands to see Caroline."

"But you could've stalled her, Kate. You could've made some sort of excuse to keep her away from my daughter. You know how I feel about Judge Vance and his wife."

Kate crossed her arms over her chest and pursed her lips together in a tight line. "I'm getting a little weary of hearing about all the things I should've done, Sam. Listen to yourself, will you? You're telling me that I should've had the sense to know that you wouldn't like spending so much money on dresses for Caroline. I should've had the sense to tell Estelle that she couldn't have Caroline for the day. I should've, I should've, I should've!"

"Well, you should've!" he roared.

"I don't believe this!" Kate shot back. "This isn't the first time that you've pointed out my flaws, you know. You're always telling me what I should've done. And personally, I'm beginning to think I should've never offered to come here with you in the first place."

"I don't know why I ever agreed to this absurd arrangement, either." His fists knotted unconsciously, and his stomach began to churn. "At least we have the assurance of knowing it can't last much longer. As soon as the Sunday newspaper hits the streets, I should be getting plenty of responses to my ad."

"Your . . . ad?" The color drained from Kate's face. "About the ad, Sam . . ."

A wave of alarm washed through him. "What about it?" he snapped.

She inhaled a deep breath. "I'm afraid your advertisement for a new housekeeper won't be appearing in Sunday's paper."

He narrowed his eyes. "I don't understand. The copy was submitted before the deadline on Wednesday afternoon, and—"

"The ad didn't get to the newspaper in time, I'm afraid." She swallowed convulsively. "You see, I forgot to stop by the newspaper office on my way home from—"

"You forgot?" Sam roared. "How in the hell did you forget?"

"I was thinking about other things. I was worried about cooking our meals, troubled about the rift in your friendship with Nathan. It didn't even occur to me to stop by the newspaper office. I'd forgotten all about it until now."

He regarded her, wary. "Maybe you didn't want to remember. Maybe you thought you could stay here longer if you conveniently forgot to submit the newspaper ad on time."

"I can't believe you have the nerve to accuse me of such deceit, Sam!" Kate bristled with indignation. "It was an honest oversight. I just made a little mistake, and I don't see why you're—"

"A little mistake?" he scoffed. "Dammit, Kate! Don't you know what this means?"

"Of course I know what it means!" she hurled back. "It means I'll have to live with the likes of you for another week!"

"If both of us survive that long," he muttered.

"You've never wanted me here in the first place." There was an accusing tone in her voice. "And you don't want me to stay any longer, do you?"

"I think it would be best—for both of us—if you went back home tomorrow, Kate. God knows, this isn't working."

"But what about . . . Caroline?"

"The longer you stay, the more attached

she'll become to you." An ache swelled in his chest. "It's best if you leave first thing in the morning."

He bolted up from the wicker chair. The verandah swarmed in front of him; a white-hot flash of pain lanced through his gut.

He grimaced, blasting himself for downing half a bottle of hot sauce at one sitting. His stomach was churning with the fury of a volcano on the verge of erupting.

Trembling with anger, Kate refused to look at Sam as he stormed into the house. She hated him, hated how he'd treated her. Samuel Springer was the most infuriating, unreasonable, ungrateful man she had ever known in her entire life, and she hoped she never laid eyes on him again.

She marched into her room, resolving to be packed and ready to leave by the first light of dawn. Yanking open the door to the wardrobe, she grabbed an armful of clothes and hurled them across the bed.

But as she opened the lid to her trunk, an ache squeezed her heart. How could she leave . . . Caroline?

A tear trickled down her cheek. How could she bear to part with the child? How could she say good-bye to a little girl who had become so dear to her?

Kate changed into her nightgown, no longer

possessing the strength nor the desire to continue packing her trunk. Shoving aside the pile of clothing strewn across the mattress, she climbed into bed with a heavy heart.

Kate had just slipped beneath the sheets when a moaning sound rippled through the air. Alarmed, she bolted from the bed and grabbed a wrapper from the still-open trunk.

She threw open the door and raced toward Caroline's room. But as she stepped into the hall, another low groan split through the night.

She froze, listening intently. The sounds were too deep, too masculine, to be the groans of a child. And they were coming from the direction of Sam's room . . .

Before she could think, she had rushed down the hall, turned the doorknob, and burst into Sam's room. But the instant she stepped inside, she stopped cold, startled by what she saw.

Sam was standing in front of the open window, stripped to nothing but his trousers. His arms were outstretched, and his hands were braced against the framework that encased the glass panes. His dark hair was clinging to his neck, and his head was hanging low. The dim light of a lantern splayed across the corded muscles of his body, and Kate could see that every sinewy line was rigid and tight.

Panic fluttered through her. "Sam?" she queried softly.

"Go away!" he bellowed, turning to glower at her. Sweat beaded his brow, and his features were contorted with pain.

"What is it?" she demanded, rushing to his side. "What's wrong?"

"I'm dying." Agony vibrated deep in his voice. "You poisoned me, Kate. And I think I'm going . . . to die."

# Chapter 14

I f the man had not been ravished by pain, Kate would have leaped to deny the ludicrous accusation. It was utter nonsense to think she was capable of poisoning anyone.

But under the circumstances, she didn't have the heart to debate the issue. How could she argue with someone who was hurting so badly?

Raking her gaze over the length of him, Kate trembled with fear. Every feature of his face was twisted in agony; every muscle in his body was contorted with pain.

At that instant, a violent shudder rippled through him. Staggering, he clutched his middle and rendered a heart-wrenching moan.

Kate wrapped an arm around his torso, attempting to brace his weight. His rigid muscles were still quaking, and his bare skin felt clammy beneath the touch of her hands. "You need to get back in bed, Sam," she urged.

"Leave me the hell alone," he growled. In spite of the pain wracking his body, he summoned up the strength to jerk away from her.

"I'm just trying to help. You need to get back to bed and—"

"I don't need your damn help. You've already done enough damage, Kate." He grimaced, hunching his shoulders and clutching his stomach. "You've poisoned me . . . the goddamn chicken . . ."

*The chicken?* Alarm raced through Kate. *Oh, God, no.* Had she served *raw* chicken for dinner? Had she been so concerned about burning the chicken that she'd removed it from the skillet before it was done?

A sickening feeling rolled through her as another horrid possibility flashed through her mind. Hadn't the chicken felt a bit warm when she'd finally placed it into the icebox? Could the chicken have gone bad before she'd ever cooked it?

Horrified by the thought, Kate squeezed her eyes shut, praying it couldn't be true. But something deep inside of her told her otherwise. She hadn't been inflicted with this horrible pain. The only person who'd eaten chicken for dinner was Sam. And Sam was the only one who was sick.

"Maybe the hot sauce didn't agree with

you," she suggested. "Maybe you ate too much of it."

"It wasn't the hot sauce," Sam snapped. "I've eaten that stuff a thousand times. And it's never caused me to puke my guts out like your damn chicken has."

She winced at the vivid images painted by his words. "If you don't want my help, I won't argue with you, Sam." She motioned toward the bed. "But I'm not leaving this room until you get back into bed. You need your rest, and you can't get rid of me until I'm certain that you're not going to collapse on your feet."

He glared at her for a long moment before turning away from the window. Trudging across the room, he grimaced in pain. Once he'd dropped onto the mattress, he shot her a begrudging glance. "Are you satisfied now?"

"I'm very satisfied," she said, straightening the rumpled covers, tucking the quilt around him.

His eyes narrowed with suspicion. "Then why aren't you leaving?"

"Because I lied." She scurried toward the wash bowl and dipped a cloth into the basin of water. Turning, she leaned over and gently placed the cool cloth over his forehead. "I'm not leaving until you're feeling better, Sam."

"I'm suddenly feeling much better," he insisted, rasping for breath. "And since I'm making such a miraculous recovery, you can feel free to leave."

She ignored the remark, knowing it was anything but true. Studying him intently, she eased her way onto the edge of the bed.

"You know, Aunt Dorinda and Aunt Odelphia fixed chicken broth for me when I was sick, and it always made me feel better. As soon as the market opens in the morning, maybe I could—"

"Don't, Kate." His eyes widened in horror. "Don't even think about it. Don't even consider the thought of cooking anything for me ever again."

He rolled to the side, turning his back to her. "Just go away and leave me alone," he muttered, burrowing his head into the pillow.

Kate massaged the nape of her neck and sighed. Considering the way Sam was treating her, he wasn't deserving of her help at all.

If she had a lick of sense, she would've been gone long before now. She wouldn't have contended with the man's sharp tongue or brutal rejections, wouldn't have stayed long enough to subject herself to his scathing remarks. The instant he'd lashed out at her, she should've turned her back on him and walked away.

But this was Sam. Her Sam. The same Sam she had known for years, the Sam who had made love to her with agonizingly sweet tenderness. How could she leave him?

Kate had no intention of allowing him to suffer through this night of misery by himself. She was responsible for his distress, and she couldn't live with herself if she turned her back on him now.

At that moment, the mattress gave way beneath Sam's weight. He rolled over, shifting onto his back, flinging his arms out to the side.

She gazed over at him, relieved he was no longer writhing in agony. Maybe the worst was over now, and he would sleep peacefully for the remainder of the night. The chiseled features of his face were more relaxed, she noticed, and his muscles were no longer quaking with spasms of pain.

As her gaze traveled over the length of his body, she found herself admiring the trim line of his belly, the taut muscles in his arms, the broad expanse of his chest. And when her gaze lingered on the dark nest of hair that covered his torso, she found herself longing to feel the touch of his furred chest beneath her fingers.

Sam shifted his weight once again, and it suddenly occurred to Kate that she was gawking at him. Worse yet, she was sitting on the edge of the bed in nothing but a thin nightgown and wrapper. And she was thinking very sinful thoughts.

But she couldn't seem to help herself. Until

now, she hadn't wanted to delve too deeply into her feelings for Sam, afraid of what she might discover. It almost seemed impossible that she could fall in love with someone like Sam, someone she'd known for most of her life.

Willing herself to banish such outrageous notions from her mind, Kate hastily rose from the bed. She settled down into a nearby chair, prepared to stay there for the duration of the night.

Sam's head throbbed with a dull ache when he awakened the next morning. Opening his eyes, he winced at the bright shaft of sunlight streaming through the open windows in his room.

"Oh, God." He squeezed his eyes shut, feeling the full effects of his restless night. His mouth was parched dry, and his stomach was tender and sore.

A soft rustling sound caught his attention, and he opened his eyes once again. Just as his lashes fluttered open, Kate appeared at the side of the bed, wearing nothing but her nightgown and wrapper.

Sam summoned up every ounce of discipline that he possessed to drag his gaze away from the enticing curves and swells of her petite frame. But as he lifted his gaze to her face, he was stunned by what he saw.

The golden strands of her hair were tangled and wild, tumbling over her shoulders in complete disarray. Dark circles shadowed her eyes, and lines of fatigue were etched into her delicate features.

And then it hit him, swift and hard. She'd stayed up all night . . . for him.

"So how are you feeling this morning?" she asked.

"Like I've been run over by a freight train." He winced, struggling to sit upright.

Kate reached behind him and fluffed up his pillows. "There," she said. "That should make you feel better. And I'll get some water for you, too. I know your mouth must be parched dry."

As she reached for a pitcher of water on the table next to his bed, Sam couldn't help but notice that she was being very nice. Too nice, considering all the things he'd said to her.

When she handed the glass of water to him, he took a hefty gulp, then leaned back into the pillow. Kate was still standing beside the bed, watching him intently. "You didn't have to stay up with me all night, you know," he told her.

"You made that point perfectly clear, Sam. As I recall, you were quite adamant that I should leave." A hint of a smile appeared on her lips. "But you should know by now that you can't get rid of me so easily."

"But after the way I treated you, after all the

things I said . . ." He paused, feeling awkward and uncomfortable. "I deserved to be horse-whipped."

"It was understandable." Her smile faded away. "You were hurting very badly."

Hearing the gentle tone of understanding in her voice, seeing the compassion shining from her eyes, Sam reeled in confusion. "Why are you still here, Kate?"

"I couldn't leave you, Sam. I just couldn't."

Sam felt something tight and restricting grip his chest. It would have been easy for her to walk away from him. So easy. He'd claimed he didn't want her here, even demanded that she leave.

But in spite of everything he'd said and done, she had stayed.

His throat tightened with emotion. How many times had he longed for someone like Kate in his life?

No one had ever remained by his side, supporting him with unwavering devotion. His best friend had betrayed him, his wife had turned her back on him. Even his own damn mother had abandoned him.

Having learned firsthand about the cruelties of human nature, Sam valued Kate's loyalty and devotion all the more. But in spite of her allegiance to him throughout the night, he expected she wouldn't want to stay with him much longer. No doubt, she'd probably had her fill of him by now.

"I wouldn't blame you if you still wanted to leave, you know," he finally said. "I'd understand if you—"

"Just a minute, Sam. I think I hear Caroline." Kate headed for the door. "I'll be right back."

When Kate returned a few moments later, Caroline was wobbling along beside her. At the sight of his sleepy-eyed daughter, Sam felt his heart roll over. She looked like an angel in white muslin, the most enchanting little creature he'd ever seen.

Kate scooped Caroline into her arms and placed her on the bed beside him. "You know, I believe we've forgotten something very important, Sam. I believe both of us have forgotten the reason why I'm here, the reason why we agreed to this arrangement in the first place."

As Kate gazed down at Caroline, Sam could've sworn the earth rattled beneath them. He wanted nothing more than to freeze this moment in time, gather both of them in his arms, and keep them in his hold forever.

All of his earlier contentions with Kate suddenly seemed insignificant and very remote. For the life of him, Sam couldn't even remember why he'd been so irritated with her.

His gaze swept up to hers. "So you'll stay on . . . for a while longer?"

"That all depends on you, Sam. Do you truly want me to stay?"

"Very much so." So much that it scared the hell out of him.

Her smile lit up the room. "Then I guess I should get busy if I intend to earn my keep around here." She held out her arms to Caroline. "We're going to let your daddy get some rest now, sweetheart. And after you and I get dressed for the day, we're going to take a little morning stroll and get some fresh air."

Sam leaned back into the pillow, grimacing from the achy sensations that plagued his body.

She hesitated a moment, raking her gaze over him with concern. "Are you sure you're feeling well enough for me to leave for a little while?"

"I'm sure," he insisted. "I'll probably sleep for a while. You take your time."

Turning, Kate held out her hand to Caroline. "Come on, sweetheart. Let's get you cleaned up and dressed so we can take our walk."

Without a moment's hesitation, Caroline slipped her little fingers into Kate's outstretched hand. A riot of tangled red curls tumbled about her face as she tilted back her head and peered up at Kate. Pure adoration sparkled from her eyes, and her face was awash with delight.

In that instant, Sam became achingly aware

of how much his daughter idolized Kate, how essential the woman had become to the child in so short a time.

As Kate and Caroline left the room, hand in hand, Sam sank back into his pillow and closed his eyes, trying to ignore the sudden wave of uncertainties flooding through him.

There was no denying that Caroline was becoming more and more attached to Kate with each passing day. No denying the child's fragile little heart would break into pieces when Kate eventually went away.

A stab of painful logic warned Sam that he should shield his daughter from the inevitable heartache of saying good-bye to Kate. Shield himself from the danger of needing her, wanting her . . . losing her.

But the only means of protection for his daughter—and for himself—was sending Kate back to Rome without a moment's delay.

And God help him, he couldn't bear the thought of letting her go.

Kate was returning to the cottage after a brisk morning stroll with Caroline when she saw Ida Mae trimming the shrubs in front of her house.

"Good morning, Kate!" Ida Mae set aside her pruning shears and crossed the lawn. "Was Sam pleased with his dinner last night?"

"I'm afraid not, Ida Mae," Kate admitted with a troubled sigh.

"Oh, dear." A frown of concern replaced the woman's cheery smile. "Whatever happened?"

"If you have a moment to sit down and chat, I'll tell you all about it. I'm afraid it's a rather long story." Kate lifted Caroline from the stroller and steadied the child's wobbly legs on the grassy lawn. "I need to run into the house for a moment, Ida Mae. Can you keep an eye on Caroline for me?"

"Of course, dear," Ida Mae said, settling down into a wicker chair on the verandah.

Kate scurried into the cottage. She swept down the hall and peered into Sam's room, relieved to find that he was sleeping peacefully. Not wanting to disturb him, she quietly closed the door and slipped away.

When Kate joined Ida Mae on the verandah, she was pleased to see that Caroline was romping merrily through the front lawn. But as Kate observed the child's lively movements, she became acutely aware of her own lack of energy. Wearily she sank into a wicker chair, silently acknowledging that her sleepless night was beginning to catch up with her.

Worse yet, pangs of guilt were assaulting her with mounting intensity. Throughout the long night and early-morning hours, she'd realized that the sole reason for Sam's agony was her ineptness in the kitchen. Now, accepting full blame for his wretched night of suffering, Kate felt terrible about causing him so much pain.

And frustrations were coursing through her, as well. After all her efforts to prepare a nice meal, the results had been nothing short of disastrous. Feeling distressed over her failure, Kate hoped that baring her soul to Ida Mae might relieve some of her inner turmoil.

But by the time Kate had recounted the events of the previous evening to her friend, she was struggling to hold back the tears brimming in her eyes. "I don't know what I'm going to do, Ida Mae. This is the first time in my life that I haven't been able to solve a problem with a charming smile or a witty remark. I'm a total disaster in the kitchen. Compared to you, I'm—"

She paused, suddenly seized by an intriguing thought. "You know, maybe this situation isn't as hopeless as I thought it might be."

"What do you have in mind, dear?" Ida Mae asked.

Kate hastily outlined her plan to the woman. Much to her delight, Ida Mae seemed delighted with the idea.

"I think you've hit upon a wonderful solution, Kate." Ida Mae rose from the chair. "See you later, dear."

As Ida Mae scurried home, Kate called out to Caroline. "Let's go inside for a little while, sweetheart."

Caroline scampered across the lawn, her red hair tumbling over her shoulders. After climbing the steps leading up to the verandah, she obediently followed Kate into the house.

Caroline was still trailing behind Kate when she peered into Sam's room. Discovering that Sam was still napping, Kate placed an outstretched finger over her lips. "Sshh," she whispered to the child. "Daddy is still sleeping, and we must be quiet."

Stifling a yawn, Kate led Caroline into her room. "While your daddy is resting, let's take a little nap, too," she suggested.

Exhausted, Kate fell asleep with little effort. When she awakened a few hours later, she felt rested and fully recovered from her sleepless night.

Shortly before noon, Kate peered into Sam's room and smiled. He was sitting up in bed, wide awake, with a book propped across his lap. "You look like you're feeling much better, Sam," she observed, sweeping into the room.

He glanced up, intending to greet her with a smile. But the instant he spied the tray of food in Kate's hand, a shudder of repulsion rippled through him. "And it looks like you're determined to kill me, one way or the other," he muttered.

"It's just chicken broth." She snatched the book from his hand and placed the tray on his lap. "And it's good for you. I promise."

"Good God, Kate! Anything that remotely resembles chicken is the last thing I want." He scowled, returning the tray to her. "I thought you understood that I didn't want you to consider the thought of cooking for me anymore. Didn't you listen to a word I said last night?"

"Your message was loud and clear, Sam." She slipped the tray back onto his lap. "But you need to eat something to regain your strength."

"I don't see how chicken broth could do any good," he grumbled.

"Aunt Dorinda and Aunt Odelphia claim that it works wonders."

"Then I guess it has to be true, then." He managed a weak smile, thinking about the elderly Hopewell sisters. "But that doesn't mean I'm going to eat this stuff."

"Would you be more inclined to eat the broth if you knew that I wasn't the one who prepared it?"

He glanced down at the bowl on the tray, then shifted his gaze back to Kate. "But if you didn't fix this . . . who did?"

"Ida Mae." A blush rose to her cheeks, dotting the creamy hue of her skin with a bright crimson. "She loves to cook, you know, and I think she's been rather lonely since her husband passed away. So I asked her if she would consider cooking our meals for a while."

Sam narrowed his eyes. "That's quite an imposition, Kate."

"But Ida Mae was thrilled with the idea! And she even offered to teach me the basics of cooking along the way. Of course, I insisted on paying for all of her work, along with all the supplies she'll be needing."

"And did you ever stop to think that I might have an opinion about this?"

A pensive expression flickered across her face. "I'm perfectly aware that I didn't consult you, Sam. But I didn't feel as though I had any choice about the matter. Obviously, my cooking abilities are less than adequate. If I'm going to be your housekeeper, it's my responsibility to serve decent meals. And after what I did to you . . ." He heard the catch in her voice, saw the dismay in her eyes. "I couldn't bear the thought of anything happening to you again."

Sam's throat tightened with emotion. It wasn't easy for anyone to face up to their faults and admit their failures in life. Especially someone like Kate, who'd rarely failed at anything she'd tried to do.

But saints above, the woman had swallowed her pride. She'd asked for someone to help her. And she'd tried to correct the error of her ways. Tried to make things right between them.

Moved beyond words, Sam reached out and grasped her hand. The brush of his fingers across hers felt like a lightning bolt searing through him.

"I suppose none of this has been easy for you, Kate." He squeezed her hand more tightly. "But I'm very, very glad that you agreed to stay. I'm not quite sure what I would do without you in my life right now."

He was still sitting there, gazing at the curves of her mouth, when Kate's voice broke into his thoughts. "Eat your broth, Sam," she urged, "before it gets cold."

With a sigh of resignation, he picked up a spoon from the tray. "Are you sure this stuff will make me feel better?"

"I'm absolutely positive."

"And if it doesn't?"

"Then you can blame Aunt Dorinda and Aunt Odelphia for giving me some bad advice." Kate lifted one shoulder in a breezy shrug. "But, of course, we both know that my aunts would never give anyone bad advice."

"They're the ones who suggested you come back to Macon with me, you know."

"Shut up and eat your broth, Sam." Kate grinned. "And just remember that the Hopewell sisters never steer anyone wrong."

# Chapter 15

**"G**oodness gracious!" Kate exclaimed when Sam entered the parlor the next morning. Setting aside the book that she had been reading to Caroline, she swept her gaze over the length of Sam's tall, muscular frame.

Judging by her expression, Sam suspected she liked what she saw. As she appraised the fit of his blue shirt and dark trousers, pure delight sparkled from her eyes.

"You look like a new man this morning, Sam," she finally assessed.

"I feel like a new man, too." He grinned. "Must have been the chicken broth."

"What else could it have been?" Kate laughed. "You should know by now that you shouldn't question the wisdom of my aunties."

"I think I've learned my lesson," he conceded, suddenly feeling famished. "Am I too late for breakfast?"

"We have some biscuits in the kitchen. Will that be enough to hold you for an hour or so? Ida Mae should be bringing our lunch soon."

"Biscuits sound wonderful." Sam leaned over and planted a kiss on top of his daughter's head, chuckling when he spotted some crumbs in her hair. "Did you have some biscuits for breakfast, Miss Caroline?"

As the child nodded, Kate laughed. "I believe it's time for a bath, sweetheart. As soon as I get your daddy's breakfast, we'll—"

"I'll heat up my biscuits," Sam offered. "You go ahead and tend to Caroline."

Sam retreated into the kitchen, pleased to find a plate with four biscuits on the table. He retrieved a jar of strawberry preserves from the pantry, and after warming the biscuits in the oven and heating a pot of coffee on the cookstove, he settled down at the table to enjoy his mid-morning breakfast.

He had just cleared the dishes from the table when Ida Mae appeared at the door, carrying a basket packed with an assortment of food.

"Let me give you a hand," he insisted, removing the handle from her grasp.

"I suppose it's a little early for lunch," Ida Mae remarked as she accompanied Sam into the kitchen. "It's just a few minutes after eleven."

"But it's never too early to think about your

next meal." Sam chuckled, placing the basket on the kitchen table.

Ida Mae laughed. "It's good to see that you're in good spirits today, Sam. I'm glad to know you're feeling better."

"Thanks, Ida Mae. Judging by the size of my appetite, I think I'm fully recovered now." Rummaging through the basket, he pulled out a square dish that held some sort of casserole. "This looks wonderful. And it smells wonderful, too. What is it?"

"It's my special ham and cheese casserole," she explained, her voice suddenly taking on a watery sound. "It was my dear Herbert's favorite dish. Every time I made it for him, he always raved about it."

"I'm sure I'll be raving about it, too," Sam assured her. "You know, Ida Mae, I really appreciate what you're doing for us here. You've been a lifesaver for us."

"It's truly a pleasure for me, Sam. Cooking doesn't seem like work to me at all. And it's even more enjoyable knowing that I'm earning a little pocket money for myself, too."

"Then I'm glad Kate came up with the idea."

"I'm glad, too." A shadow of concern flickered across the woman's weathered face. "But I sensed it wasn't easy for Kate to ask for my help. When she presented the idea to me, I got the feeling that it was an admission of defeat for her."

"That's because Kate usually accomplishes what she sets out to do," Sam explained. "I suspect she must be learning that she can't always depend on a witty remark and a charming smile to provide solutions for the difficulties in life."

"Maybe so." Ida Mae pulled a loaf of bread from the basket. "Still, she was terribly distraught that you weren't feeling well because of something she'd done."

At that instant, Caroline scampered into the kitchen, Kate following close behind her. The child's freshly washed hair was shiny and bright, still bearing the marks of a comb, and she was wearing a plaid dress with a dainty lace collar.

Ida Mae leaned over and admired the green ribbons dangling from Caroline's hair. "How pretty you look, Caroline!"

Something akin to delight sparkled from the little girl's wide eyes before she turned and buried her face in the folds of Kate's skirts.

Kate brushed her hand across the soft crown of the child's head. "I do believe you've just won a special place in Caroline's heart, Ida Mae," she observed with a smile.

After Ida Mae left the cottage, Kate prepared to serve lunch on the sun porch. Just as she spooned a generous helping of ham and cheese casserole onto Caroline's plate, Sam sat down at the table.

"You know, I believe Caroline has taken quite a liking to Ida Mae," Kate remarked. "Did you see the way her eyes lit up when Ida Mae told her how pretty she looked today?"

Nodding, Sam gazed fondly at his daughter. "I'm glad she's getting to know her. Caroline needs the influence of a grandmotherly type in her life." A shadow of darkness shaded his face. "And my mother certainly doesn't want to be part of Caroline's life. Or mine, for that matter."

Kate felt an ache swelling in her chest. Sam's mother wouldn't be the kind of influence that he would want for his daughter, even if the woman had maintained contact with him over the years.

"You know, I never knew my grandmothers, either," Kate remarked. "Or my own parents, for that matter. I was so little when my father died that I don't remember very much about him. But I've been very fortunate having Odelphia and Dorinda in my life. They've always seemed more like grandmothers than aunts to me."

"I've always considered Odie and Dorie as my grandmothers, too." A trace of bittersweet sadness skated across Sam's face. "I wish Caroline could have more contact with them. But I guess she'll never know what it's like to be part of a large family, considering I don't have any relatives . . . other than my adopted family at Hopewell House, of course."

An ache of sadness filled Kate's heart. "I don't understand why the Vances have to be so hateful to their own granddaughter." She wiped the remains of Caroline's lunch from the child's chubby cheeks. "I'd say they don't know how fortunate they are to have a grand-daughter like Caroline."

Rising, Kate stacked up the soiled dishes from their meal. "So what are your plans for this afternoon, Sam?"

"I'm intending to sort through some books that are packed away. I'm looking for one particular volume that I'll be needing to prepare an upcoming case."

"I could help you, if you'd like," Kate offered. "The bookshelves in the parlor are collecting dust, and I'm sure your books would look nice on the shelves."

It was an offer Sam couldn't refuse. "I'm ready when you are."

"Just let me find a dust cloth for wiping off the shelves."

By the time Sam brought the first carton of books to the parlor, Kate was diligently dusting the tall mahogany bookcases, stretching up on her toes and wiping each shelf with a rag. Dust mites were floating through the air, tickling her nose and her eyes.

"These are real dust-catchers," she mumbled, her nose itching from the tiny particles of dirt drifting around her.

When Sam placed the carton of books on the floor, Caroline scampered up beside him. As soon as Sam opened the carton, the little girl leaned over and peered inside. Pulling out a small book, she toddled over to the bookcase and handed the leather-bound volume to Kate.

"What a good helper you are, Miss Caroline!" Kate praised.

At that instant, a tickling sensation assaulted Kate's nose. She had just retrieved a handkerchief from her pocket when the tickly feeling became a full-blown sneeze. "Ah-ah-choo!"

The laugh of a child, girlish and carefree, rang through the room.

The sound was so stunning, so unexpected, that Kate reeled in disbelief. She snapped around, startled to see a broad smile on Caroline's lips.

"Did you hear that, Kate?"

Kate nodded. But before she could reply, another sneeze assaulted her. "Ah-ah-choo!"

Caroline laughed again.

Sam dropped his books to the floor and caught his daughter in his arms. Spinning, he lifted the child above his head and whirled her around. All the while, Caroline was shrieking with delight.

"So you think Kate's sneezes are funny, do you?" he teased.

After they collapsed, breathless and dizzy, into a heap on the floor, Sam turned to Kate, his expression suddenly turning serious.

"Do you know how long I've been waiting to hear this child laugh? She's been so sullen and disagreeable since her mother died that I was beginning to think I'd never hear her laugh again." He paused. "And I don't think this would have happened if it hadn't been for you, Kate."

His green eyes shimmered with gratitude, soul-deep gratitude, and a wondrous burgeoning of hope.

Kate ached with the beauty of his gaze, rejoiced with him for his daughter.

But she couldn't help but wonder what it would be like to see those eyes aglow with love for her, shining with the love of a man for a woman.

Kate was unpacking the last carton of books when Sam answered a knock at the door. Just as she placed the final book on the shelf, Sam returned to the parlor.

"You have company, Kate," he announced, his voice brimming with irritation.

Kate spun around, surprised to see Peyton Ransom standing next to Sam. "Well, what a surprise!"

Peyton's smile was charming and warm. "I couldn't resist the temptation of dropping by to see you today, Kate. I haven't been able to stop thinking about what a wonderful time we had together the other night."

Kate's heart plummeted to her toes. Dear heavens, so much had happened since Peyton had brought her home from the concert. She stole a glance at Sam, not surprised to find that his jaw was clenched, his face red with fury.

"It was a wonderful evening," she agreed. "But I'm not—"

"Considering how well we get along, I thought you might agree to spend another evening with me," Peyton said. "I understand the library association is sponsoring a gala on Saturday evening. From what I've heard, it's supposed to be the most spectacular event of the year. And I would like nothing more than to escort you to the ball, Kate. After all, I know how much you like to dance."

"It sounds wonderful, Peyton." She couldn't help but smile at the prospect. "I truly enjoy social events, especially dances, you know. And I—"

"I'm afraid Kate won't be able to accept your invitation, Peyton," Sam cut in smoothly.

The man's eyes narrowed in confusion. "What do you mean?"

"She has already agreed to accompany another gentleman to the ball on Saturday evening," he said in a clipped, crisp tone.

Disappointment shadowed Peyton's face. "I should've expected as much, I suppose." He turned back to Kate. "I should've realized that you had already made arrangements for the ball. No doubt, most of the men in town are lining up for the chance to escort you to various social events."

"Actually, there isn't—"

"Her social calendar is quite full," Sam interjected.

Peyton's gaze lingered on Kate for a long moment. "I must I admit that I'm quite envious of the man who will be accompanying you to the ball. Would I know him, perchance?"

"I'm not certain," Kate admitted. "You see, I don't actually—"

"You know him, Peyton," Sam broke in. "I'm the man who will be Kate's escort on Saturday evening."

Peyton's brows narrowed in confusion. "I wasn't aware of your interest in your housekeeper, Springer."

"Well, you are now," Sam shot back. "And I don't suspect you'll be having any reason to call on her again in the future."

Doubt and skepticism shimmered from Peyton's gaze. "Is Sam expressing your true feelings about the matter, Kate? Or is he speaking out of turn?"

"Things have changed since we attended the concert together, Peyton. Sam and I . . ." Kate hesitated, groping for the right words. "Sam and I have realized that our feelings for each other are growing into something more than fondness and friendship."

"I see." A strained smile appeared on Peyton's lips. "Well, then, I suppose there's nothing more for me to say . . . except to wish all the happiness in the world to both of you."

Kate gazed fondly at the man, admiring his dignified manner and gallant acceptance of the changes that had transpired since their last meeting. "Thanks, Peyton," she whispered in a choked tone.

Sam briskly escorted Peyton to the door, then returned to the parlor with a frown on his lips. "You were seriously toying with the notion of accepting Peyton's invitation to the ball, weren't you?"

Kate's eyes widened in disbelief. "Whatever makes you think that, Sam?"

"Good God, Kate, I'm not a damn fool! When Peyton asked to escort you to the fundraiser, I saw the excitement in your eyes, heard that little tremble of anticipation in your voice."

"For heaven's sake, Sam! Why shouldn't I get

excited about the prospect of going to a ball? You know I adore formal social functions!"

"Enough to go with Peyton?" he demanded, his voice rough with emotion. Before she could answer, he raged on. "Dammit, Kate! Have you forgotten what happened between us the other night?"

"Of course I haven't forgotten," she returned. "Accepting Peyton's invitation was never even a consideration with me, Sam. It was the thought of attending the dance that excited me—not the notion of going with Peyton. But you wouldn't give me the chance to explain that. In fact, you wouldn't give me a chance to say anything while Peyton was here."

"What in the hell did you expect, Kate? I had no intention of allowing you to encourage that man's affections. I don't even want any other man looking at you. I can't even bear the thought of any other man touching you, dancing with you . . ."

His voice became husky and low. Pulling her into his arms, he crushed her against him so tightly that she could scarcely breathe. "You're mine, Kathryn Carey, all mine," he warned, claiming possession of her lips with a hungry, demanding kiss.

A late-afternoon shower brought some respite to the heat of the July day. When the rain had subsided, Kate grasped Caroline's hand. "Let's enjoy the cooler temperatures while we can," she insisted, leading the child into the backyard.

Sam trailed behind them, watching with amusement. Caroline and Kate were scampering across the grass, playing with a red ball. Each time Kate rolled the ball across the ground, Caroline scurried after it, laughing and shrieking with delight.

Sam couldn't resist the temptation of joining them in their play. But after a half hour of sprinting across the lawn, he called for a brief rest. "Let's sit down and catch our breath for a few minutes, Kate," he suggested.

They sauntered over to the flower garden at the edge of the property. As they settled down beside each other on a stone bench, Caroline remained on the lawn, contentedly tossing the ball into the grass and chasing after it.

"You haven't said anything about the gala at the Johnsons' house since you volunteered to take me," Kate remarked.

Sam shrugged. "What more is there to discuss?"

"Something tells me that you've consented to attend the ball just to appease me," she chided. "Based on your lack of enthusiasm, I suspect that you don't really want to go."

"I'm not very fond of attending formal

events," Sam conceded. "In fact, I usually try to avoid them. The atmosphere at those affairs can get awfully stuffy at times."

"But I'm sure many of your clients will be attending the fund-raiser," Kate pointed out. "Your attendance would confirm to everyone that your law firm is supportive of community endeavors."

"Maybe so, but . . ." He hesitated a moment, then heaved a disgruntled sigh. "Hell's bells, Kate. I've always hated going to these blasted things because I've never learned how to dance."

Her eyes widened in surprise. "You don't know how to dance?" she echoed.

"Why do you look so stunned? For God's sake, I've never had a reason to learn how to dance. I was just a kid when I lived at Hopewell House, and dancing was the last thing on my mind back then. After I got to college, I was too busy to even consider it. When I wasn't working to pay for my tuition and books, I was studying for my classes."

"Then it's about time you learned," Kate insisted. She grasped him by the hand and pulled him up from the bench. "You want to make a good impression on everyone at the ball, don't you?"

He scowled down at her. "I offered to escort you, Kate. Nothing more."

"But don't you think it's a good idea to rub elbows with your clients at a charitable function?"

"Yes, but—"

"And don't you think your attendance would show that your law firm supports the library association?"

"Yes, but—"

"And don't you think that you'd feel more comfortable attending the ball if you learned how to dance?"

He laughed. "All right, Kate. You win. Teach me how to dance."

She beamed up at him. "It's very easy, once you get the hang of it. I promise. We can practice out here on the lawn and keep an eye on Caroline at the same time."

They'd taken only a few steps across the yard when Sam stumbled to a halt. "But what about music?" he asked.

"I'll hum a few tunes as we go along," Kate assured him. "That's all we need for now."

Sam chuckled. "Whatever you say, teacher."

Standing directly in front of him, Kate grasped his left hand with her right one. "Now, this won't be difficult at all. In fact, I'm sure it will be easy for you."

"Are you willing to make a wager on that?" he taunted.

"Not really," she conceded, grinning sheepishly. Taking a deep breath, she placed his right hand on her waist, then peered up at him with a smile so dazzling that his breath caught in his throat. "Ready?"

"As ready as I'll ever be."

"All right, then," she said. "Here we go. It's very simple, you see. You lead, and I follow. You step to your left, and I'll fall into place beside you."

They practiced in time to Kate's chants for a few moments. "One, two, three, one, two, three . . ."

"This isn't as hard as I thought it would be," Sam finally admitted.

"I knew it wouldn't be difficult for you," Kate insisted.

She hummed a lively tune under her breath as Sam swept her around the lawn. Approaching Caroline, Kate called out to the child. "Look at us, Caroline! Your daddy and I are dancing!"

Giggling, Caroline clapped her hands with approval.

"I didn't think I looked that funny," Sam grumbled goodnaturedly. "Do you think people will laugh at me while I'm dancing with you at the ball?"

"Of course not!" Kate grinned. "But I'm sure the other guests will be looking at you very closely. After all, you are a very handsome man, Samuel Springer."

"But what if I'm possessed by the urge to kiss

you while we're dancing?" he teased. "Will people laugh at me then?"

Her eyes sparkled with a mischievous gleam. She slid her hands up the length of his shirt, then curled her arms around his neck as he continued to guide her across the yard.

"It all depends on how you kiss me," she said very slowly. "Perhaps you could demonstrate your kisses for me, and I could tell you which ones would be most appropriate for the ball."

"You already know how I kiss," he countered, his voice teasing and warm. "But in case you've forgotten . . ."

He bent his head and captured her lips with his own, intending for the kiss to be playful and light, a mere extension of their bantering. But the instant he tasted the sweetness of her lips, all of his good intentions disappeared.

He plunged his tongue into her mouth, exploring, tasting, searching. Bolts of desire were shafting through him like hot lightning, and his loins were pulsing with an aching need.

God help him, he couldn't get enough of her. Every part of him was aching, yearning, demanding more. He was drowning in the touch of her satin-soft lips, mesmerized by the feel of her breasts rubbing against his chest, enchanted by the scent of rosewater that drifted around her.

Just as he plunged his hand into her hair,

pulling her closer to him, a shriek ripped through the silence of the summer afternoon.

Startled and shaken, Sam tore his lips away from Kate's. Fear pounded through his veins. He snapped around, his gaze darting across the yard, frantically searching for his daughter.

But she wasn't difficult to find. Caroline was sitting in the middle of the flower garden, sobbing uncontrollably. Drenched with splatters of mud, she was struggling to pull herself upright.

Sam raced across the yard, realizing that Caroline had tripped and fallen in the garden. And she'd landed flat on her bottom in the middle of a puddle of red Georgia clay.

He was only a few feet away from Caroline when he heard the shriek of a woman behind him.

"Dear Lord in heaven, whatever has happened to you, Caroline?"

Recognizing the voice of Estelle Vance, Sam groaned. "Just what I need," he muttered in disgust.

# Chapter 16

~~~~~~~~~⌒◯⌒~~~~~~~~~

**K**ate cringed in dismay at the sight of Estelle marching across the lawn, heading straight for Caroline. Judge Vance stomped behind his wife, his face red with fury.

"What rotten timing," Kate muttered. She hiked up her skirts and sprinted toward the garden, dreading to hear what the Vances had to say about their granddaughter wallowing in the mud.

She had just stepped up beside Sam when Estelle clutched her throat and shuddered in horror. "Oh, my," the woman moaned.

Sam lunged for his daughter, but Kate reached out and grasped his arm, holding him at bay. "I'll get her," she insisted.

Before Sam could protest, Kate hunkered down and plucked the frightened child from the mud. Mindless of the red Georgia clay seeping into the folds of her own dress, Kate pressed Caroline to her breast.

"It's all right, sweetheart," she soothed. "You're not hurt at all. You're just a little muddy and—"

"This is dreadful, simply dreadful," Estelle lamented, still swooning at the sight of the muddy toddler.

"How in the hell did this happen?" Judge Vance demanded.

The harsh remarks evoked another loud wail from Caroline. Kate gathered the child close. "You're going to be just fine, Caroline. Everything will be all right. There's nothing to be afraid of."

Turning, Kate trudged through the mud and settled down on the stone garden bench with Caroline. She was wiping the mud from the child's face with the hem of her skirt when the judge lashed out at Sam.

"How do you explain this, Springer?"

Sam whipped around to face the man, scowling with annoyance. "For God's sake, can't you see it was an accident? Caroline simply slipped and fell in a mud puddle."

"But it could have been avoided," Estelle admonished. "This would have never happened if someone had been watching her."

"Kate and I were keeping a close eye on Caroline," Sam snapped.

"But not close enough, apparently," the judge contended.

Estelle pursed her lips together in a tight line. "All along, I've suspected that Miss Carey has no comprehension of what a nanny is supposed to do. I'm convinced the woman is an imposter, if I've ever seen one."

"That's the most preposterous notion I've ever heard," Sam growled. "Good God, take a look at Kate right now, would you? She's doing everything she can for Caroline!"

Estelle dismissed the remark with a haughty toss of her head. "She puts on a good front, I'll admit. But you're too smitten by the woman to see her for what she really is, Sam. I'm convinced she's much more concerned about finding a husband for herself than taking care of my granddaughter."

"If you could have seen her at the concert this week, you would have no doubts about her reasons for coming to Macon, Springer," the judge added. "It was obvious that she was trying to snare the attention of every man in town."

"You've already made that point perfectly clear, Judge." Sam clenched his jaw. "And I'm damn tired of listening to these ridiculous accusations. Truth is, Kate has totally devoted herself to caring for Caroline since she's been here. Never for one instant has she neglected my daughter."

"Then you certainly could've fooled me," Judge Vance muttered, glancing toward the muddy tyke.

"If you have any more complaints about Kate, I suggest you keep them to yourselves," Sam warned in a low, menacing tone. "If either of you had a lick of sense about you, you'd realize that Kate isn't the real source of your anger, anyway. I'm the one you despise. But you're too consumed with hatred for me to discern that you're unjustly condemning Kate. You're too busy venting all of your rage on her to realize that you're focusing your anger on the wrong person."

"Still, you're not providing a healthy environment for your daughter as long as Miss Carey is living in your home, Sam," Estelle warned.

"And you're cutting your own throat with this living arrangement of yours, Springer. It's highly inappropriate, to say the least," Judge Vance noted. "Tongues are already wagging about the woman living under the same roof with you."

"Frankly, I don't care what people are saying—and that includes both of you," Sam snapped, promptly closing the discussion. Wheeling, he motioned to Kate. "Let's take Caroline back to the house and get her cleaned up."

"Come on, Estelle." Judge Vance grasped his

wife's arm. "We'll visit with our granddaughter some other time."

As the Vances stormed across the lawn, Kate retreated into the house and hastily prepared a bath for Caroline. After bathing and dressing the child, Kate stripped off her own soiled gown and washed the mud and grime from her face and hands. By the time she'd finished dressing, Ida Mae had arrived with their evening meal.

Sam remained unusually quiet throughout dinner, making no further mention of the unsettling visit from the Vances. But after tucking Caroline into bed for the night, Kate was determined to break the silence between them.

She sauntered into the parlor, finding Sam slumped into a chair. His long legs were stretched out in front of him, and a book was propped in his lap.

He glanced up as she entered the room, but the tight clench of his jaw and the somber look in his eyes told Kate that he wasn't particularly overjoyed to see her. Something was disturbing him, something she couldn't identify.

Hoping to lift his spirits, she flashed a bright smile in his direction. "I thought our dinner tonight was the best meal that Ida Mae has ever prepared for us. Didn't you think so?" she asked, settling down into a comfortable chair.

"It was very good," Sam responded blandly.

"And the pie!" Kate made a soft cooing sound. "Pecan pie has always been my favorite, but I do believe Ida Mae's was the best I've ever tasted in my life. Wouldn't you agree?"

"I enjoyed it," Sam mumbled, restlessly flipping through the pages of his book.

"Then what's disturbing you, Sam?" Kate asked, genuinely concerned.

His head snapped up. "Nothing is wrong with me, Kate. After our pleasant visit with Caroline's loving, devoted grandparents this afternoon, what could possibly be wrong?"

Kate heaved a frustrated sigh. "Maybe the entire incident could have been avoided if I had been paying more attention to Caroline. She probably wouldn't have tripped and fallen in the garden if I'd been watching her more closely."

Sam snarled. "Quit trying to fool yourself, Kate. If Caroline hadn't fallen into the mud, the Vances would have found something else to gripe about."

"Estelle certainly seems to thrive on criticizing me," Kate conceded. "When she dropped by the cottage the other morning to pick up Caroline, it seemed as if she were deliberately trying to provoke me. She insisted I was a terrible influence on her granddaughter, and then started hurling all sorts of accusations at me."

The line of his jaw hardened. "Judge Vance has been harassing me, too. He actually had the audacity to threaten—"

Halting in mid-sentence, he gave his head a shake, as if he'd caught himself saying something he shouldn't.

But Kate had heard enough to know what had transpired between Sam and the judge. "Judge Vance threatened you?" she whispered, her voice strangled and low.

"Let's just say he issued a warning to me. And if I don't comply with his demands, he assured me I would regret it."

An ache swelled in Kate's chest. "What does he want, Sam? What do the judge and his wife expect from you?"

"I suspect they don't even know themselves, Kate. I think they're just determined to make my life a living hell for as long as they can."

"Then they won't stop harassing you until they come to terms with Abigail's death," Kate contended. She frowned, troubled by the prospect. "I'm tempted to set them straight about their daughter's true character. They need to know what she was really like."

"You'd only be wasting your breath," Sam admonished. "When Abigail was alive, the Vances thought their daughter could do no wrong. Now that she's dead, nothing you could say or do would change their opinion about her. In their eyes, Abigail was a damn saint."

"But their grief over Abigail's death doesn't justify what they're doing to you now, Sam."

"It doesn't justify what they're doing to you, either. In case you haven't noticed, they've been directing most of their accusations at you. And I'm afraid they're going to find fault with everything you do as long as you're here. I suspect they don't relish the idea of you filling their daughter's shoes."

"But every time one of them hurled an accusation at me this afternoon, you leaped to my defense. In fact, I thought you did an admirable job of setting them straight about me."

"Still, you don't need the hassle of being badgered by anyone, Kate." He raked a hand through his thick, dark hair. "I should be horsewhipped for getting you into this situation in the first place. You don't deserve this sort of treatment."

He lapsed into a troubled silence, offering nothing more. After a few moments, Kate attempted to change the subject. "So are you ready for another dancing lesson?" she asked, her voice bright and cheerful.

"I don't think so, Kate," he returned in a somber tone. "I think it would be best if we forgot about dancing lessons. In fact, I think we should forget about going to the ball."

Her eyes widened incredulously. "What do you mean?"

"I think it would be better for you if I didn't escort you. You don't need someone like me complicating your life."

A tiny pulse of suspicion beat through her veins. "You're not buckling beneath all the pressure from the Vances, are you?"

Anger flared from his eyes and his voice. "For God's sake, Kate! Do you think I'm nothing more than a spineless fool?"

"Of course not," she denied hastily. "But I can't understand why you've suddenly changed your mind about attending the ball."

He inhaled a deep, shuddering breath. "Contending with all the harassment from the Vances this afternoon, I realized that you don't need me in your life, Kate. I can't offer you anything but problems and heartaches."

"I should be the judge of that, Sam. Not you."

"But you can't make rational decisions about anything based on emotions and feelings." He clenched his jaw with determination. "Maybe you should reconsider Peyton's offer to escort you to the ball."

"What makes you think I would attend the ball with Peyton?"

"From everything I know about him, he's the perfect match for the man of your dreams. You claim you like the adventurous type, the sort of man who can sweep you off your feet and whisk you away to places you've never even dreamed of visiting. And it seems to me that Peyton fits that description quite nicely.''

Enraged and deeply offended, Kate trembled with fury. ''Then why don't you consider taking Harriet Gordon to the ball?'' she shot back. ''She's quiet and shy, sweet and thoughtful. She's not bossy or controlling or demanding. She's everything you said you wanted in a woman. And since she's everything I'm not, I'm certain you would find her most appealing.''

''Escorting Harriet to the ball makes a helluva lot more sense than taking someone like you,'' he snapped.

''And I'd much rather attend the dance with Peyton than to be accompanied by someone like you,'' Kate insisted. ''Peyton is dashing and charming, and he knows how to have a good time.''

Sam lunged to his feet. ''Fine, then. Go to the damn ball with Peyton.''

''Since he has already expressed interest in taking me to the ball, I'm certain he won't hesitate to escort me.'' Kate darted up from the chair, determined to have the last word. ''But I can't imagine why Harriet would agree to go anywhere with you, Samuel Springer,'' she muttered, picking up her skirts and leaving the parlor in a rush of fury.

\* \* \*

For the next four days, Kate was sorely tempted to seek out Peyton Ransom and inform him that she would be delighted to accompany him to the library fund-raiser.

But the gnawing ache inside her heart held her at bay. In all honesty, she didn't want to go anywhere with Peyton Ransom. And Sam had bruised her spirits so badly by refusing to escort her to the dance that she couldn't even summon up the desire to provoke his temper by attending the function with Peyton.

Worse yet, the tension in the cottage had become almost unbearable. Sam was barely speaking to her, practically avoiding her at all costs. Kate kept her distance from him, too wounded to initiate any confrontations.

By the time Perlina dropped by the cottage for a visit on Friday morning, Kate was genuinely glad to see her friend's smiling, cheerful face.

"I can't stay too long, dear," Perlina said, sinking into a parlor chair. "I'm on my way to the Johnson home to help decorate for the ball tomorrow evening."

"I'm sure it will be a lovely affair." Kate gave a wistful sigh. "You'll have to drop by next week and tell me all about it."

Disappointment clouded Perlina's bright eyes. "I thought perhaps you and Sam would be attending the gala."

"Sam doesn't particularly like formal functions, I'm afraid," Kate explained.

"But that doesn't mean you can't attend the fund-raiser, you know. There will be plenty of females at the ball without escorts. In fact, you're welcome to go with Harriet and me. We're going by ourselves."

A hint of smile blossomed on Kate's lips. "Are you sure you wouldn't mind?"

"We'd love to have you join us, dear. We'll come by for you about eight." Rising, Perlina turned to leave. "See you then, dear."


"So is this your first visit to Macon, Miss Carey?"

"I do hope you're planning to stay for the remainder of the summer season, Miss Carey."

"May I freshen your drink, Miss Carey?"

Standing on the sidelines of the crowded ballroom, Kate flashed a dazzling, artificial smile at the gentlemen surrounding her.

"I've visited Macon several times in recent years, but this is the first time that the duration of my stay has extended beyond a few days. Unfortunately, however, I'm afraid I won't be staying here for the rest of the summer. And, yes, I would love to have another drink," Kate finished, handing her glass to the young man standing next to her.

Waves of laughter surged across the overcrowded ballroom at that moment, drowning out the murmurs of conversation and the sounds of music. Kate glanced across the room, impressed by what she saw.

Undoubtedly, it was one of the most elegant affairs that Kate had ever attended. By any standards, the Johnson home was palatial. The guests were friendly, the food was scrumptious, the music divine. All in all, it was a wonderful evening.

And Kate had never been more miserable in her life.

Since she'd arrived at the fund-raiser, her appearance had prompted dozens of lush compliments and approving glances. She'd worn her most flattering gown for the event, an alluring mauve evening dress trimmed with lace and pearls, and styled her hair into ringlets that tumbled across her bare shoulders and cascaded down her back. But not even the flattering remarks and admiring stares could boost her dismal spirits.

A few moments later, she was whirling across the ballroom floor in the arms of a dreadfully boring stranger. By the time the musicians had played the last notes of the selection, Kate could scarcely wait to leave the man's side.

As she worked her way through the crowd, she suddenly noticed the presence of a tall man with auburn hair in the throng. Her heart leaped into her throat. *Sam.*

Never had he looked more handsome. His tailored black evening attire hugged his broad shoulders and long legs, contrasting beautifully against his white shirt.

His gaze drifted over her with blatant approval, and her pulse quickened beneath his warmly intimate appraisal. It took every ounce of determination that Kate possessed to keep from rushing up to him.

Steeling herself, she tried to ignore him, tried to pretend he wasn't there. But no matter how hard she attempted to forget about him, Kate was acutely aware of his presence throughout the evening.

When dinner was served, Sam took a seat at one of the long, narrow tables in the dining hall. Kate purposely seated herself on the other side of the room. Though the meal seemed exquisite, Kate was chagrined to discover that her appetite was sparse, the food tasteless and bland.

By the time Kate left the dining room, the lump in her throat and the ache in her chest were so large that she could scarcely catch her breath. God help her, she didn't want to be acting like some mindless fool, but she couldn't seem to help herself.

She cared for Sam, cared for him more than

she'd realized. And somewhere along the way, she'd fallen in love with him.

But never had he ever mentioned love to her, and Kate suspected he never would. He knew as well as she that they weren't suited for each other.

Returning to the ballroom, Kate couldn't help but notice that Sam was chatting with Harriet. She lifted her chin, trying to ignore the stab of jealousy coursing through her. But Kate couldn't deny that she wanted Sam all to herself, and she didn't want to share him with anyone.

Yet, deep in her heart, she knew she could never have him. After all, she wasn't the type of woman with whom he wanted to share his life. He'd already made that perfectly clear to her.

But if they were so wrong for each other, why did the prospect of returning to Hopewell House fill her with so much sadness? And why couldn't she set aside her worries and fears and enjoy herself this evening?

The musicians played another tune, and Kate was swept up in the arms of yet another stranger. Gliding past Sam and Harriet, Kate purposely forced a bright smile on her lips.

Watching Kate sweep across the dance floor, Sam took a hefty gulp of his drink. It took every effort he possessed to quench the insane urge to tear her away from the arms of her partner. He wanted everyone to know she was his, wanted to claim her as his own.

The soft purr of a feminine voice interrupted his thoughts. "So have you known Miss Carey for very long?" Harriet asked politely.

Sam ripped his gaze away from the dance floor and forced a smile onto his lips. "For most of my life. We grew up together in the same household."

"I see."

An awkward pause dangled between them until Sam motioned toward the ballroom floor. "Would you care to dance, Harriet?"

A blush rose to her cheeks. "I'm flattered that you've asked me. But in all honesty, I've never cared for dancing very much."

"A lot of people would agree with you. Personally, I think there are many things in life much more enjoyable than dancing."

As the evening wore on, Sam discovered that Harriet Gordon was polite and thoughtful, quiet and kind, everything a woman ought to be. They even shared common interests in books and children, quiet evenings and close friends.

But she didn't make his heart pound with fury or thunder with desire. She didn't provoke his temper or soothe his frazzled nerves. And she couldn't pull his attention away from Kate.

No matter how hard he tried, he couldn't

ignore her. But by the end of the evening, every muscle in Sam's body was fraught with tension. Weary of watching Kate sweep across the ballroom floor in the arms of other men, Sam could endure no more.

After politely bidding good evening to Harriet, Sam pivoted on his heel and strode from the room.

Shortly after midnight, the hack driver came to a stop in front of the cottage. Kate thanked Perlina for the ride home, then stepped down from the vehicle and quietly slipped into the house.

Though she hadn't seen Sam leave the Johnsons' home, she had instinctively known that he was no longer present. His presence had seemed like a tangible force, and his absence had been just as noticeable.

Regretting she'd ever entertained the notion of attending the function in the first place, Kate wearily trudged into her room. Mentally and physically exhausted from the ordeal, she tossed aside her evening gown, slipped into her night wear, and tumbled into bed.

But the tumultuous emotions careening through her held sleep at bay. She was still tossing and turning when the whimpers of a child shattered the silence of the night.

Kate rose from the bed and grabbed her wrapper. When she reached the hallway, Caroline let out a heart-wrenching cry. Alarmed, she rushed into the child's room.

She had just hurled open the door when Sam rushed up behind her. "What's going on?" he demanded, his eyes wide with alarm.

"I think she's having a bad dream." Kate scooped the child into her arms and held her close, kissing the tears streaking down her cheeks. "It's all right, sweetheart. It was just a bad dream, and it's all over now. Your daddy and I are here, and everything is going to be all right. We won't let anything happen to you."

She sank into the rocking chair beside Caroline's bed, still whispering her soothing words of reassurance to the frightened tot. Caroline nestled close, sniffing back her tears. Within a few moments, the little girl's whimpers had subsided.

Sam sagged against the wall, relieved that his daughter's outcry had been nothing more serious than a nightmare. But he was somewhat astonished by Caroline's immediate response to the comfort of being held in Kate's arms.

Yet, wasn't that what every child needed? The contentment of knowing someone cared? The peace that came with knowing that one special person would always be there?

Something tight and restricting gripped Sam's chest. Why was it so difficult for him to admit that he needed that same type of assurance in his life?

At that instant, Kate rose from the chair and returned Caroline to her bed. Drinking in the sight of her, following her every movement, Sam reached out for her.

"Come here, Kate," he whispered.

Before she could answer, Sam grasped her hand and pulled her into the hallway. And then, without another word, he led her into the privacy of his room.

# Chapter 17

Sam closed the door behind them. "I've been waiting all night for the chance to have you all to myself."

She peered up at him, startled by the emotions written on his face. His eyes were dark with passion, his expression filled with stark need. Just looking at him, Kate felt her chest swell with longing.

"I've been wondering why you didn't ask me to dance at the ball tonight," she finally said. "And I've also been wondering why you decided to go. I was surprised to see you there."

"I didn't intend to make an appearance. But after you left the cottage . . ." He swallowed thickly. "I couldn't bear the thought of you being there . . . with Peyton."

"I didn't even see Peyton tonight, Sam. As far as I know, he wasn't there." She nervously

313

moistened her dry lips with her tongue. "But I was well aware of your presence."

He lifted his hand to her face, brushing back a stray curl dangling along her temple. "I couldn't take my eyes off you, Kate. Couldn't stop telling myself what a fool I've been. Couldn't stop wanting you, no matter how hard I tried."

"But you seemed to be enjoying yourself with Harriet," she noted.

"Harriet Gordon is a wonderful woman, Kate. She's everything you said she would be, everything I claimed to want in a woman. But . . ." He drew in a ragged breath. "But she's not you, Kate. You're all I've ever wanted. There will never be anyone else for me except you."

Her heart leaped into her throat. "Then why did you pull back from me, Sam? Why did you insist that you weren't the right man for me?"

He winced. "I've never felt as if I've deserved you, Kate. Never felt as though I could give you the kind of life you want for yourself."

"I've learned some things about what I want, too, Sam." She reached up and threaded her fingers through his thick, dark hair. "I've found out that I don't really like the dashing, adventurous sort that has no inclination to settle down. I've found out I need someone like you in my life."

She heard his sharp intake of breath, saw the

desire glimmering from his eyes. "God help me, Kate, I needed to hear you say that."

He crushed her against him, devouring her lips with his own. Kate squeezed her eyes shut, trying to drive away her doubts and fears and enjoy the magic of the moment.

There was so much she wanted to hear, so much she wanted him to say. He'd never once told her that he loved her, and she longed to know that he wanted her by his side for the rest of his life.

But she would be a fool to let the moment slip beneath her fingers, a fool not to seize the time they had. For now, Kate didn't want to think or worry or fret or complain. All she wanted to do was lose herself in loving Sam.

Later, she would have plenty of time to think about the consequences of her actions. A lifetime to remember what they almost had.

With a boldness that belied her doubts and fears, she slipped her arms around his neck and thrust herself against him.

"Ah, Kate," he whispered against her mouth. "I can't kiss you without wanting more . . . so much more . . ."

Lost to the sheer abandon of the moment, Kate felt as if time itself was grinding to a halt. Want, hot and scorching, sizzled through her, spiraling downward into the deepest part of her. And her need was so driving, so tangible, that she could feel it pulsing through her veins.

Restlessly she tugged at the collar of his shirt. "Too many buttons," she muttered.

She swiftly unbuttoned the garment. As the material parted, she slid her hand over the muscles of his chest. His skin was warm, and she reveled at the feel of the dark hair beneath her fingers.

Her thumb skimmed across one hard, male nipple. Sam jerked in reaction to her touch. "My turn," he warned, his fingers moving to the neckline of her gown.

Within a few moments, their clothing was scattered across the floor. Driven to ease the relentless urgings riveting through her, Kate pressed the length of her body against his hard, male frame.

Throwing caution to the wind, she pressed him against the sheets. Slipping her body over his, she positioned her knees on either side of him. He arched his body and entered her with one, powerful thrust that rocked her to the core.

She rocked urgently against him, meeting each of his thrusts with cries of pleasure, staring down into his eyes as violent shudders quaked through both of them.

Later she lay silently at his side, spellbound by the afterglow of their joining. It felt so right, so natural to lie here with Sam.

But even as she savored the beauty of the

moment, she felt that gnawing sense of apprehension invading her thoughts once again.

Though they had expressed their adoration for each other through the union of their bodies, much had been left unsaid between them.

Kate was sitting at the kitchen table, dawdling over a cup of coffee, when Sam shuffled into the kitchen the next morning.

Leaning forward, he planted a kiss on her cheek. "My bed seemed awfully cold when I woke up this morning without you, Kate. You've got to stop this foolish nonsense, you know."

She nodded across the table toward Caroline, who was busily licking strawberry preserves from the tips of her chubby fingers. "Hungry little girls can't wait too long for their breakfast."

He chuckled, grabbing a mug from the shelf and pouring himself a cup of coffee. But his grip tightened around the handle of the mug when he noticed the Sunday newspaper on the table.

"Have you taken a look at the paper this morning?" he asked.

She gave a curt nod. "You can find your ad on page six. It has a good placement, and I'm sure you'll get lots of responses this week."

Was that a trace of sadness in his eyes? A hint

of regret shimmering from his gaze? Did he feel the same sense of dread that was pounding through her veins?

"Odd, isn't it?" His laughter was forced and strained. "All along, I've wanted nothing more than to see this ad in the paper. And now . . ."

His gaze swept up to hers, and Kate trembled when she saw all the turbulent emotions written there. So much had changed between them, she thought. So much.

Yet, the newspaper ad was a grim reminder that nothing had changed at all. As soon as Sam found a housekeeper, she would have to leave. It had been inevitable from the start. But facing the truth was much more difficult than Kate ever dreamed it could be.

"I'm not really in the mood to interview potential housekeepers this week," Sam admitted.

"But you'll need to hire someone eventually, Sam." Though the admission was painful, Kate knew they had to face what was certain to come between them.

"I know." The bleakness disappeared from his eyes, replaced with a faint glimmer of hope. "Could you stay just a little while longer, Kate? Maybe a week or two. It's all I'm asking. And then if you want to go back to Rome, you'll be free to leave. I promise I won't ask anything more."

One more week? How could she endure the

agony of knowing it would be their last week together? Yet, how could she walk away, knowing all the memories she would be leaving behind? She would have to live on the memories of their time together for the rest of her life.

"I think we would just be delaying the inevitable, Sam. As much as I want to stay, I know I shouldn't. It would only be more difficult when I eventually have to leave. It would—"

"Let's not worry about next week or next month or next year, Kate. Let's just enjoy what we have for now."

"I suppose I can stay on for another week or so," she finally conceded. "But once you've hired a new housekeeper, I'll have to return to Rome."

During the next few days, Kate immersed herself in the daily routines of life, trying not to think, not to feel, not to worry about anything other than each passing moment. She forced herself to cast aside her doubts and fears in the comfort of Sam's arms each night, refusing to entertain any thoughts other than the blissful joy she found in their passion-drenched lovemaking.

By Friday afternoon, however, she became acutely aware that the week was rapidly drawing to a close. But to her knowledge, Sam had not yet interviewed any potential candidates for a housekeeper, and she wasn't willing to leave Caroline until she knew for certain that someone would be caring for her.

She was still pondering the situation when she heard an impatient rap at the door. Scurrying into the foyer, she intended to welcome the callers with a bright, cheery smile. But the curve on her lips disappeared when she swung open the door.

The Vances were standing on the verandah. Judge Vance's face was tight and drawn, and his wife's expression was nothing short of formidable.

"We need to see Sam," the judge announced stiffly.

"If you'll have a seat in the parlor, I'll get him for you," she said.

After ushering the Vances into the house, Kate called Sam into the parlor. When he entered the room, he scowled with dismay.

"I assume that spending some time with your granddaughter is not the intent of your visit," he mumbled, making no attempt to hide his irritation.

"Quite frankly, Sam, we have decided that we should spend a great deal more time with our granddaughter," Estelle revealed.

"On a permanent basis," the judge added.

Sam frowned. "What do you mean?"

"We found our last visit here to be quite distressing," the judge explained. "This week, we have been giving a great deal of thought and discussion to the matter."

"And we feel that you're raising our granddaughter in an environment that is far from suitable for her," Estelle added.

"We don't think it's wise to expose Caroline to a living arrangement like the one you have here." Judge Vance scowled. "In fact, we find the entire situation despicable."

"You've already expressed these sentiments to me. More than once, I might add." Sam's voice was hoarse and strained. "But I'm the one responsible for my daughter. I'm the one who decides where she lives and who she lives with."

"Not necessarily," the judge contended. "If a court of law finds that you're not providing a suitable environment for the child, then—"

"I know what the law says," Sam shot back, his face reddening with fury. "And I know that Caroline is thriving here in this home with me. Nothing I've done—or ever will do—will cause my daughter any harm."

"But a court may see things differently. A court may consider the fact that an attractive, unmarried woman is living here with you."

"As Caroline's nanny, for God's sake!" Sam roared.

"But is that the only role she has assumed since she's been living here, Sam?" Estelle cast a scathing glare at Kate, the implications of her question quite obvious.

Infuriated, Sam bolted to his feet. "God help me, I should demand that both of you leave these premises at once. I should—"

"I'm the one who should be leaving, Sam," Kate interjected. "Not Caroline's grandparents. I'm the cause of all their anger and dismay, all of the squabbling between you."

He snapped around to face her. "You have every right to be part of this home, Kate. These people can't waltz in here and tell me what to do or how to live my life. They don't have the right to do so."

"We'll let a court of law decide the issue for us, then." The judge sprang to his feet and pulled some papers from the pocket of his jacket. "We're filing for custody of Caroline, Sam. Here are the papers that I intend to file with the courts on Monday morning."

Sam stared in disbelief at the documents in the judge's hands. "You son of a bitch."

"We want her to live with us on a permanent basis," the judge continued on. "And I have every reason to believe that the courts will grant permission for us to move the child into our home—especially if they realize that Miss Carey is living here with you under these circumstances."

"You're wasting your time, Judge." Sam edged closer to Kate, draping an arm around her narrow shoulders. "By the time you file those papers in court, you won't have a leg to stand on."

"What do you mean?"

Sam gazed down at Kate. "Miss Carey will be living here under different circumstances very soon. She will be living here as my wife."

The judge's eyes widened incredulously. "You intend to marry this woman?"

As Sam nodded, Kate spoke up. "And I intend to marry him," she confirmed.

The judge's shoulders sagged with disappointment. "I must say, that puts a different light on the matter entirely."

"Don't be so hasty to believe everything you hear," Estelle warned her husband. Her eyes narrowed with suspicion. "They could be lying to us, you know. They could've conjured up this whole thing just to keep us from filing for custody of Caroline."

"If you want proof of our marriage, I will be glad to provide you with a certified copy of our marriage certificate," Sam volunteered. "Would that be enough evidence for you?"

"I suppose that would do," Estelle conceded with reluctance. "But just when is this ceremony supposed to take place?"

"We're still confirming our final arrangements," Kate explained. "The wedding will take place in our hometown of Rome, Georgia, but we haven't yet settled on a specific date."

"But we know it will be soon," Sam added. "Very soon, in fact."

The judge cast a defeated glance at his wife. "I suppose we should leave, dear. There's no use pursuing this matter any further now."

After the Vances had left the cottage, Sam let out a sigh of relief. "Thanks for standing by my story," he said. "I don't know what I would've done without you to back up my claim."

"It was the least I could do." She managed a weak smile, her heart splintering into pieces.

On Monday morning, Kate entered the law firm of Gentry, Springer, and Pierce. Approaching the dark-haired woman seated at the desk in the reception area, she flashed a friendly smile. "Good morning, Miss Dunbar," she said.

"Why, good morning, Miss Carey!" The woman rose and scurried around her desk. Kneeling, she brushed her fingers through Caroline's mop of carrot-red curls. "And good morning to you, Miss Caroline!"

"I have a very important favor to ask of you, Miss Dunbar," Kate explained. "Yesterday, Sam ran an advertisement in the newspaper for a housekeeper, and the applicants are supposed to reply at the address listed in the advertisement. Of course, Sam listed the law firm's address as the place of application for the respondents. And I was wondering—"

"We haven't had any respondents yet, Miss Carey." Miss Dunbar returned to her desk.

"But if someone comes to respond to the ad, will you please send them to the cottage? I'll be there for most of the day, and I'd like to screen the applicants for Sam. I believe it would save him a lot of time and worry if I could talk to the women first."

"I'll be glad to refer them to you," Miss Dunbar agreed.

"Thanks. I appreciate your help."

Kate left the office with Caroline in tow, hoping Miss Dunbar couldn't detect that her heart was breaking into pieces.

It was time for her to leave Macon. It was time for her to return home, to put the past behind her and move on with her life. If Sam had truly wanted to marry her, he would have asked her long before now. And he had the perfect chance when he'd concocted the story of their upcoming marriage for the sake of the Vances. He could have insisted that they follow through with their plans.

But she couldn't totally abandon Caroline. She had to make certain that the child would have the love of a caring, giving woman when she was gone.

She returned home with a heavy heart, knowing what she had to do.

Shortly after noon, a heavyset woman knocked at the door. "I understand you're looking for a new housekeeper," the woman said.

"Please come in," Kate invited, swinging open the door.

"This is a very nice house," the woman remarked, gazing around the room.

"It's not very large, so it's easy to keep clean," Kate assured her. "But the person I'm looking for has to be very fond of children. Little girls, in particular, I might add."

"Little girls?" The woman's eyes sparkled with delight.

"Actually, there's just one. And her name is Caroline."

"What a beautiful name!"

"I think so." Kate edged toward the hall. "Come here, Caroline. We have someone here that I'd like for you to meet."

The child scampered out of her room and flew straight into Kate's outstretched arms.

"She really adores you," the woman observed.

"It's going to be very difficult for me to leave her," Kate admitted in a choked tone.

At that moment, the front door hurled open and Sam entered the house. An expression of surprise flickered across his face when he saw the heavyset woman standing in the parlor.

"Good afternoon, ma'am," he said to the woman. "I'm Samuel Springer."

"Gertrude Jones here, Mr. Springer." The

woman flashed a pleasant smile in Sam's direction. "You have a very nice house here."

"Thank you." Sam turned to Kate. "Is Mrs. Jones one of your new friends?"

"Not exactly," she admitted. "You see, Sam, Mrs. Jones is here to apply for the housekeeping position that appeared in yesterday's newspaper."

A frown wrinkled his brow. "A housekeeper?"

"There has been a bit of confusion here, Mrs. Jones," Kate interrupted hastily. "Would you mind coming back in an hour or so? I would like to talk with you privately at that time, if you don't mind."

"I'd be happy to, ma'am."

As soon as the woman had left, Sam turned to Kate in confusion. "What's going on here, Kate?"

She heaved a weary sigh. "I'm afraid you'll be needing a new housekeeper after all, Sam."

# Chapter 18

❝**H**old on a minute here.❞ Sam's confusion gave way to a heated rush of anger. "Why in the hell do I need a new housekeeper?"

"Because it's time for me to leave, Sam. We agreed I would stay until—"

"But I thought you were happy here. We haven't even discussed the possibilities of you leaving!" He stiffened noticeably. "And besides, conducting interviews for a new housekeeper should be my responsibility. Not yours."

"Well, you don't seem to be very eager to talk to anyone about the position," Kate reasoned. "Yesterday was the second Sunday that your advertisement has appeared in the paper, and you haven't interviewed a single woman for the job."

"But interviews take up a great deal of time,

Kate. I just haven't had the chance to fit them into my schedule. I've been preparing several cases for upcoming trials, and my work load has been rather full."

"Don't give me that, Sam. I have the sense to know that Caroline is much more important to you than your work."

"But my schedule has been busy of late."

She heaved a weary sigh. "I promised I would remain here until I know for certain that you have someone to take care of Caroline. But I can't stay here forever, Sam. I've already stayed here for far too long."

"And you're so anxious to leave that you decided to take it upon yourself to interview some applicants for the housekeeper position," he surmised.

"Well, you're obviously not going to take the initiative," she countered. "Someone has to find a new nanny for Caroline. And it might as well be me, I suppose."

He shook his head in frustration. "When are you ever going to learn, Kate? When are you ever going to realize that you can't keep overstepping your bounds like this?"

"And when are you ever going to learn that you can't keep procrastinating about hiring a new housekeeper? For heaven's sake, Sam! Don't you think it's time you took some action?" She rolled her eyes heavenward. "I'm beginning to think you don't even want to hire anyone for the position."

"And maybe you're right." His lips twitched with the hint of a smile. "I'll admit it, Kate. I haven't been anxious to interview any applicants. I haven't been at all eager to hire someone for the position. In fact, I've wanted to delay the entire process for as long as I can."

"But . . . why?"

"Because I don't want you to leave." His voice became husky and low, and his eyes took on a warm, provocative gleam. "I want you to stay. Caroline and I . . . well, we need you in our lives, Kate. We need you very badly."

A heavy weight filled her heart. Common sense warned her that love wasn't the reason why Sam wanted her to stay. Never once had he professed his love for her. Logic said he only wanted her to stay because he needed a mother for his daughter. He was thinking of Caroline, and nothing more.

"It's a wonderful feeling to know that you and Caroline need me," she finally choked out. "But I need more than that, Sam."

"Then what do you want?"

Couldn't he see? Was the man so blind that he couldn't see she was crazy in love with him? That she wanted to spend the rest of her life loving him and his daughter?

"Oh, for heaven's sake, Sam! You can be the most infuriating man in the world at times."

"All I did was ask you to stay. What's so wrong with that?"

"Not a blasted thing, I suppose, if that's what I wanted to do."

"You don't want to remain here?"

"I'm not going to stay here under false pretenses any longer, Sam. Everyone may think that I'm simply your housekeeper and your daughter's nanny, but both of us know that I'm warming your bed every night, too. As things stand between us now, I'm not much more than a live-in mistress. And I can't continue to go on this way. It's time for me to go back to Hopewell House, I'm afraid."

"Fine, then," he snapped. "Leave, if that's what you want to do."

"Then you're not listening to me, Sam! I didn't say I *wanted* to leave." She gave her head a shake. "And I still don't know what you're going to do about the situation with the Vances. Eventually, they'll begin to wonder why they haven't received a marriage certificate from you, and they'll—"

"Why can't I send them a marriage certificate?" he challenged.

"Because we're not getting married!"

"And why not?"

"Because you haven't asked me to marry you!"

He stilled. "Then it's about time I did."

Taking her by the hand, he led her out onto

the verandah. Seating her in a wicker chair, he dropped to his knees in front of her. "Will you marry me, Kathryn Carey? Will you become my lawfully wedded wife?"

She gazed into his face, and her heart swelled with love. God help her, how could she refuse? She loved the man. Loved him with all of her heart and soul, with every fiber of her being. She'd loved him since she was a little girl, and she knew she'd never stop loving him, never in a million years.

But could she settle for what he was offering her? Could she live with the man for the rest of her life, knowing he'd only married her out of concern for his daughter? Could she endure the torment of his unwillingness to proclaim his love for her?

"No, Sam," she whispered in a choked voice. "I can't possibly marry you."

Bewilderment flickered across his face. "And why in the hell not?"

Her throat was so clogged with emotion that she could barely speak. "B-B-Because you h-h-haven't . . . b-b-because I n-n-need t-to—"

"For God's sake, Kate!" Sam bolted to his feet. Frowning, he wiped off the dust from the knee of his trousers. "I'm not playing games here. I'm dead serious. And I don't want to argue with you about this. We argue enough as it is. Will you—or will you not—marry me?"

She swallowed, hard, to clear the knot in her throat. "That all depends."

"So now you're setting conditions on marrying me?" he asked.

"I don't intend to place any demands on you." She heard the quiver in her own voice. "I just need to know *why* you want to marry me."

"Why? I've already told you, Kate. Caroline and I need you."

"But that was the reason you gave for wanting me to stay here. You haven't told me why you want to marry me."

He slowly fell to his knees once again. Grasping her hand, he gazed into her eyes with such intensity that Kate's breath snared in her throat.

"Why do I want to marry you, Kate? Because I can't imagine my life without you. You've brightened every dark corner of my home— and my heart—with your joy and laughter. And I can't bear the thought of letting you go. I can't bear the thought of a future without you by my side."

Her hand was trembling as she reached out and brushed her fingers across the line of his jaw. "I'm deeply touched, Sam. Truly, I am. But I can't possibly marry someone who doesn't love me."

"And what makes you think I don't love you? For God's sake, Kate, I *adore* you!"

"But you've never *told* me that you love me, Sam."

"But haven't I shown you how much I love you? Can't you tell that I'm crazy about you?"

"But I need to hear you say the words. I need the assurance of knowing that your heart belongs to me—and only me. And if I hear those three simple little words—I love you—I'll know your feelings for me are different from your feelings for anyone else."

"I feel very much like a fool, Kate. I should've told you that I love you long ago. But I've never . . ." He swallowed with difficulty, and his voice became clogged with emotion. "But I've never known how to say those words. In all honesty, I've never heard anyone say those words to me. Love has never been a part of my life . . . until now."

Sudden understanding assaulted her. Sam's life had been so bereft of love that it was little wonder he'd never learned how to verbally express his emotions.

An ache squeezed her heart for the little boy whose mother had cast him aside, for the man who had endured the pain of a woman's heartless disregard, the agony of a friend's cruel betrayal.

His fingers tightened around her hand. "But I do love you, Kathryn Carey. God help me, I love you more than I ever dreamed I could love anyone."

She blinked back the sudden surge of moisture swelling in her eyes. "And I love you, Samuel Springer."

The happiness glowing from his eyes filled her with more joy than she'd ever known. "Then I'd like to propose a question to you. Will you marry me, Kate?"

She hesitated, wanting to savor the moment, wishing she could freeze it in time, trying to hold on to all the wondrous feelings soaring through her.

But an impatient frown marred Sam's brow. "I'm not going to repeat myself again, Kate. I've already posed the question to you three damn times."

A hint of a smile curled on her lips. "Yes, Sam. I'll marry you."

His smile warmed her heart. Springing to his feet, he swooped her into his arms. "Yes!" he bellowed. "She said yes!"

He whirled her around, kissing her, loving her, shouting for joy. "Yes, she said!" he exclaimed once again.

At that instant, the front door slammed. Startled, Sam stilled just as the sound of tiny footsteps pattered across the verandah.

Caroline rushed up to them, her face awash with curiosity. "Yes?" she echoed.

Laughing, Sam bent down and snatched up his daughter. As he pulled Caroline into his arms, he drew Kate closer to him, enfolding both of them in the circle of his embrace.

"Yes, Caroline," he said, smiling down at her. "Kate is going to marry me. She's going to stay right here forever."

Caroline was giggling with delight when Kate noticed that someone was walking across the lawn. She glanced up, surprised to see that Mrs. Jones was returning to the cottage.

"Are you still interested in hiring a new housekeeper?" the woman asked.

Kate's gaze lingered on Sam and Caroline for a moment, and her heart swelled with love. Unable to suppress the joy coursing through her, she flashed a dazzling smile in the woman's direction. "I'm very happy to say that the position has just been filled."

Sam tightened his hold around his future wife, grinning unabashedly. "On a permanent basis, I might add."

# Epilogue

"**I** always knew they were meant for each other," Dorinda Hopewell insisted, a wistful little smile curling on her lips.

"Pshaw, Dorie." Odelphia rolled her eyes heavenward. "Those two never said one civil word to each other when they were children. They were constantly fighting and arguing."

"My ears are still ringing from the memory of their squabbles." Tyler chuckled. "Who would've ever dreamed that they would end up as husband and wife?"

"That's the wonder of love, I suppose." Julia leaned closer to her husband, sighing contentedly as she gazed across the front lawn of Hopewell House. "Have you ever seen a happier couple?"

At that moment, the swell of music filled the air. Surrounded by an admiring crowd of wedding guests, the groom pulled his new bride into his arms and swept her across the emerald lawn.

The bride's white lace veil, caught on the wings of a warm September breeze, fluttered through the air, swirling around them like a heavenly cloud as they whisked their way across the grounds.

Kate smiled up at Sam, beaming with joy. "You've become a remarkable dancer, Mr. Springer."

He grinned. "I had a remarkable teacher."

She gave a wistful sigh. "I've always dreamed about this day, you know."

"As I recall, you've been planning it for quite some time. Perhaps about ten years or so?" he taunted.

"At least you didn't stand me up at the altar this time," she conceded, unable to suppress a smile. "But, then, I didn't really expect that you would."

"And what brought about this confidence, Mrs. Springer?" he chided.

"If my memory serves me correctly, you once told me that when you decided to marry someone, you wanted to be the one who does the asking. And since you took the initiative to pose the question to me this time, I assumed you were truly sincere about your offer."

"You're damn right I was sincere." He chuckled under his breath. "But then, you should've known that, Kate. If you remember, I popped the question to you on bended knee three damn times before you gave me the right answer."

"What can I say?" Kate fluttered her thick, dark lashes in a most beguiling way. "I wanted to make sure you knew what you were getting yourself into."

Laughing, he pulled her closer against him. "I should've known to expect nothing less from someone like you."

She feigned innocence. "Someone like me? Why, whatever do you mean?"

"I should've known you possessed the power to drive me to my knees—three times, no less, in the course of one afternoon."

"But you couldn't have possibly known what would happen between us," she insisted. "You were too busy arguing with me to notice that I'd fallen in love with you."

"Thank God I finally came to my senses." The smile on his lips was tender and warm, and love shimmered from his gaze. "I love you, Mrs. Kathryn Springer. And I'm absolutely certain that I'll never regret this day, never in a million years."

"I intend to make certain that you never regret it." She smiled up at him, her heart swelling with love. "But, then, with someone like you as my husband, I suspect that won't be difficult for me at all."

"And with you as my wife, I suspect our lives

will never be boring." He pulled her closer
against him, whirling her across the lawn, the
deep rumble of his laughter close and warm
against her ear. "But, then, I wouldn't expect
anything less from someone like you, my dar-
ling Kate."

# Discover Contemporary Romances
## at Their Sizzling Hot Best
## from Avon Books

**THE LOVES OF
RUBY DEE**       *by Curtiss Ann Matlock*
*78106-9/$5.99 US/$7.99 Can*

**JONATHAN'S WIFE**       *by Dee Holmes*
*78368-1/$5.99 US/$7.99 Can*

**DANIEL'S GIFT**       *by Barbara Freethy*
*78189-1/$5.99 US/$7.99 Can*

**FAIRYTALE**       *by Maggie Shayne*
*78300-2/$5.99 US/$7.99 Can*

## Coming Soon

**WISHES COME TRUE**       *by Patti Berg*
*78338-X/$5.99 US/$7.99 Can*